"The Black Sheep knitting series has it all: Friendship,
kniting, murder, and the occasional recipe
create the perfect pattern. Great fun."
—*New York Times* bestselling author Jayne Anne Krentz

Praise for *While My Pretty One Knits*

"The crafty first of a cozy new series. . . . The friendships
among the likable knitters. . . . help
make Canadeo's crime yarn a charmer."
—*Publishers Weekly*

"Fans of Monica Ferris . . . will enjoy this engaging
amateur sleuth as much for its salute to friendship as
to Lucy's inquiry made one stitch at a time."
—The Mystery Gazette

"Delightful. Enchanting. Humorous. Impressive. Witty.
Those are just a few adjectives to describe Anne Canadeo's
effervescent cozy debut, *While My Pretty One Knits*."
—Book Cave

"[A] unique murder mystery. . . . Fast-paced
and electrifying. . . . First in a new series
you are sure to enjoy."
—Fresh Fiction

Meet the Black Sheep Knitters

Maggie Messina, owner of the Black Sheep Knitting Shop, is a retired high school art teacher who runs her little slice of knitters' paradise with the kind of vibrant energy that leaves her friends dazzled! From novice to pro, knitters come to Maggie as much for her up-to-the-minute offerings like organic wool as for her encouragement and friendship. And Maggie's got a deft touch when it comes to unraveling mysteries, too.

Lucy Binger left Boston when her marriage ended, and found herself shifting gears to run her graphic design business from the coastal cottage she and her sister inherited. After big-city living, she now finds contentment on a front porch in tiny Plum Harbor, knitting with her closest friends.

Dana Haeger is a psychologist with a busy local practice. A stylishly polished professional with a quick wit, she slips out to Maggie's shop whenever her schedule allows—after all, knitting is the best form of therapy!

Suzanne Cavanaugh is a typical working supermom—a realtor with a million demands on her time, from coaching soccer to showing houses to attending the PTA. But she carves out a little "me" time with the Black Sheep Knitters.

Phoebe Meyers, a college gal complete with magenta highlights and nose stud, lives in the apartment above Maggie's shop. She's Maggie's indispensable helper (when she's not in class)—and part of the new generation of young knitters.

Knit, Purl, Die

Anne Canadeo

Pocket Books

New York   London   Toronto   Sydney

Pocket Books
A Division of Simon & Schuster, Inc.
1230 Avenue of the Americas
New York, NY 10020

First Pocket Books trade paperback edition January 2010

POCKET and colophon are registered trademarks of Simon & Schuster, Inc.

For information about special discounts for bulk purchases, please contact Simon & Schuster Special Sales at 1-866-506-1949 or business@simonandschuster.com

The Simon & Schuster Speakers Bureau can bring authors to your live event. For more information or to book an event contact the Simon & Schuster Speakers Bureau at 1-866-248-3049 or visit our website at www.simonspeakers.com.

Manufactured in the United States of America

10   9   8   7   6   5   4   3   2   1

Library of Congress Cataloging-in-Publication Data is available.

ISBN 978-1-4165-9812-1
ISBN 978-1-4391-2694-3 (ebook)

To Nick Deane—
who lived large, loved life, and was loved by all who knew him.
We were privileged to be your friend.

Acknowledgments

I wish to thank attorney Dwight Vibbert of Peabody, Massachusetts, for a thorough review of the estate probate process. Thanks also to Chief Gavin Keenan of the Ipswich Police Department in Essex County, Massachusetts, for his explanation of police procedure at the scene of a drowning.

I would also like to thank Crystal Palace Yarns and designer Lisa Dykstra for permission to include a link to the mist lace scarf pattern, and Wendy D. Johnson, author of *Socks From the Toes Up*, for permission to include a link to Sprucey Lucey Socks pattern and WendyKnits.net.

I'd also like to thank my editor, Kathy Sagan, for her sage advice and encouragement, and my agent, Bob Mecoy, for his unflagging "yes, we can!" spirit.

Last but not least, my family must get some credit for putting up with all that takeout food and a frightening lack of clean laundry as I staggered toward the finish line.

*Everyone is a moon and has a dark side
which he never shows to anybody.*
—Mark Twain

Chapter One

*H*emingway was wrong. The rich *are* different." Lucy gazed out the passenger-side window of her friend Maggie's car as gated entryways, privacy hedges, and lawns as lush as country club greens rolled by. "They definitely have longer driveways."

"And better haircuts, usually," Maggie agreed. "But Gloria isn't different from us. Not really."

They were on their way to Gloria Sterling's house, driving down tree-lined roads deep with afternoon shade, traveling from the heart of the village to The Landing, a neighborhood of gracious old homes that flanked not-so-gracious minimansions and a variety of architectural styles in between.

Maggie had known Gloria a long time, but Lucy had met her only recently.

"Gloria wasn't born with money. Just the opposite," Maggie reminded her. "It's nice of her to have us all over tonight. She's not even part of the group."

Their knitting group—five friends in all—normally met on

Thursday night at one another's homes, or at the Black Sheep, the knitting shop Maggie owned. Gloria had just jumped into the rotation like a sidelined player in a volleyball game. She wasn't an official member of their circle, more like a "guest star," Lucy thought.

Since Gloria had returned to Plum Harbor a few months ago, after a long stay at her house in Florida, she'd been spending a lot of spare time at Maggie's shop. If Gloria happened to be hanging around when one of their meetings started up, it seemed rude to exclude her. She was always interested in Maggie's demonstrations of a new stitch or technique. Or just happy to stitch and chat.

Gloria's irreverent humor and "live large" style had taken some getting used to, for Lucy at least. But the plain-talking blonde bombshell definitely kicked up the evening a notch. And they all liked her husband, Jamie.

Gloria Sterling and Jamie Barnett were pretty much a package deal. Newlyweds, joined at the hip. Or so it seemed at times. Jamie was Gloria's third run at matrimony, clearly the trophy husband. Gloria, the iconic cougar, wasn't coy about it. "I've put in my time with men my age. This one is dessert," she'd told them one night.

The invitation had been for cocktails, knitting, and supper, poolside. Perfect for a surprisingly warm night in June. Would Gloria actually make the meal herself, or have it catered, Lucy wondered. She didn't seem the cooking type and probably had a housekeeper. There was always Jamie.

"Maybe Jamie is doing the cooking." Lucy turned to Maggie and smiled. "Those macaroons he brought to the meeting last week were intense."

"I've had dinner there. He *is* a good cook. Among his other talents." Maggie was still watching the road, but Lucy caught her small smile.

Jamie was a man of considerable talents. He cooked, he baked, he even knit with the group from time to time, all without seeming to feel any threat to his masculinity.

Who would question his masculinity? No woman Lucy knew, that was for sure.

A big, broad-shouldered, dirty blond hunk of guy, he had less guile than a golden retriever and even more devotion when it came to Gloria. They did seem amazingly happy together, both blissfully unaware of their age difference. Which was in the double digits, Lucy guessed.

If Gloria were a man and had hooked a babe ten, fifteen, or even twenty years younger, no one would think twice about it. But with the roles reversed, the pair did raise a few eyebrows around town. Plum Harbor's Main Street was not exactly Rodeo Drive.

Of course, the fact that Gloria could easily pass for forty made the math less obvious. But Lucy had to wonder how long anyone could keep that up. How many mindless treadmill miles or gallons of Retinol cream did it require? How many discreet nips and tucks and cellulite suctions?

How much money did it take to hold back time's handiwork? The inevitable changes had to catch up sooner or later. At least on the outside.

But Lucy didn't want to take a pessimistic view. The connection between Jamie and Gloria seemed more than skin deep and they seemed to have made some separate, private peace with what others might view as a fatal flaw in the partnership. They even joked about it.

No, it was the real thing. You could tell by the way they

looked at each other. She delighted in him. Everything Jamie did was charming to her. And Jamie acted the same way about Gloria, even her flaws, her impatient and demanding side, seemed amusing and even endearing to him. You only had to be around them for a short time to see it. Lucy had witnessed enough relationships, good and bad—including her own failed marriage—to know the difference.

"I think the turn is coming up soon, on the right," Maggie said. Then she suddenly swerved into a narrow lane. The sign read "Sugar Maple Way."

"Here we are. Number five." Maggie steered the little car up a long, gravel-covered drive. Lucy noticed that their other friends Dana and Suzanne had already arrived; their cars were parked farther up, near the front door. Phoebe, a college student who worked part-time at Maggie's shop and who was also part of the group, wasn't coming tonight. Her boyfriend's band had a gig at a bar in Gloucester. Phoebe was needed to clap loudly and help move the equipment.

Which was probably just as well, Lucy decided, eyeing Gloria's impressive house and property. Phoebe was likely to have an attack of social conscience in this setting and act out in some countercultural, college-student way.

Maggie hadn't said much about Gloria's house. Lucy had pictured an older home, beautifully decorated and meticulously maintained. Just like Gloria herself. But it wasn't quite what she expected.

The house was a large, abstract-looking structure with clean, stark lines, constructed of wood and glass. A style very popular in the 1970s. Considered "modern" back then, though the years since had continually redefined that term.

Maggie parked on the drive and Lucy reached into the

backseat for her knitting bag and a knapsack that held a bathing suit and towel, though she doubted she'd swim. At this time of year, she was reluctant to bare too much skin. Her legs especially looked pale and doughy, she thought, like slices of Wonder Bread. When Lucy got out and headed for the stone path that led to the front door, Maggie waved her back.

"I hear them in back. We'll just go 'round the side. Follow me."

Lucy followed Maggie up the driveway and then around the far side of the house. From behind a tall white fence she could hear the sound of voices, splashing water, and music. Was that Latin jazz? Her friends always kicked back at a knitting night, but Gloria's version already seemed like a real party.

"Sounds like they started without us," Maggie said, pushing open the gate.

"Don't worry, we'll catch up," Lucy whispered as she followed.

"Welcome, ladies, come right in. We've been waiting for you."

Gloria was sitting at a round, wrought-iron table shaded by a white market umbrella, along with Dana and Suzanne. She stood up and came to greet them. The other women both looked up from their knitting for a moment and waved. Lucy saw tall cocktail glasses and knitting paraphernalia already spread out around them.

The table was one of three, set on a multilayered stone patio that flanked a kidney-shaped pool. The pool and patio were bordered by flower beds and thick green shrubs. At the far end of the pool, Lucy noticed a waterfall, about six feet high, the water tumbling over large rocks into the deep end.

It was a gorgeous setting, like something out of one of those "houses to drool over" TV shows.

Gloria approached, high-heeled slides clicking on the smooth stones, her wrap-style sundress swinging around her legs and clinging in all the right places. The halter-style neckline displayed a deep tan, killer cleavage, and a perfect figure.

Lucy had once read that the Barbie doll's body was anatomically impossible. Designed by a man, of course. So was Gloria's. Lucy tried to remember that any time she felt a twinge of envy. Gloria was a poster girl for cosmetic, surgical intervention—and every boy's dream.

Gloria gave them each a hug hello. Lucy stared at the pattern on her dress. A designer logo of interlocking letters she couldn't quite translate. It was either Calvin, Coach . . . or Le Shopping Channel?

"So glad you could come. Ready to knit the night away? Jamie's grilling. Shrimp and chicken saté with spicy peanut sauce and grilled vegetables."

"Sounds delicious." Maggie smiled and offered a bottle of wine she'd brought as a hostess gift.

Lucy silently agreed. A gourmet, lo-carb meal. She had expected no less.

Jamie stood at the far side of the patio, manning a huge stainless-steel grill, equipped with several cooking areas and rows of shiny black controls and dials. It could probably send and receive e-mail and had a GPS system, Lucy thought.

He checked something under the large dome lid, then turned to wave hello, his hand covered by a hot mitt.

Lucy and Maggie waved back. Lucy smiled quickly and looked away, aware that she'd been staring. Bare chested, he wore a black chef's apron over red bathing trunks. The

incongruous outfit reminding Lucy of those male pin-up cal-
endars passed around during bridal showers. Tacky . . . but
effective.

Gloria leaned over and took Maggie's arm. "Come and sit.
I'll get you both a drink."

They walked to the patio where Suzanne and Dana were
busily chatting and knitting. "Hi, guys. Join the party." Suzanne jumped up and pulled out the chair next to her for Lucy.

Suzanne, a Realtor and mother of three who lived by her
BlackBerry, seemed very relaxed tonight, Lucy noticed. Whatever she'd been drinking had done a good job unwinding her.

"What can I get for you two?" Gloria asked Maggie and
Lucy. "We made a big pitcher of caipirinhas. Jamie and I had
them every night on our honeymoon. We brought the cachaça
back from Brazil. Want to try one?"

"Highly recommended," Dana said, taking a small sip from
her frosty glass.

"I'll try one," Lucy answered bravely. "I may not be able to
knit a straight row after, though."

"Possibly. But you won't worry about it, sweetie," Gloria
promised.

"Just white wine for me," Maggie said.

"Whatever you like. But you still need to be in the samba
contest."

Samba contest? She was kidding . . . right?

"Be right back." Gloria grinned and trotted toward the
house.

"Don't worry, Lucy. There's no samba contest. Not that
we've heard about." Dana glanced her way and smiled. Lucy
guessed her expression had given her away.

She watched Dana turn her project over, a pale yellow vest

with an argyle pattern on the front. She was making it for her husband, Jack. Knitting a pattern with so many colors was a bit advanced, but Dana could handle it. She was a very careful, methodical knitter who rarely started one project before finishing another. Not like most people Lucy knew, who had plenty of UFOs—unfinished objects—lying around at any given time.

A psychologist with a busy practice in town, Dana's office was just a few blocks down Main Street from Maggie's shop. She often stopped in at the shop for a knitting break between appointments with her clients, a routine she claimed kept her own sanity intact.

"I know everyone's in the middle of something," Maggie began, "but I found a project I want to show you."

She pulled out a few pages that looked like they'd been printed off the Internet. "I heard about this organization called Warm Up America. I went to the site and found a project we can make together. It's very simple. We each knit squares, seven by nine inches. Just a garter stitch. Then we put all our squares together to make a blanket and send it in. Warm Up America will give it out to someone in need, in a hospice or a homeless shelter. Or to a family who has lost their home in a fire or flood."

"What a great idea. Sounds easy, too." Suzanne took the pages from Maggie, eager to look at the instructions. "I was thinking of trying a pullover for Kevin. I figured if I started now, I might be done for Christmas."

Suzanne held up a photo of a classic but complicated fisherman knit sweater, then passed it over to Maggie.

She was an ambitious knitter, Lucy had to hand her that. Though she often tackled more than she could successfully stitch her way through.

Maggie thought the same, Lucy guessed, but didn't want to discourage Suzanne. She glanced at the sweater photo and handed it back. "The blanket squares will go quickly. You'll have plenty of time before Christmas to try that one."

Gloria had returned and set down a tray that held a frosted glass filled with the exotic cocktail du jour, and a wineglass. Alongside the glass, Lucy spotted a plate of vegetable crudités and a white creamy dip.

"Did I hear something about a group project?" Gloria handed a caipirinha to Lucy and then the white wine to Maggie.

"We're talking about making a blanket for charity. Everyone knits a few squares and we put it all together. I think we should decide on a palette and each take our own color."

"That sounds fun. Can I make some? I'm almost done with my scarf." Gloria's tone was eager and excited, sounding more like a middle schooler than a woman in her fifties.

"Of course you can." Maggie didn't even glance at the others. She knew they would all agree. The Black Sheep wanted to spread the joy of stitching, not hoard it for themselves.

"The pattern on the website calls for forty-nine squares. We're six, counting Phoebe. So that works out fine, eight squares each, and one person makes an extra. I thought we could figure out something special for the center," she suggested. "I have copies of the pattern for everybody, too," she added, pulling out another pile of papers from the bag. "But you each need to make a template for the squares, like this one . . ."

She held up a rectangle cut from cardboard. Lucy had used a template once before, when she'd worked on an afghan. The tension in everyone's stitches was different, a little tighter or looser, and measuring against a template, as well as counting stitches, kept pieces of large projects uniform.

"Just write everything down. Jamie will take care of it. He's good with things like that." Gloria stretched out on a chaise longue next to the table, white wrought iron with thick yellow cushions.

She extended her long tanned legs and picked up her knitting bag, a chic black tote with a tortoiseshell handle. Then she drew out her project with care, a beautiful fine-gauge, lace-stitch piece that she called a Mist Lace Scarf.

The yarn was a brilliant shade of tangerine, very Gloria; Gloria knew what looked good on her and the scarf was a great choice, Lucy thought. With her long blonde hair and green eyes, the delicate lace would look perfect draped over her bare shoulders on a summer night.

Gloria was a surprisingly deft knitter, Lucy had noticed. Her long polished nails—probably add-ons—didn't seem to hamper her progress one bit.

"Anybody want to jump in the pool?" Jamie called from the grill. "Dinner's going to be a few more minutes."

"You guys go ahead if you like." Gloria encouraged her guests with a wave of her hand, bangle bracelets jangling. "I'm not a big pool person. The hot tub, okay. Once in a while. When the mood strikes," she added, glancing at her husband. "But those chemicals . . ." She rolled her large, mascara-edged eyes. "You might as well soak yourself in battery acid. I swear, I come out looking like the Queen of the Crypt Keepers."

Jamie laughed. He had left his cooking post and now stood behind his wife. He reached down and rubbed her shoulders. "She looks like Venus, rising out of the foam in a Renaissance painting."

"Jamie, please . . . give me a break." Gloria shook her head, though Lucy thought she enjoyed the comparison. A hint of pink flushed her cheeks.

"She does. I want to paint her out here in the water, just floating like a water lily with her hair around her head." He squeezed next to Gloria on the longue chair and slipped his arm around her shoulders.

She glanced at him and smiled, but didn't miss a beat in her knitting. "I'm not the water lily type, babe. More of a tough old . . . geranium."

Her comparison made everyone laugh.

"A tiger lily, then." Jamie replied, kissing her hair.

"How is your painting coming along, Jamie?" Maggie asked.

Maggie had been a high school art teacher before opening her knitting shop about three years ago. She still loved visiting the museums and galleries in Boston, though fiber art was a big interest now.

"Pretty good. Really good, actually," Jamie answered with a hesitant smile. "Of course, I have my muse here. She keeps me in line." He gave Gloria's shoulder another squeeze.

"I bring some bread and water to his cell every few hours, and remind him to come to bed when he's working too late. He's made big progress since we moved back up here. I think New England has been good for him. Very good," she added. Then she glanced at her husband, her love as evident in that look as a beam of light, Lucy thought. "Can I tell them?" Her tone was eager and unexpectedly sweet.

Jamie looked flustered. "All right . . . but nothing's solid yet. It might just be a lot of talk," he explained to the group.

"It's practically a done deal, Jamie," Gloria insisted. "Think positively." She turned to her friends. "Jamie's going to have a show at a gallery in Boston. A very good gallery. All his own work, too. Not some group grope thing. Isn't that great?"

"I *might* have a show," he corrected. "We haven't really nailed it down."

Maggie peered at the couple over the edge of her reading glasses. "That is great news. Congratulations," she said sincerely.

The others quickly chimed in. But Jamie was quick to tamp down their enthusiasm. "It looks good, but we still haven't signed anything. So I'm not breaking open the champagne yet."

"But we will, sweetie. Very soon," Gloria assured him. "I might hop into the hot tub for that celebration," she added, making her friends laugh.

"When will you know for sure?" Dana asked.

"I'm going to Boston tomorrow to meet with the gallery owner. He invited me to the opening of a new exhibit. There are some people coming by who he wants me to meet."

"That sounds promising." Suzanne had already put aside the fisherman knit pattern and was studying the instructions for the blanket squares.

"Very promising," Lucy agreed. Her work as a graphic designer for advertising agencies and publishers didn't put her in touch with the gallery scene much, but she did have a few friends who were still trying to make it in that realm. It was a tough, often disappointing road. It sounded to her as if Jamie was making enviable headway.

"When will this possible art show happen?" Suzanne asked.

"In the fall probably," Jamie answered. "I've started a new

series. I'm going to bring a few pieces with me to show him. But I still have a lot of work to do to put together an entire show."

"He's very productive when he has a goal." Gloria patted her husband's leg. "He'll stay in that room for hours. Working and working. So . . . intense."

Lucy didn't think of Jamie as intense. In fact, that was one of the last adjectives she'd use to describe him. She would have never taken Jamie for an artist, either, he was so down to earth and modest. Not at all the pretentious, downtown type she'd often been drawn to in her younger days. But maybe that was because Jamie was the real thing, an unspoiled, even naïve talent. Not posing, or playacting.

She'd never seen his work, but assumed he did have talent if a good gallery had shown interest in representing him. Art was still a business, and gallery owners had to be savvy salespeople to survive, and without seeming so, either. Jamie obviously had something worth marketing in his work, in addition to his movie star looks.

"I think the food is ready. I'll be right back." Jamie touched Gloria's cheek as he stood, then headed back to the grill.

"I'm so happy for him," Maggie told them in a quiet voice, one that Jamie probably couldn't hear. "For both of you. You must be very excited."

"I am. And very proud, though he hates when I say it," Gloria told them in an even quieter voice. "He has so much talent and he works so hard. He just needs a break. A show at a good gallery that can promote his work. I'm really hoping this is it. If he does get it, and I'm sure he will, we'll hire a publicist and all that. You'd think the art world was different. But that's what it takes these days to get noticed. Publicity, marketing. Your name in the newspapers."

"And on the Internet," Lucy added.

"Exactly. And Jamie is so naïve about business," Gloria whispered, glancing over at her husband as he worked at the grill, arranging the food he'd prepared on several large platters. "Not that it's a bad thing," she added with a small, tender smile. "I'd never want to change that about him."

Jamie brought over the trays of saté and grilled vegetables and set them on a buffet table, where large yellow plates, cloth napkins, and silverware stood ready and waiting. Gloria went into the house and emerged with bowls of cold sesame noodles and a shredded cabbage salad with rice wine vinegar dressing. Quickly clearing the table of their knitting projects and equipment, the group rose and helped themselves to dinner.

"Everything looks delicious, Jamie," Lucy complimented him as she returned to the table with a heaping dish. "Thanks for doing all this cooking."

"No big deal. I really like to cook. Helps me unwind after I've been in the studio all day."

Gloria sat next to her husband, dropping just a tablespoon or two of food on her dish, Lucy noticed. "We use the term 'studio' very loosely around here. It's really just a spare room. Not nearly big enough now for all his things, and the light in there absolutely stinks. Even I can see that."

Jamie dipped his skewer of shrimp saté in some peanut sauce and took a bite. "It's fine for now, Glo. I'm not exactly Picasso."

"He needs a real studio," she continued, ignoring him. "He was going to use one of the stores I own in town. A few are vacant right now. Then we decided to just sell this place and find something new. I've always liked this house," she added, "but it's just not right for us."

Lucy knew that Gloria had inherited the house from her second husband, George Thurman, a successful entrepreneur who had mentored and launched Gloria into the business world. Lucy had heard from Maggie that George had taught Gloria everything she knew. She'd been a junior accountant at one of the firms he owned when they met, and he'd divorced his wife to marry her. George had died of cancer about fifteen years ago. Gloria had nursed him at home, until the end.

Lucy imagined there were a few ghosts wandering around these cedar and glass walls. The newlyweds probably wanted a fresh start.

"So you want to find a house with a little cottage on the property. Something like that?" Suzanne asked curiously. Lucy could practically hear Suzanne mentally sifting through her thick file of listings.

"Exactly. My very talented husband needs his space and solitude to create. I know it's not a great time to sell—" Gloria winced at the thought of the money she stood to lose in the down market. "But it works both ways. We might find a real bargain on the other side, right?"

"Exactly. I think you definitely can," Suzanne quickly agreed. Lucy saw her practically spring up in her seat, her fork full of sesame noodles hanging in midair.

"Are you going to stay in Plum Harbor?" Dana asked them.

"We want to. We love it here." Gloria glanced at her husband and he nodded.

"Gloria's business is here. All of her friends. It's close to the city but quiet enough to get real work done. I really like it," Jamie added.

"Do you have any special part of the village in mind?" Suzanne asked.

"Something on the water would suit us, I think. I bet those houses down on Bayview have terrific light," Gloria added, naming one of the most exclusive streets in town. "And we both love the beach."

Lucy noticed Jamie reach over and cover Gloria's hand with his own. Their fingers intertwined and he turned to smile at her. "There are some beautiful properties down there," Suzanne agreed. "I have a few listings I can show you. At least one or two have little outbuildings for studio space. I can put it all into the computer and see what pops up," she offered with supersaleswoman cheer.

"That would be terrific. Give me your card and I'll call you," Gloria promised. "Maybe you could help us put this place on the market. I guess I could move on a new property, if it seemed right." Meaning she didn't have to sell this house in order to afford another, Lucy translated. "But we need to get the ball rolling here, too, right?"

"Yes, you definitely should. This is the perfect time of year. With all the beautiful landscaping and the pool, this place will really show well." Suzanne nodded in agreement.

The prospect of two commissions on top-drawer properties seemed to sharpen Suzanne's appetite. She dug into her saté with abandon.

Not bad work for an evening out. Lucy had the impulse to give her pal a high five, but instead just exchanged a discreet glance of glee.

Jamie wiped his mouth with a napkin and stood up. "It's

been fun, ladies. But that cramped, dark little spare room calls."

Lucy was surprised. Jamie often sat and knitted with them, or just hung out while everyone else knit and chatted.

Gloria seemed surprised, too. "Really, honey? I thought you were going to take a break tonight."

"I have to finish the blue piece, so I can bring it with me tomorrow," he reminded her.

"Oh, right. That one is strong. You should bring it."

He smiled at her, then leaned over and kissed her cheek, his hand cradling her face for a tender instant. "Don't fall asleep out here in that chair," he warned her in a firm but loving tone. "And come say good night before you go to bed?"

She didn't answer, but held his gaze a moment and just smiled. Then he stood up again and briefly waved. "Good night, everyone. Have fun."

"We definitely will," Maggie promised him.

"Thanks again for dinner, Jamie, it was delicious," Dana said.

"You are all very welcome. Come back soon." With another sunny smile, he turned and headed into the house.

The backyard had grown dimmer and cooler, though the sun had not quite sunk from view. The outdoor lights had come on, glowing under the shimmering blue water in the swimming pool, bright spots over the patio, and even little white lanterns under the umbrella that surprisingly provided enough light to knit.

Gloria had lit a bowl full of votive candles in the center of the table; the flames glowed warmly. The women worked together to quickly clear the table, placing everything from dinner on a tea cart.

Then Gloria set out dessert, a sumptuous-looking fruit salad and a pile of home-baked cookies. Lucy spotted Jamie's chocolate-laced coconut macaroons, which probably packed about a million calories a bite, she figured. But were too good to resist.

"Can I get anyone another caipirinha or a glass of wine?" Gloria asked.

"I'd really love some coffee, if it's not too much trouble," Maggie replied.

"Me, too," Lucy seconded the motion. The tropical cocktail had gone straight to her head. Lucy took out the new pattern for the blanket square but couldn't quite focus on the simple instructions. She did have the right size needles and thought she'd just make a sample swatch, instead of jumping right in, the way she usually did. Swatching this time was the right thing to do, a moral imperative. It was different when you worked on a group project, she thought. She didn't want to throw the whole thing off on her first square.

"So you're not going into Boston tomorrow with Jamie, I gather," Maggie said to Gloria.

"He asked me to come, but I don't want to butt in. Even if I promise myself to keep my mouth shut, sooner or later, I just lose it, and I butt in. This is his deal. He's doing great so far, and I think it's important for him to reel this in on his own."

"That's very wise of you. You probably would be tempted to say something, or give advice, if you were there." Maggie had known her the longest, and if anyone was able to honestly acknowledge Gloria's assertive side, Maggie would be the one.

"I'm just praying it works out. On any terms at all. He's trying to stay low-key, but I know he'll be crushed if this guy has just been stringing him along." Gloria sighed. "I know you haven't seen his work, but trust me, he's really good. He deserves a break. He just hasn't had time to focus. Until we got married, I mean. He had to take all these odd jobs to make ends meet. Hard, menial jobs that tired him out and depressed him. When we met he was tending bar at some beach resort, for goodness sakes. It's very difficult for people with artistic talent. Our society doesn't reward that effort. You have to be lucky. And persistent . . . and have some help. At least at the start."

"That's very true. There are a lot of very talented people out there who never make it." Lucy was thinking of many friends who she knew from college.

"That's right. They get worn-out and give up. Jamie was nearly at that stage when we got together. I told him when we got married he had to focus on his work, give it his best shot, and I would support him."

Lucy glanced at Maggie. She appeared to already know this story. Lucy had never heard it before, though, and guessed the information was also new to her other friends.

"That was very generous of you," Dana said. "Very . . . loving."

"I love him something awful," Gloria stated flatly. "But it's not even about that. I believe in him. It would be a pity to see his talent go to waste. He's not used to that kind of unconditional encouragement. It's taken him a while to feel comfortable with it. He didn't have any growing up. A terrible family life, to tell you the truth." She glanced over her shoulder, at the house. Lucy saw a light glowing in a window on the upper floor but the window was closed tight.

"He's up there, but he can't hear me. I don't think he would want me to tell you this," she said quietly, as if wondering if she should. She paused a moment, then finally continued. "His father left the family when he was just a baby, he doesn't even remember him," Gloria confided, lowering her voice to nearly a whisper. "His mother was overwhelmed. She drank herself sick and neglected him. So he was sent to live with relatives, moved around. Sent to foster homes. Got in some trouble . . . yes." She nodded her head and sighed. "Could you blame him? When he was a teenager, he just took off on his own and has barely spoken to his family since. No one ever gave him a thing. Not love or attention. Not even the women he's been involved with. Needy, needy head cases. One after the next. No one has ever *really* loved him, or taken care of him. Except for me," she added. Gloria's voice held a sharp, determined edge.

An angry edge, Lucy noticed. Angry at all the people in Jamie's past who had neglected him. They'd better stay out of sight, if they knew what was good for them, Lucy realized. They didn't want to meet up with Gloria.

"It's amazing he turned out with such a sweet personality, after going through all that." Suzanne's tone was sympathetic.

"Yes, it is," Gloria agreed. "But he's just built that way. He's a special person."

"Every child deserves a loving home. Kids are so defenseless," Dana said. "It's just not fair what some children have to go through."

"Not fair at all. But you know what?" Gloria looked up from her knitting, glancing at each of them. "When I told him, 'Jamie, this is your chance. I want you to just go and paint,' he wouldn't do it. He gave me an argument. Said he didn't feel it was right and what would people say, and so on and so forth." Gloria laughed, skillfully slipping a double stitch onto a long wooden needle. "As if I ever cared what people said about me. But it was sweet of him," she noted. "He didn't want to take advantage. He finally said we would give it a year and see if he'd made any progress. If not, he might go back to school and get some sort of degree. Cooking, maybe. That's his second love. But I know that's not where his heart is. I hope it doesn't come to that."

Neither did Lucy. Jamie loved to cook, but she didn't think he was cut out for commercial kitchens. He did have a great personality and good social skills. He'd probably do very well in some sort of sales job, Lucy thought. If the painting didn't work out, that is.

"How long has it been, Gloria, since he began painting full-time?" Dana asked curiously.

"Let's see . . . we were married in December. Christmas Eve, down in the Keys, very romantic. So it's almost six months. So far, so good."

"Yes, very good," Maggie agreed. "If it doesn't work out at this gallery—I mean, it seems like it will, but you never know—it sounds like he'll have other opportunities."

"I've tried to tell him that, too. But I've got my fingers crossed. I hate to see him disappointed. He gets so blue and down on himself. Then he doesn't want to touch a paintbrush for weeks and starts questioning everything. Oh, God. Sometimes I really forget how young he is." Gloria lifted her head and gave a little laugh. "If there's one thing I've learned, don't waste time with a lot of self-doubt and existential bellyaching. It's useless. When disaster strikes, just pick up your skirts and plow on, ladies. That's my motto. That's what gets the job done."

"When disaster strikes, just keep knitting. That's my motto," Maggie countered, making her friends laugh.

It was true. Whenever Maggie faced one of life's lashing storms, she'd just hunkered down and knit her way right through it.

"Same philosophy." Gloria waved her hand; the rings on her slim fingers twinkled in the dark like fireflies. "You have to stay focused and productive. Not give in to that poor-little-me mind-set. There are always going to be problems in life. You're always going to hit a few speed bumps and potholes. When you least expect it, too. That's one good thing about getting older. These little setbacks don't throw you as much as they used to."

Gloria seemed to be talking about something entirely different now than Jamie's art show, or even their marriage, Lucy thought. Gloria sighed and gazed down at her knitting. Lucy had a feeling she was deep in thought about some unexpected speed bumps she'd either recently hit, or spotted on the horizon.

Then Gloria suddenly looked up, realizing she'd been distracted.

"Just between us," she confided in a softer voice, "my dearest love will have a show in Boston before the year is out, if I have to buy the gallery and hang every one of those darn paintings myself."

Everyone laughed at her declaration. But Lucy wasn't sure that their hostess was actually joking.

Chapter Two

*L*ucy opened her eyes Friday morning to find herself nose to nose with her dog, a mostly golden retriever mix named Tink.

Tink was not allowed on the bed, but never tired of negotiating that question. As long as she managed to keep her back paws on the floor—sometimes, only one paw . . . or one doggy toenail—Lucy didn't have the heart to scold her.

Her front half was now up on the mattress, her muzzle flat on the quilt, slowly inching up to the pillow. As Lucy stared into her eyes, Tink's tail wagged behind like the propeller on a single-engine airplane, warming up a runway.

"Oh geez . . ." Lucy sighed and rolled over. Tink interpreted that response as "come on up!" and landed squarely in the middle of Lucy's chest, pinning her to the mattress. Then she began methodically licking off any remnants of face cream Lucy had applied the night before.

"Okay. I'm getting up. See? Just let me out of the bed, dog."

The sixty-pound hound finally released her and Lucy sat upright. She grabbed around the tangled bed linen for her robe, while Tink picked up a slipper in her mouth and dashed downstairs.

I'm dating a vet. Shouldn't this dog be better trained by now? Lucy pondered the question as she stumbled down the stairs in one slipper.

While the dog was definitely more work than she'd expected, Tink had made her solitary life more interesting and made the cottage she lived in feel more like home. Lucy and her sister, Ellen, had spent summers in the cottage with their aunt Laura all through their childhood. When their aunt had died a little over a year ago, she'd left the place to her two nieces.

Married with two children, Ellen would be a perfect candidate for *Real Housewives of Concord, Massachusetts*, if such a show was ever aired. Plum Harbor was not her style anymore and Ellen was happy to have Lucy in the house, instead of some unknown renters.

Ellen and her husband, Scott, preferred the Vineyard or the Cape for summer weekends with their family, though Plum Harbor was a coastal village with beautiful beaches, boating, and a quaint Main Street that looked like a set from a Frank Capra movie. Neither a suburb nor a truly rural place anymore, Plum Harbor was something in between, an exburb, Lucy had heard it called. Either way, it suited her fine. So far, at least.

At the time of her aunt's death, Lucy was still reeling from her divorce and had just quit her job at a big advertising agency to start her own graphic design business. She'd decided to move out to Plum Harbor for the summer for some peace and quiet and a change of scene. And had ended up staying long past Labor Day. She still sometimes felt like a visitor here, but now that nearly a year had passed, the move did seem to be a permanent one.

Down in the kitchen, as Lucy put together a pot of coffee, she felt a dull headache coming on. Her stomach felt queasy and her mouth was as dry as chalk.

Stomach virus?

Then she remembered . . . Gloria's Brazilian cocktail. She should have known she'd regret it.

She managed to gulp down a mug of black coffee, then made her way upstairs and into the shower. She dressed in shorts, a T-shirt, and sneakers and returned to the kitchen. Tink danced around the slippery floor, waving a shoe in her mouth—universal canine sign language for "I need to relieve myself. Now." Lucy finally clipped a leash on her collar and they launched into the neighborhood.

The dog had been shortchanged on her walk the night before, when Lucy got home late from Gloria's. A long walk into town would do them both good, Lucy thought, as long as there was another huge cup of coffee and some pain relievers waiting on the other end. And she knew just where she might find some at this early hour, too.

Starting off from her cottage, the streets to the village all led downhill, which Lucy truly appreciated this morning. She hung onto Tink's leash and let gravity do the rest as the dog pulled her along a winding route that led to the harbor and green.

Instead of walking all the way to the harbor this morning, as they usually did, Lucy steered Tink on a shortcut to Main Street and emerged on a corner about two blocks from

Maggie's store. It was only half past eight, but Lucy thought Maggie might be there by now. She often came in early to straighten the stock and get organized for her day. And she always put up a big pot of really good coffee, first thing.

As Lucy drew closer to the Black Sheep, she spotted Maggie's green Subaru parked on the street in front. Maggie was in, no question. Even Tink seemed to know where they were headed and picked up her pace for the final stretch.

When Maggie was looking to open the Black Sheep knitting shop, she had found the perfect spot, the first floor of a freestanding Victorian building in the middle of the town's main thoroughfare. The brick path that led from the sidewalk was bordered by flower beds, where Maggie had planted a lush array—clumps of yellow daylilies, dark pink snapdragons, and inky blue petunias.

There were more blooming plants along the front of the building—roses, hydrangea, peonies, and others that would blossom as the summer drew on. Window boxes hung from the porch railings, filled with more colorful flowers and long trailing vines.

The shop couldn't have looked more inviting and did not disappoint in the least once you went inside, the array of flowers outside matching the colorful displays of all types of yarn.

Lucy led Tink up the porch and tied her leash to a post on the porch railing in a spot where the dog would be visible through the big bay window at the front of the shop. Lucy took a bottle of water and a portable dog dish out of her canvas bag and gave Tink a drink. Then Lucy dropped Tink's favorite Nyla bone nearby, in case her little pal got bored and decided to taste test some of Maggie's wicker furniture. Tink lapped the water noisily, then lay down with a deep sigh. She was used to their routine by now.

"Be a good girl. I won't be long," Lucy promised.

The door was open and Lucy walked in. The shop covered several small rooms and knitting nooks, a love seat and comfortable chairs to the left of the entrance. Armoires and baskets brimming with yarns stood near the counter in the center of the store and a big work table, used for classes and demonstrations, filled most of the back room. A cabinet full of buttons and other needful knitting items stood against the rear wall. Lucy took in the familiar surroundings with a glance. Maggie, however, was nowhere in sight.

"Anybody home?" Lucy called out.

"I'm back here, making coffee," Maggie called from the storeroom. "Would you like some?"

The storeroom had been a kitchen at one time and still had the basic equipment, which Maggie frequently put to use.

"Yes, please. The largest cup you have. With a bottle of Advil, on the side."

"Sounds like you have a hangover," Maggie diagnosed.

"You guessed it."

"Eat a banana. That always helps," a third voice advised.

Lucy turned to see who had come in behind her at this hour. It was Edie Steiber, her big body covered in a loose-fitting cotton dress, a circa-1960s flower-power print. Large earrings shaped like daisies and bright bangle bracelets—definitely thrift store or garage sale finds—provided the perfect accessories. Lucy couldn't help thinking that dear Edie looked like a flowered minivan . . . but the older woman did have her own fashion sense, you had to grant her that. A yellow cardigan, embellished with more daisies, was slung over her shoulders, her knitting bag firmly clamped under one thick soft arm.

Edie had obviously overheard their shouted conversation out on the porch. "Bananas help a lot of things—warts, muscle cramps . . . constipation—"

"I'll have to remember that," Lucy said quickly, cutting off Edie's list of ailments.

Edie owned the Schooner, a diner on Main Street that was practically a historic landmark, certainly the favorite hangout of everyone Lucy knew in town. Aside from Maggie's knitting shop.

She wondered why Edie wasn't in her usual post at this hour, behind the cafe's long Formica counter, watching over the cash register and the waitstaff with the vigilance of the three-headed dog at the gates of hell. Then again, she'd opened at the crack of dawn, so it was practically lunchtime on her clock, and Edie often went up the street to the Black Sheep when she had an emergency with a project . . . or a particularly juicy bit of gossip to share.

Lucy wondered which of these compelling reasons had brought her by this morning.

"Hello, Edie . . . I didn't know you were here." Maggie emerged from the back room with the coffeepot, creamer, sugar, and a few mugs on a tray, which she set down carefully on the big farm table at the back of the shop.

"Lucy has a big head. I told her to eat a banana."

"I don't have any bananas in the back. I did find some headache pills."

"Thanks, I think I will have a few." Lucy picked up a mug of coffee and the little white bottle.

"I've heard the best cure for a hangover is drinking lots of water," Maggie offered. "Gloria's exotic elixor?"

"You guessed it." Lucy shook two red pills into her palm and then downed them with a gulp of coffee. "You were smart to avoid that potion."

"Yes, I was, wasn't I? But I've know Gloria a lot longer." Maggie cast Lucy a sympathetic smile, then turned to Edie. "We were at Gloria Sterling's house last night. She invited the knitting group for dinner. It was lots of fun."

Edie didn't seem impressed, Lucy noticed. She sat down at the table with a low grunting sound and helped herself to a mug of coffee, which she fixed with a long pour of milk and two spoons of sugar.

"Is she still married to that guy she picked up in Florida? Most people bring back a box of oranges."

Maggie looked amused by the question. "Yes, it's still going strong. Almost six months now, I think."

"She ought to enjoy herself while she can. I have food in my walk-in that's going to last longer than that hookup."

Lucy wasn't sure if this advice was a comment on the durability of Gloria's marriage, or the questionable food handling practices at the Schooner.

"They seem very happy together," Lucy said, feeling that Edie was being unfair.

"Of course they're happy. She's a plain fool with truckloads of money and he's a boy toy who likes the good life. It's a perfect match, honey," Edie argued with her. "He'll take her for whatever he can get and when he's tired of being tied down to some Botoxed-up old bag—who people keep mistaking for his mother—he'll dump her for someone his own age."

"Or they'll stay together and prove you wrong?" Maggie offered.

"Right. When pigs whistle. Hey, I'll bet you fifty bucks that guy has his Louis Vuitton packed within a year," Edie insisted.

"Okay, you're on, my friend." Maggie offered Edie her hand. Edie took it and shook, but still didn't look satisfied.

"Did she make him sign a prenup?" Edie asked bluntly.

Lucy noticed Maggie hesitate before answering. "I really don't know."

"Oh . . . don't give me that. You know. That means she didn't, I'll bet," Edie said. "I'm not the type who wishes other people ill. But what goes around comes around and that Gloria Sterling has plenty coming around to her. That guy is going to take her for every penny and she'll get what she deserves."

Edie was never one to mince words or edit her opinion, but it did seem that the mere mention of Gloria had struck a sensitive nerve.

"Well . . . let's hope not," Lucy said, gamely speaking up again in Gloria's defense. She liked Gloria, for all her flash and over-the-top style. She liked Jamie, too. She wished that they proved everyone wrong—everyone who held the same opinion of their marriage as Edie—and stayed together forever.

"You don't understand," Edie said, turning to Lucy. "You're new around here. Maggie knows what I'm talking about," Edie said, turning back to Maggie.

"Well . . . I'm not exactly sure, Edie. What *are* you talking about?" Maggie challenged her.

"The Queen of Mean, that's what. When she was married to George Thurman, they terrorized this town. 'Thurman-ized' us, we used to say. She made the Wicked Witch of the West look like Christie Brinkley. I'm going back about twenty years now, I guess. It was the early nineties, a big recession. They bought up property like they were playing Monopoly. Raised the rents, threw people out. Hardworking people who had been in business for ten, twenty years in the same spot. Then suddenly, they couldn't afford the new jacked-up leases."

"I didn't know that," Lucy said honestly. She glanced at Maggie, wondering how much of this tale was fact and how much was Edie's emotion-fueled hyperbole.

"Oh . . . well . . . I guess I've heard something about that, but I was still teaching back then," Maggie reminded her. "I was pretty much out of that loop. I only opened this shop a few years ago. And I only got to know Gloria after George died," she added.

"Okay, I see your point," Edie replied evenly. She added another spoonful of sugar to her coffee and stirred slowly. "You weren't on the front line, that is true. But it wasn't pretty, believe me. The Thurmans were heartless. I was lucky. My father bought the Schooner when he had the chance, so I didn't have to worry. But there are some people in this town who won't even say her name out loud. You think I wish her ill? I really don't. I'm just observing the way the world works. Over time. Sooner or later, what you put out comes back to you. Washes back up in the tide. It's just the way it is," Edie concluded with a shrug.

She sat back and sipped her coffee, a flower-covered Buddha, schooling the unenlightened.

She had spewed a lot of venom, even for Edie, but she did have a point, Lucy thought. It did seem true that a person's deeds, good or ill, did come back to them. If you lived long enough to see it.

But while Lucy didn't know Gloria very well, or for very long, it was hard to believe that Gloria had been so hard-hearted and unfeeling in business matters. She was smart and tough. Nobody's fool, that was sure. But cold and heartless?

Hard to buy it, Lucy thought knowing Gloria even as briefly as she did.

Gloria was certainly the perfect magnet for envy from many who wished that they were riding around town in a white Mercedes, had a closet full of designer clothes, size two, and piles of jewelry. And lived in a big expensive house in the Landing with a handsome younger man, waiting there with a home-cooked dinner after a busy day in the office.

Heck, when she thought of it that way, even Lucy felt jealous of Gloria.

"What about George Thurman?" Maggie said finally. "He'd been wheeling and dealing long before he met Gloria. I'm sure he was the one pulling the strings in those days. I don't think she really had much to do with those evictions and all of that. I think it was all George," Maggie said in her friend's defense.

Edie made a snorting sound. "Think what you like, it's a free country. I know she's your friend. It might have been all George back then, but it's all Gloria since she buried him. She certainly learned her lessons well, I'll say that for her."

Maggie didn't answer. "How's that headache, Lucy?" she asked instead.

It had actually gotten worse, with all the arguing, but Lucy didn't want to make a big thing about it. "Coming along," she told Maggie. "That's really nice yarn," she added, trying to change the subject.

She picked up a ball of fine, multicolored ribbon yarn that was sitting in a basket on the table and examined a strand. "Is it new?"

"Just came in yesterday. I'm going to use it for a class this morning," Maggie told them.

"Very pretty," Edie agreed. "That would make a nice baby

blanket. Which reminds me why I came in here in the first place. I need some more yarn for that blanket I'm working on. My niece Miranda, down in Framingham who got married last summer? Well, she's expecting," Edie explained. "First couple I've heard of in thirty years that doesn't want to know the baby's sex. We have to be surprised. But what's the point now? I don't get it." Edie shook her head. "Maggie found some self-striping yarn for me—powder blue, pink, and yellow. That about covers it, right?"

"Absolutely," Lucy agreed, though she wondered what the yellow stripes stood for. Undecided?

"Whoops, looks like someone is spying on us . . ." Lucy followed Edie's glance to the bay window at the front of the shop. Tink was staring inside, her paws up on the window ledge, her nose pressed to the glass.

But Lucy quickly determined the dog was not pining for her negligent owner. She was stalking the window display. Maggie had found some black sheep stuffed animals in the toy store down the street and had set three in the window on some fake grass, among piles of yarn and knitting equipment. A few attractive projects hung from a clothesline strung across the top.

Tink stared at the sheep with the same concentration she focused on squirrels she spotted out in the garden. Lucy could practically see her hot breath fogging the windowpane.

"She's so cute, Lucy. You can bring her in. I don't mind, as long as there are no customers here," Maggie said.

"You don't mind because she's never been in here," Lucy reminded her. "Believe me, it wouldn't be pretty." Lucy finished her coffee and stood. "I have to get home and start working anyway."

"I have to run, too." Edie slowly lifted her bulky body. The little chair she'd been sitting on creaked with relief. She came unsteadily to her feet, then balanced on her large, white walking shoes that looked as soft as marshmallows.

"Let me find that yarn you need, Edie." Maggie stood up too and walked up to the front of the shop. "So long, Lucy," Maggie added. "Hope your headache goes away quickly."

"Think I'll go home and try a banana."

"Good idea. It couldn't hurt," Edie advised as Lucy slipped out the door.

Lucy walked home with Tink, choosing the quickest route. As the dog tugged her along tree-lined streets, she couldn't help thinking about Gloria. Edie's diatribe had shown their new friend in a completely new light. Not a very flattering one, either.

Lucy had to wonder if Gloria's reputation as the Queen of Mean was really deserved. Or was it guilt by association, her husband George Thurman being the real evil genius?

George had been dead now for fifteen years Lucy knew, and the title still clung. Was it simply because Gloria was a woman and not rewarded for playing hardball in the business world? These days, women were in a no-win situation, expected to succeed, to be tough and shrewd . . . but still be "nice." It seemed to Lucy that Gloria was subject to this ambiguous measure.

She was also sure that Gloria had heard all the claims and grudges against her and didn't give a flying fig what Edie Steiber, or anyone else in town thought of her. Which probably annoyed that faction even more.

Whatever else you wanted to say about Gloria, she was her own person. Lucy definitely admired her for that.

When Suzanne finally reached her office at Premier Properties—after driving her kids to school, dropping off the dry cleaning, swooping through the drive-thru bank window, and leaving the dog off at the groomers—she wondered if she should call Gloria first thing, to follow up on the lead from last night. Or did that seem too . . . desperate?

She carefully considered the question and took a long sip of the Cranberry Detox Fat Flush Juice drink she'd brought from home. The first installment of about ten gallons of pale pink liquid she was supposed to absorb today, the only nutrient of her new diet.

She heard Gloria's voice on her message machine and stopped midsip.

"Hi, Suzanne, it's me, Gloria. I'm just calling about the house. I'd like you to stop over so I can give you the grand tour and we can talk about an offering price and all that. Let me know when you are available. My schedule is pretty open."

Suzanne fumbled for the phone receiver, nearly dropping the plastic bottle in her lap. She found the number and quickly hit the redial button. Gloria picked up on the third ring. Suzanne greeted her cheerfully.

"Hi, Gloria, it's Suzanne. I just got in the office and I found your message. I was just about to call you."

"Good, we're on the same wavelength. That's what you want in a real estate person," Gloria replied smoothly. "I'm just sending Jamie off," she reported. Then in a whisper added, "I swear, you'd think he was eight years old, going off to sleepaway camp for the first time. It's cute, but I have a life, know what I mean? Oh . . . just a sec. He's calling me again about something. What is it, hon?" Suzanne heard Gloria shout. "I left them out for you, right by the bed."

Then she said to Suzanne, "I'm sorry. Can you hold on a minute?"

"Sure. No problem."

I'll hang on until Christmas, Suzanne nearly told her, if it means getting your business, Gloria.

Gloria often joked about Jamie needing attention and help from her, like a little boy, but Suzanne thought she secretly enjoyed mothering him. Gloria never had children of her own, Suzanne knew. Though she'd never said too much about it to the knitting group, Suzanne sensed Gloria felt a real lack in her life, having missed out on that experience.

"I'm back. I think he's finally packed. I'm just going to ignore him if he calls me again." She took a deep breath. "Now, where were we?"

"Figuring out a time when I can come by to look at the house and talk about the market?" Suzanne reminded her.

"Oh, yes. Right. I'm working from home today. What's your schedule like?"

Totally open for Gloria, was the truth of the matter.

Not wanting to sound too eager and as if she didn't have any other hot deals going, Suzanne delayed with a little humming sound, as if she was checking her very packed schedule, trying to fit Gloria in.

"Hmm. Let me take a look . . . okay, I see something. How about . . . eleven? Does that work for you?"

She did need to answer her e-mails and call up a long list of open house walk-ins. Suzanne was pretty sure she wouldn't have a nibble there. The owners of the house in question—seniors, trying to downsize—thought they were selling the Taj Mahal. The three-bedroom bungalow was anything but, crowded with knickknacks, overstuffed furniture, and about

a thousand pictures of grandchildren. The kitchen and bath-
rooms were a total disaster and the entire place smelled like
they used meat loaf-scented air freshener.

Most of the phone numbers jotted on the open house
sign-in sheet would be fake, of course. So the task would not
take very long at all.

"Eleven would be fine," Gloria said.

"I'll pull up some recent sales in your area, so we have
some comps to look at. And I have a few very nice listings on
the water you might be interested in looking at, too. We can
get a photo tour of most of those on my laptop."

"Sounds terrific, Suzanne. I think we're going to have a
great time doing business together."

"Looking forward to it." Suzanne assured her. They said
good-bye and she hung up the phone.

This could be good. This could be very good. Good for the
twins, who already needed to start with the orthodontist, and
the final payment due on the fancy drama and dance camp
that her daughter, Natalie, was headed for in August.

The market had been absolutely dead these last few
months. It had gotten so bad, Suzanne had even considered
jumping ship and trying something new, though she wasn't
sure what. Her husband Kevin's construction business wasn't
nearly as busy as it had been the last few years and they relied
on her income to make ends meet.

The ends weren't meeting so well lately, as much as Suzanne tugged and stretched, like trying to fit herself into some
beloved, prepregnancy pair of jeans.

Then out of the clear blue, Gloria comes along and drops
this Godiva gift basket of sales commissions right in her lap.

All Suzanne could say was, "Bless that woman. Bless every

highlighted hair on her head and every synthetic, inserted part of her."

Suzanne's appointment with Gloria took over two hours, longer than she'd expected. But the grand tour of the house—she had only peeked at the interior the night before on a trip to the bathroom—was even better than she'd imagined, with huge rooms and stylish decorating that complemented the architectural features perfectly. This place was going to show like a room set in *Better Homes Than You'll Ever Live In*.

The meeting wore on and they hit their stride, sipping iced tea poolside, with Gloria positioned on her favorite chaise, busily working on her knitting. Suzanne had left her knitting bag in the car. She never brought it to a meeting like this and even though Gloria encouraged her to fetch it, she was content to focus on business.

Good thing, too. Because just as Suzanne thought they had wrapped up the conversation, discussing the sale of Gloria's house and her purchase of new property, the Godiva gift basket of commissions got even bigger.

"Does your office handle commercial property, Suzanne?"

"Yes, we do. Absolutely. We do a lot of that, in fact."

Ca-ching! Suzanne hoped the dollar signs weren't showing too boldly in her wide, surprised eyes. She slipped on her sunglasses just in case.

"I have a few properties in town I'd like to put on the market. There's a condo in the Windward Shores development, you know, near the golf course?"

Gloria turned her project to the other side and examined her work. The fine lace shawl was getting longer, covering her lap and slim, tan legs, down to her knees.

"Know it well." Suzanne nodded.

A condo in Windward Shores? Sweet . . . there was always demand for that development, even in a down market.

"It's a nice unit, on an upper floor with a great view. I've been renting for a few years, but it's so much work. Tenants moving in and out. And if they're troublemakers, I just don't have the time to deal with all the headaches and phone calls from the condo board. Now that I'm married, I can't just work my life away, twenty-four/seven. There has to be time for Jamie."

"Absolutely," Suzanne agreed sympathetically. "Once your married, it's a whole different ball game."

Though she was not quite in the same ballpark where Suzanne played, Suzanne could see how Gloria's workaholic tendencies might get the best of her. If she didn't have Jamie, what was there besides work to distract her? No children. No family nearby. No intense hobbies, besides knitting, not that Suzanne had ever heard about. She had an active social life, plenty of friends and invitations. But a lot of that was work related, as well.

"There's also a building in town. Two stores on the bottom and a floor above with three apartments." Gloria mentioned the street address. "The same story, too many headaches. Tenants driving me crazy. I hired a management company to deal with it, then *they* were calling me night and day. I know it's a slow market, but there are still people out there with money, looking for good, sound investments. Don't you think?"

"Plenty of them," Suzanne agreed. There had to be. Suzanne was determined to find those people, too, if she had to track them down with bloodhounds and high-tech surveillance equipment.

"That's good to hear," Gloria said with another warm, approving smile.

Be still, my greedy little heart! Suzanne could not imagine what she'd done to deserve this bounty of good fortune. All in one morning?

"I think we're going to do a lot of business together, Suzanne." Gloria smiled at her.

"Bring it on." Suzanne laughed. She was trying not to sound too eager. But it was a challenge.

Chapter Three

Suzanne climbed back into her family-size SUV a short time later, a victory prize tucked into her slim leather case—the signed contract for exclusive sales representation on Gloria's house. And Gloria's promise to work with Suzanne on finding a new home for herself and Jamie was another reason to leave Sugar Maple Way with a smile.

Gloria had been interested in at least two of the properties Suzanne had showed her, via virtual tours, and wanted to see them right away. Meanwhile, Suzanne had clients on her list that had been looking for a new house in The Landing for a long time and were likely possibilities as buyers. She was going to make calls and set up appointments as soon as she returned to her office.

And the icing on the cake was the condo and commercial building that Gloria wanted to sell. Suzanne was not experienced with commercial property and would need some help on the building, but she was happy to share that commission, which would be a mother lode if it ever came through.

Not "if." *When*, she reminded herself.

It's going to happen. It is going to happen for me, Suzanne chanted to herself, remembering her sales motivation CDs.

All in all, it was shaping up to be a good day, a good way to wind up an otherwise totally flat-ass, boring week.

Suzanne felt so good as she cruised back to town, she decided to ditch her detox juice fast—which she had kept now for a full . . . five hours?—and celebrate with a BLT. She was allowed a break for lunch and she decided to bring her sandwich over to Maggie's shop so she could share her good news.

She picked up a tasty sandwich at her favorite deli, then drove up to the knitting shop. Perfect timing, too, she realized. As she parked near the Black Sheep, she spotted Dana, sitting in a wicker chair on the porch, eating lunch and working on her argyle vest.

Phoebe was also outside and waved as Suzanne walked up the flower-edged path. Maggie's helper was tending to the window boxes with a watering can, sprinkling most of the water on her long Indian-print cotton skirt and sandal-covered feet. Probably a welcome relief on such a hot day, Suzanne thought.

With her long dark hair bunched up in a ponytail, Phoebe's magenta streak was pulled taught, glinting in the sunlight and reminding Suzanne of a pink zebra stripe.

"Hey Suzanne," Phoebe greeted her. "I hear you guys really partied last night at Gloria's. Sorry I missed it."

"We missed you, too, Phoebe," Suzanne said sincerely. "But it wasn't that wild. We weren't dancing on the tables or anything."

"That's not what I heard. Maybe you don't remember that clearly? Dana says she has pictures . . . for a price."

Suzanne finally realized Phoebe was teasing. "That's

supposed to scare me? You should see the ones my kids take. The twins sneak up with their camera phones while I'm wrestling with the trash bag, or crawling around, looking for stuff under the beds. Or sometimes they catch me asleep on the couch and get right up under my nose and . . ."

Suzanne heard Dana laughing. Phoebe held her hands up. "Too much information."

"No problem," Suzanne replied with exaggerated charm.

Phoebe drifted to the far side of the porch with the watering can and Suzanne took a seat near Dana. "Nice job. I like your technique."

"Don't mess with me. I'm invincible today. I'm Super Real Estate Woman, able to leap gated communities in a single bound."

Dana seemed impressed. "Any particular reason for this power surge? Or is it just a hormonal swing?"

Suzanne pulled out her BLT, set it squarely on the wicker side table, and inhaled its enticing aroma before peeling back the paper wrapping.

"I just got back from Gloria's. She gave me an exclusive on her house, and I'm making appointments to show her two properties on the water this weekend."

"Good work." Dana put down her knitting. Her face lit up with a smile.

"Wait, there's more. I was just about to wrap up the visit when she asked if our firm handles commercial property. She has a building in town she wants to sell and there's a condo at Windward Shores that she wants to unload, too."

Dana looked really surprised now. "Sounds like she's really downsizing. That wasn't just talk last night, was it?"

Suzanne shook her head and took a bite. She relished the

taste of the cold lettuce and tomato against the warm toast and bacon, all mingling with the creamy mayo. Dear Goddess of Carbs, Fat Grams, and Empty Calories, please forgive me for my sins, she prayed silently.

After a big swallow, she said, "No, it wasn't just talk. She called first thing in the morning to get together and put her house on the market. She signed the sales contract on the dotted line. Once she makes up her mind, that woman doesn't waste time."

"She always seems very decisive to me," Dana agreed. "She's very social and outgoing, but has a very analytical mind. Processes information quickly, I've noticed."

"She's a sharp cookie," Suzanne translated from shrink-speak.

"Exactly." Dana smiled at her. She put her salad aside to pick up her knitting again. She hadn't started her quilt squares yet, Suzanne noticed, but the vest was coming along nicely.

Dana planned to give Jack the vest for Father's Day, which was a little more than two weeks away. But she'd have it done in time, Suzanne was sure. She knit like a plow horse. Slow but steady.

Dana tied a marker at the end of a row. "Why is she selling all this property now? It isn't very good timing."

"She owns a lot more than those places, believe me. She says she just doesn't have the time to spend managing the rental side, or to deal with the managing agents and the condo board. Now that she's married again, she has to change her workaholic ways. She wants more time for Jamie."

"Oh . . . I see." Dana nodded, examining her stitches, which were enviably even and clung to the needle with just the right tension. Suzanne also noticed that Dana did not sound convinced by this explanation. A certain note in her "I see" reply gave her away.

"I hope you close all those deals, Suzanne. That would be a real estate agent's equivalent to winning the lottery, wouldn't it?"

"As close as I'll ever get." Suzanne finished the last bite of her sandwich, then licked a bacon crumb off her fingertip.

Several women strolled out of the shop at once, chatting as they walked down the porch steps. It seemed that Maggie's class had ended. Suzanne thought to go inside and say hello, then noticed Maggie in the doorway, coming out to visit them.

"I thought I spotted you two. Did I miss the lunch break?"

"Just about." Dana glanced at her watch. "I can hang out a little longer. Suzanne has big news. She's celebrating with a BLT."

"Didn't you just start that Cranberry Flush Fast thing this morning? Not that I think you need a diet," Maggie added.

"Of course I do. But some diets were made to be broken. What can I say. Besides, I had to celebrate."

"Suzanne is Super Real Estate Saleswoman today. You just don't recognize her without the cape," Dana explained.

"Those positive-thinking CDs kicking in?"

"Must be." Suzanne shrugged and grinned. "Gloria Sterling gave me an exclusive on her house and she wants me to find her a new one—"

"Oh right. You settled it already? Good work," Maggie cut in.

"And she has two other properties in town she asked me to handle. One is that big commercial building on Main Street with two stores in the bottom and apartments above."

"Wow, you did sweep the table this morning," Maggie said. "That should keep you busy for the rest of the summer."

"It will definitely keep me out of trouble. Especially with the twins' orthodontist."

"Which building on Main Street?" Maggie asked.

Suzanne gave the number address. "The one with the new dress shop on the street level."

"I'm glad it's not my building. I'd hate to have the rent on my office raised right now," Dana said honestly.

"It would be tough," Maggie agreed.

Suzanne's BlackBerry buzzed and she quickly checked it. "Duty calls, gang." She gathered up her trash and handbag. "I've got to get back to the office. I have a big afternoon of gloating ahead, and making my coworkers crazy jealous."

"All in a day's work for a superhero." Dana rose, too, and packed up her knitting.

"What can I say? It's a tough job, but somebody has to do it." Suzanne grinned at her friends as she gave them all a wave good-bye and practically floated off the porch.

It had been a good day. A very good day. With any luck, the first of many that were on the way.

Lucy worked steadily through the afternoon, getting up from her computer only once or twice for a cup of tea, more headache pills, and to let Tink out for a backyard break. She did need to check her e-mails from time to time, just to keep her sanity. She quickly opened one from Suzanne that arrived around 4:00. Suzanne ecstatically reported she had snagged Gloria as a client and was going to do about ten deals for her at once.

Lucy was happy for her. Suzanne was working hard but the real estate market in town had been a dead zone lately. Suzanne could definitely use this windfall of commissions.

Lucy wrote a quick note back, cheering her on, and then

checked a few more messages from her clients. The editor of her current project was checking in before the weekend and Lucy was happy to report that the project was coming along on schedule. For once.

Lucy knew she wasn't the greatest with keeping to a deadline. Life was always getting in the way, it seemed, and everything took longer than she expected. But somehow, she got the jobs done within reason.

She had almost finished inputting final changes on a children's book project, a nonfiction title in a series about nature topics.

It was nearly 5:00 before she noticed. Time to shut down the computer and get ready to meet her boyfriend, Matt, in town for dinner. When Lucy finally got up from her desk chair, her back and neck felt stiff and she did a little yoga stretch, looking forward to a long hot shower to get the rest of the kinks out.

Lucy wasn't a real clock-watcher and worked as many hours in the day as she needed to in order to deliver projects on time. Or, *almost* on time. Sometimes she worked late into the night if she had a particularly tight deadline. Being single, she could do that without worrying about getting up early the next day to make breakfasts or bagged lunches, take children to school, or any other family responsibilities.

She did want to marry again and have children, but it was too soon after her divorce to worry about that, wasn't it? She needed to go slowly this time. She couldn't let herself feel pressured by some sort of self-imposed timetable.

Her sister was no great help on the subject. Ellen, who had popped out babies in her twenties—as if the schedule was noted in her Day Timer—often hinted that Lucy's eggs were getting stale, approaching the expiration date stamped . . . somewhere. And she had to start thinking about these things.

"Can we have a conversation that doesn't include my ovaries?" Lucy had once asked her. That shut Ellen up on the topic . . . for a while.

Since Lucy had started seeing Matt, back in March, Ellen had finally stopped engineering fix-ups with her husband's single coworkers and golf buddies, possibly the dullest group of men on the eastern seaboard.

Matt was different. Lucy had known that from just about the first time they'd met, when she'd brought Tink in with a mysterious stomach ailment. One thing had led to another. The hideous specimen Matt removed from Tink's stomach had turned out to be a major clue in the murder of Amanda Goran. Matt had turned out to be just as kind, intelligent, and funny as she'd imagined from that first meeting. He laughed at her jokes, even when she wasn't trying to be funny. What else could you ask for?

You could ask for a guy who was actually, completely, legally free from his first marriage? a little niggling voice reminded her.

Well . . . let's not get picky, Lucy thought as she quickly dressed.

The delay was all on his wife's side, to hear him tell it. She just wouldn't make it easy for him. Especially now, that he'd started seeing Lucy.

She'd heard stories, of course, of women who got involved with almost divorced men who eventually returned to their wives. Or women who did the same thing, for that matter. She didn't want to think she was wasting her time in this relationship . . . or falling for someone who wouldn't stick around.

The hot humid weather had made her long dirty blonde hair a wild mass of waves. She scooped it up and pinned it into a loose twist, then put on a pair of silver hoop earrings and matching bracelets.

So she tried not to think of it at all. It was too early to confront him about it, she thought. He was trying his best . . . wasn't he?

Lucy was meeting Matt in town at their favorite restaurant, the Main Street Café. She drove into town so she wouldn't be late and luckily found a parking spot right in front.

A popular spot on the weekend, especially in the summer when boaters tied up at the dock adjacent to the green and came into the village for dinner.

The cafe had a large, old-fashioned-looking bar in front, with a pressed tin ceiling and wainscoted walls, covered with black-and-white photos. The gallery was vast and wide ranging, showing the town and famous locals, dating back to the 1800s. There were celebrities and national figures, too. Many sports heroes and newspaper headlines.

There was a lot to look at while you waited for a table, not to mention people watching. Lucy stood at the bar, shoulder to shoulder with other patrons, and looked around for Matt.

"You can't get a caipirinha in here, sorry. But they do make a mean martini," a familiar voice informed her.

Lucy turned to find Gloria, looking particularly vivacious and summery tonight in a yellow off-the-shoulder top and slim white capris.

"Hi, Gloria. It's so crowded in here, I didn't even see you."

"I don't think you were looking for me, either," Gloria teased her. "Meeting your boyfriend?"

"Yes, I am. Are you here alone?" Lucy asked, wondering if Matt would mind if she invited Gloria to eat with them.

They didn't have much time together, so he might not like the idea. But once he laid eyes on Gloria, he'd probably decide it wouldn't be complete torture, Lucy thought.

"I'm waiting for some friends," Gloria replied. "Are you surprised that I'm not home alone, pining for Jamie?"

"No, of course not," Lucy said quickly. Did she looked surprised? She actually was, but had tried not to show it.

"How did his meeting go today? Any word?"

"Everything is going perfectly. That's why I didn't run into Boston to join him for that party. He asked me to come. A few times. But I want this to be his own thing. He needs some space, even though he doesn't always think so. Know what I mean?"

Lucy nodded. It was wise of Gloria to see that, Lucy thought. There was probably a danger in their relationship of Jamie feeling overwhelmed. Her strong personality coupled with the difference in their finances was a solid combination punch.

Lucy was impressed that Gloria seemed aware of that. She was no dumb blonde, that was for sure. Not when it came to handling men.

Gloria's words were slightly slurred, sounding as if she'd already had a martini . . . or two. Or maybe she was just feeling emotional talking about Jamie, the way she'd been last night. She was very dramatic sometimes, all her emotions bubbling to the surface. That was part of what made her so interesting to be around.

The crowd at the bar shifted and Lucy spotted Matt in the doorway. When their eyes met and he smiled, she felt that funny little ping in her chest.

Yes, she'd wait for him to get a divorce and she wouldn't nag. She'd wait three months . . . six . . . a year . . .

"Is that Matt? He's a babe. I had no idea."

Lucy smiled, she couldn't help it. "Thanks . . . I think so."

"Well, here's to love." Gloria tipped her glass. "It's worth everything. Believe me."

Gloria took a long sip of her cocktail and peered at Lucy over the rim. Her green eyes glinted knowingly.

Matt made his way through the crowd and Lucy introduced him to Gloria. But before they could engage in any small talk, the hostess announced that their table was ready.

They said good night to Gloria and headed off for dinner.

"Perfect timing." Matt rested his hand on her shoulder as they walked to the back of the cafe.

"You came in just on cue," Lucy told him.

Marcia and Ken Bueller were ripe to make an offer. Suzanne could smell it on them.

Or maybe that was just the pile of shin guards and abandoned lunch boxes—God only knew what was left in them—that she'd hastily tossed in the cargo area of her Mom mobile before chauffeuring her clients around to view various properties on Saturday morning.

Gloria's house was the grand finale. Saving the best for last was an old sales trick . . . but it worked. Suzanne had a feeling it would work on the Buellers. The thirty-something DINKS—double income, no kids—had just lost out on a very similar house in the area.

The Buellers longed to live in The Landing and were primed to jump all over Gloria's stunning contemporary. Suzanne was nearly tempted to hand around a box of hand wipes; the couple was practically drooling as she turned down Sugar Maple Way. It was moments like this that made her job fun and Gloria's glorious property was going to be love at first sight. Suzanne just had a feeling. She was relieved Gloria wouldn't be at home for the showing. Suzanne operated much better without the buyer anxiously hovering.

Gloria, of course, would have played it cool. But wouldn't it be a thrill to tell Gloria that she had a buyer, a mere twenty-four hours after their meeting yesterday? And before the house had even officially gone on the market?

Suzanne had been so excited on her way to the office this morning, she had to play her sales CD, the one about fear of success. She silently reviewed the affirmations, just for good measure.

I am fearless. I am a winner. I am surrounded by a white protective light. Nothing stands in my path. I am going all the way today . . .

"Oh, I love the windows in front . . . and look at that beautiful tree, Ken. What kind of tree is that?" Marcia Bueller's high-pitched voice cut into Suzanne's mental pep talk.

"It's a Japanese maple. Very rare," Suzanne noted. "All the landscape design was done by Quinn and Rottman, a very exclusive firm. Wait until you see the back."

"Very nice," Brad Bueller said in a bland tone from the backseat. "Must need a lot of special maintenance though."

Brad played his cards close to his chest, Suzanne knew. But she could tell he liked it, too. Besides, it seemed that Marcia was the real decision maker here. Brad was just the front man.

Suzanne pulled her SUV around the U-shaped driveway and parked at the front door, so her clients got that "Honey, I'm home!" feeling.

She led them to the cupola entrance and searched around for the keys, then quickly unlatched the door. All the while she heard the Buellers behind her, murmuring in approval about the impressive architectural lines.

Suzanne had the code to shut the alarm system, but when she checked the box near the front door it seemed Gloria had forgotten to turn it on. So much the better, Suzanne thought. She hated fooling around with those things and was always afraid to set off some sales-curdling siren.

She turned to the Buellers, who stood in the middle of the foyer, gazing around with gratifying awe. It was impressive: a round, light-filled space with a two-story high ceiling and a long, curving stairway that led to the upper floors. The shiny black granite floor and entry table, topped by an arrangement of fresh flowers, made the passageway seem like the entrance to a luxury hotel.

"Very elegant," Marcia cooed. "A much more open feeling than that house on Tyler Street."

"Yes, much more open," her husband echoed.

Suzanne abstained from comment. She knew they would hate the house on Tyler Street. That one had been a setup.

She led them into the stadium-size living room next, decorated in a stark, minimalist style and practically nonexistent colors—off white, putty, and gray.

The Buellers were suitably impressed, necks craned back as they gawked at the ceiling height and stone fireplace. But Suzanne was surprised that Gloria had not made much effort to clean up. The room looked far from magazine-spread perfect. A bad sign at a first showing. It usually took a few weeks before the sellers fell into a "love it or leave it" attitude.

A pile of magazines was spread out on the floor next to a pair of leopard-print slides. The headline on the cover of *Cosmo* shouted in hot pink type, "Our Best Ever 'BIG O' Issue!"

Suzanne discreetly kicked it under the couch. Was Gloria still reading that stuff? To look at her, you'd think she knew it all by now.

Suzanne leaned over and discreetly fluffed some smashed pillows, then spotted two empty wineglasses, stained with dull red rings, sitting in clear sight on the slate end table. They gave off a vinegary smell, too. The exact opposite scent of the apple pie theory, which some of her colleagues swore by—have the seller stick something coated with cinnamon and sugar in the oven a few minutes before the potential buyers arrive. The comforting, homey scent sends subliminal messages to the buyer's brain.

What message did dirty wineglasses send? More like the party's over, Suzanne thought.

"I'll just take these into the kitchen," Suzanne murmured, "be right back."

Suzanne scooped up the glasses, quickly carried them into the kitchen, and rinsed them with some hot water and stuck them in the dishwasher. Then she made a note on her BlackBerry to bring Gloria some cinnamon-scented candles or sachets.

On her way back to the living room, Suzanne glanced through the glass doors that framed the patio and pool. Another mess outside, darn it. Sitting on a little table in clear view, another dirty wineglass and Gloria's knitting bag, tipped over on the floor.

There seemed to be a blank spot, Suzanne realized, where

Gloria's favorite chaise longue usually sat, the top portion shaded by a standing umbrella. Then she spotted the chaise down near the end of the pool, left at a random angle. It was a heavy piece but had wheels on one end, so it was not impossible to move, she realized. Gloria must have rolled it away from her usual spot for some reason.

Suzanne resisted the urge to run outside, clean up, and rearrange the lawn furniture. She wasn't Gloria's maid, for goodness sakes. A few dirty dishes weren't going to throw the deal, she thought. I'll just have to remind her for next time . . .

"Do you know how much it costs to heat that pool?" Ken stood by the glass doors, gazing outside. "The waterfall must run on some sort of electric motor . . . right?"

Suzanne had planned on showing the outside last, after they toured the house. But it was usually better to go with the flow if the clients were hot about the property.

"I need to check with the owner on those costs. I'll make a note, Brad. Why don't we go outside and take a look. All the stone and tile is imported from Italy, and there's a beautiful mosaic at the center of the pool."

The glass door was unlocked. Ken Bueller pulled it open and politely let his wife step out before he did. Suzanne hung back a moment, checking her specs. Ken Bueller had so many questions, he must have been a quiz show host in a past life.

"Oh my God!" Marcia Bueller stood in the middle of the patio and squealed. Suzanne looked up and saw her through the glass, pointing at the pool.

She loves that mosaic, Suzanne thought.

Then she watched Marcia's hand rise to cover her mouth. She turned to look at her husband, her expression hardly one of delight. More like shock and horror.

"Hey, what is that? . . . is there someone . . . in there?" Her husband also stared at the pool, then trotted down to the patio's lower level.

"Good Lord . . . Marcia . . . don't come any farther. Don't look," he shouted back, waving his hand at her.

Suzanne raced outside to the pool. Shards of sunlight glinted off the sparkling blue water, making it hard to see clearly.

She cupped her hand over her eyes and stepped closer to the edge.

Something was floating in the water at the far end. She couldn't quite tell what it was. She walked closer, down the side of the pool toward the waterfall.

She could see it now. It was a body . . . facedown. Perfectly still. Except for a slight bobbing motion caused by the current from the tumbling water.

Suzanne ran the last few steps to get a better look.

It was a woman. A loose yellow top billowed around her middle, exposing her bare waist up to the band of her bra. She wore white capris below that clung to her bottom and thighs, the waterlogged fabric practically transparent.

Long blonde hair drifted around her head like water weeds, with dark roots showing near the scalp in back.

A tangle of orange yarn floated nearby.

Suzanne staggered backward, gasping for air. "Oh my God—it's Gloria! Call nine-one-one. Get some help. Please!"

The folder of papers Suzanne held slipped from her grip . . . and everything went black.

Chapter Four

*L*ucy? I'm at Gloria's. There's been a terrible accident . . ."

"Suzanne, what's the matter? What happened?"

Lucy had just walked in after a visit to the beach with Tink. She scrambled to pick up the phone in time. All she could hear now were Suzanne's muffled sobs.

"It's so awful," Suzanne managed, choking on her words. "Jamie will be back soon . . . and the police have to tell him . . ."

"Tell him what? Did something happen to Gloria?"

Suzanne burst into tears again. "Gloria's dead. She must have fallen into the swimming pool . . ."

"Oh my God! No . . ." Lucy dropped into a kitchen chair, unable to believe Suzanne's words. "How can that be? I just saw her in town last night."

"I spoke to her last night, too," Suzanne said. "They're still trying to figure out when it happened . . . and what happened exactly. The police said I could call someone. I tried to call Kevin, but he didn't pick up."

Suzanne's voice dissolved again into a burble of sobs.

"How can I help? What do you want me to do? Should I go to your house and check on the kids?"

"Kevin took them all to the Cape to visit his parents this weekend. I didn't know whom to call. The police aren't supposed to let anyone else in, but Detective Walsh just came . . ."

"Detective Walsh?" All the Black Sheep knitters knew Detective Walsh, though they hardly had warm feelings for him. He'd investigated the murder of a village shopkeeper, Amanda Goran, just a few months ago and Maggie had been his lead suspect.

"Yes, it's Walsh. Small world, right?" Suzanne added in a lower voice. "He can see I'm a basket case, so he said I can have someone come over and stay with me. For support. Are you free?"

"Sure, I'll come. I'll leave right this minute," Lucy told her. "Sit tight, I'll be right there."

Lucy hung up, then wondered if she should tell any of their other friends about poor Gloria. Maggie, Dana, and even Phoebe were going to be terribly upset by this news. Lucy didn't even want to imagine it. Somehow, she and Suzanne would have to get word to them. The most important thing now was to help Suzanne.

Lucy's old running shoes were full of sand and her T-shirt was stuck to her skin with a combination of salt air and perspiration, but she didn't want to waste a minute changing. She quickly grabbed her handbag and keys, then headed for Gloria's house, driving on autopilot.

But how could Gloria be dead? She just saw her last night at the restaurant, all cheery. It was impossible. It must be some huge mistake, Lucy's heart argued. But she sensed there had been no mistake. Life was fragile; a shaky proposition. A minute-to-minute arrangement. Of course, we couldn't think about it that way. We couldn't function very well, constantly holding in mind the image of our fragile mortality, dangling from a thread.

The truth was, there were no guarantees for anyone. Every day, every hour could be the last.

Poor Gloria, Lucy thought. Why here, why now, when she'd finally found some happiness? It didn't seem fair.

As she drove toward The Landing, memories of Thursday night came to mind, cruising down these same roads, sheltered by the arching boughs of towering old trees, the big houses that looked so grand and solid, seeming immune to the troubles of ordinary lives. Was that only two nights ago? It seemed light-years now, Lucy reflected.

Despite her knowledge of the sad situation, the scene in front of Gloria's house still surprised her. Three police cruisers, two local and one state, and an ambulance with a swirling red light on top, stood parked at the top of the drive.

She parked farther down and quickly walked up to the front door. A uniformed policeman stood at the doorway, eyeing her as she approached.

"I'm Lucy Binger, a friend of Mrs. Cavanaugh's?" Lucy pointed to Suzanne, who was standing in the living room, talking to a tall, bald man who wore glasses. An investigator, she guessed.

"Detective Walsh said she could have someone with her. For support," she added.

The uniformed policeman's expression didn't change. "Can I see some ID?" Lucy handed him her license. He looked it over, then handed it back. "Print your name and sign over there." He handed her a clipboard and pointed to the spot she needed to fill in. The sheet showed a list of names and times for arrival and departure. She noticed Suzanne near the top as she scribbled her signature.

"You can go in. Just don't touch anything."

"I won't," Lucy promised.

Was this a crime scene? Gloria's death had been an accident. But the police had to inspect the place to confirm that, she guessed. They had to investigate to eliminate the possibility of foul play. She knew as much from watching police dramas on TV.

As Lucy walked into the living room, she saw Suzanne standing alone by the fireplace. Suzanne glanced her way and her big brown eyes lit up. She ran over and Lucy gave her a tight hug.

"Are you okay?" Lucy eyed her with concern. Her poor friend looked as if she'd been put through the spin cycle.

Suzanne's eyes were red rimmed and puffy from crying, her eye makeup smeared and her long dark hair flying off in all directions.

"Oh Lucy . . . it was horrible to find her like that . . . you can't imagine . . ."

"You found her?"

Suzanne nodded bleakly, then blew her nose on a wadded-up tissue. "My client, Marcia Bueller, saw the body first. But I was the one who got really close and . . . recognized her."

Lucy sighed and squeezed Suzanne's hand. Poor Suzanne. That was even worse than she'd imagined.

"You don't have to talk about it now if you don't want to," Lucy told her.

"It's okay. I want to tell you. I really need to talk to someone who knew her. Another friend. You know."

Lucy nodded, but didn't say anything.

"I brought my clients, the Buellers, over to show the house," she began. Then she went on to explain how the couple went outside first to the patio while she stayed in the living room, brushing up on the specs. Then she heard Marcia scream and by the time she got outside, both Buellers had spotted Gloria floating in the pool.

"We didn't even realize what it was at first. She was on the far end. So I ran down and took a closer look . . . and saw her. Facedown in the water. But once I looked closer, I could tell . . ."

Suzanne's voice trailed off again and Lucy saw her eyes fill with tears.

"How horrible," Lucy said quietly. Suzanne nodded bleakly. "What did you do, call the police?"

"I blacked out," Suzanne admitted. "I mean, the shock and all, seeing her like that. Ken Bueller called nine-one-one and Marcia splashed some cold water on my face. Then we just waited and the police came. Uniformed police came first and they called the detective and said we had to wait to talk to him. And we've been waiting ever since. They questioned each of us separately, in the kitchen. But they said we can't leave yet."

"I guess it won't be too much longer," Lucy said. "Where is . . . Gloria?" she managed to ask.

"Last I checked, she's still out there." Suzanne tilted her head in the direction of the patio. "But they may have taken her away by now. I asked what was going to happen after Detective Walsh questioned me. He said he couldn't move the body until the medical examiner came, or something like that. But I think that guy has gotten here. They've been taking photographs and looking around the house and the property.

I guess they need to be very official. But it seems pretty obvious. She fell into the pool and drowned."

"I guess," Lucy murmured. Gloria had expressed her disdain for the pool's chlorinated water the other night because she hated what it did to her skin and hair. Lucy wondered now if she even knew how to swim. Maybe she was a weak swimmer and panicked when she fell in the deep end?

"Maybe she tripped and hit her head on something," Lucy offered.

"Maybe." Suzanne sighed. "They didn't tell Jamie over the phone. They just said it was an accident."

"When did the police call him?"

"Not too long after Walsh came. Nearly two hours ago," Suzanne added, glancing at her watch.

They both knew what that meant. Boston was only about two hours. If you were lucky with traffic and pushing the speed limit, you could make it out to Plum Harbor even faster. Jamie would walk through the door any moment. Lucy felt her breath catch just thinking about it.

Suzanne glanced across the room. "The Buellers are traumatized. Ken Bueller won't even look me in the eye. Could you imagine it, though? You go out house hunting on a sunny Saturday afternoon and this happens? They may never make an appointment with a real estate agent again."

They'd never make one with Suzanne, Lucy felt pretty sure of that. But she didn't want to make her friend feel even worse. In the big picture, what did that matter?

"Don't worry about them. They'll recover. They didn't even know Gloria. Not the way we did." Lucy rested her hand on Suzanne's shoulder. "Why don't you stay over tonight? You probably don't want to go home to a big empty house, right?"

"Can I, Lucy? That would be great. Thanks. I was really dreading going home later." Suzanne drew in a deep shaky breath.

Lucy was about to answer but the scene outside drew her attention. Suzanne cast her a curious look.

"What is it?" Suzanna turned and followed her gaze.

Down at the end of the pool they saw some officers lift a long bundle in a heavy plastic bag and place it on a gurney. Gloria, wrapped in a body bag. Lucy's breath caught in her throat as the gurney was wheeled out of view.

"I can't watch." Suzanne shook her head and started crying again. Lucy patted her hand "I still can't believe it. I'm really worried about Jamie. You know how close they were. Still in that honeymoon stage, for goodness sakes. He'll be devastated."

"Devastated" was one word that came to mind.

"Crushed," "overwhelmed," "grief stricken" were a few more.

As if their anxious thoughts had summoned him, Lucy suddenly spotted Jamie standing in the foyer.

He was flanked by two uniformed policemen who stood on either side as he walked toward the living room.

"Suzanne . . . Lucy . . ." he called out to them, sounding surprised to see them there.

He turned, started to walk over to them, but one of his police escorts held him back. "You can speak with your friends later, Mr. Barnett. Detective Walsh is waiting to see you outside," the officer said simply.

Would they have Jamie identify the body right here? How awful. Lucy hoped not.

Jamie nodded, and continued walking. He looked haggard and disheveled. As if he had dressed in a hurry and hadn't slept very well. But he'd been at an art scene party last night, boozing and schmoozing. Probably bar hopping after the party ended, too. He had probably been sleeping late and the phone call from the police would have seemed like a nightmare.

Once Jamie went outside, Lucy and Suzanne drifted over to the glass doors. They didn't say a thing to each other but both knew what the other was feeling. They couldn't help themselves. They felt compelled to watch the unbearable scene unfold, like being unable to turn away from the scene of an accident.

They watched Jamie walk down the length of the pool.

Detective Walsh appeared and walked up to meet him. Lucy recognized him easily, even at a distance. A tall, thin man with a long, sad face. He rarely smiled and when he did, it appeared to pain him. That's how she'd describe Walsh.

She saw Walsh speak quietly to Jamie for a moment, with his characteristic deadpan expression that Lucy remembered so well, then reach out and briefly touch Jamie's arm.

Then Lucy heard Jamie scream, "No . . . no . . . oh my God . . . please, no . . ."

He covered his face with his hands and fell to his knees. The uniformed officers gently tugged Jamie up and maneuvered him to the chaise longue that stood nearby.

Jamie sat holding his head in his hands, his big body shaking with sobs.

"Poor Jamie. What a shock." Suzanne shook her head and pressed her hand to her mouth, looking as if she was going to cry again. "I knew he'd take it hard. And now the police are going to ask him a million questions. The poor guy."

Lucy guessed Suzanne was right. Even though it had been an accident, the police didn't seem to be in any hurry to depart. Thank goodness the police had taken Gloria's body away and he didn't have to see her like that, Lucy thought.

"Maybe we can sit with him a while?" Lucy said.

"I don't think so. They barely allowed you in here," Suzanne reminded her. "I think we just have to wait."

Suzanne was right. Detective Walsh stood outside with Jamie a long while, asking him questions and writing on a notepad.

"Gosh, this is taking a long time. What could Walsh be asking him?" Suzanne sounded annoyed.

Lucy just nodded. She felt bad for Jamie, too, and wished the police could wait until tomorrow with their questions. That's all Jamie needed now was some dragged-out interview.

Finally, Detective Walsh was done. Jamie got up and slowly walked back into the house. Suzanne reached him first, putting her arms around his shoulders. "Jamie . . . I'm so sorry," she said quietly. "It's so horrible. So . . . unbelievable."

He nodded, closing his eyes. "I can't believe it," he gasped. "It just can't be . . ."

Lucy came up to him next and also gave him a hug. "I'm so sorry, Jamie. How can we help you?"

Jamie stepped back, his blue eyes blank and stunned. "They won't let me see Gloria. They're taking her to a hospital somewhere in Boston. Mass General, I think he said? I have to go there to identify the body."

Probably a morgue where Gloria's remains would be autopsied, in order to confirm that she drowned, Lucy guessed. Or maybe she had a heart attack and that's why she fell in?

It was useless to speculate. They would find out the facts soon enough.

Suzanne rubbed his arm in a soothing gesture. He didn't seem to notice. "We can drive you there."

"That's okay . . . they say I can't see her until tomorrow. . . . But I can't stay here tonight. They want to just keep looking around." He gazed around, seeming totally disoriented. "It would be hard anyway," he added.

Lucy swallowed. She didn't know what to say. "You can come to my place. Suzanne is going to stay over, too. Her family is away."

Jamie looked surprised by the suggestion and she almost thought he'd accept. Then he shook his head. "Thanks, Lucy. But I just . . . just need to be alone right now."

Being alone at a time like this was probably the worst thing for him, Lucy thought. But she couldn't argue.

"It's still so hot out. Come into the kitchen. We'll get you a cold drink," Suzanne said, coaxing him.

Jamie stood up and allowed himself to be led toward the kitchen. Lucy had never seen anyone sleepwalking, but she imagined they would look a lot like Jamie did right then.

Suzanne led him to the long oak table. He sat down, put his head in his hands, and started sobbing again. Deep, uncontrollable sobs that shook his entire body. Lucy put her arm around his shoulder. He barely seemed aware of her. She glanced at Suzanne, who scuttled around the kitchen, fixing Jamie a glass of ice water, though the gesture seemed pointless, they both knew.

"I must have called her twenty times yesterday. I think she finally shut her phone off. I tried last night and there was no answer . . ." he sobbed. "I thought maybe she went out . . . or went to bed early. I had no idea . . ." he gasped.

"Of course you didn't. How could you have known? It was

a freak accident." Suzanne set the glass in front of him. The ice cubes tinkled.

He lifted his head and looked at each of them in turn, wiping his tears with the back of his hand. "I asked her to meet me in Boston. I wanted her to come to the party. But she just wouldn't," he said, sounding sad and frustrated. "She was so stubborn sometimes."

"I saw her in town last night," Lucy said. "She told me that you wanted her to join you. But she really wanted to give you some space," she tried to explain.

"I didn't need my space . . . I needed her," Jamie sobbed. "If only she'd come with me, this wouldn't have happened. . . . I don't know what to do. I don't know if I can live without her . . ."

Lucy and Suzanne stared at each other. Neither of them knew what to do. Suzanne leaned over and patted his back again. "Jamie, honey . . . please . . ."

That's all she could say. Lucy understood. She couldn't say, "Don't cry. It's going to be okay." It wasn't going to be okay. He loved Gloria and in the blink of an eye, she'd been taken from him. He was reeling, like a wounded, stunned animal.

"Maybe we should call Dana," Lucy whispered, thinking their friend could help with professional grief counseling right now.

"I tried her right after I called you. There was no answer," Suzanne whispered back. "I left a message on her cell," she added.

Lucy nodded, hoping Dana would call back.

Detective Walsh walked in. "How's he doing?" the detective asked Lucy.

"Not good. He's really shaken." A vast understatement, she knew, but she didn't know how else to describe it.

The detective looked at Jamie. "This is the medical examiner, Dr. Cowald. He'd like to ask you a few more questions, Mr. Barnett. It shouldn't take very long."

Jamie stared at him bleakly. Then nodded. "Might as well get it over with."

The detective looked relieved, Lucy thought. He probably wanted to wrap it up and file his report. He asked Lucy and Suzanne to wait in the next room. He'd call them when he was through.

They sat down together in the living room again. Two uniformed policemen lingered, milling around, but some others had gone, Lucy noticed.

"I guess they finally let the Buellers leave," Suzanne said, looking around for her clients.

"Looks like the police are almost done here," Lucy replied. "I think we ought to make some calls while we're waiting. Maggie and Dana need to know."

Suzanne nodded her chin, trembling as she pulled out her cell phone. "Yes, we need to tell them. It's too bad it has to be over the phone. I'll try Dana first," she said, dialing the number.

"Do you want me to talk?" Lucy offered. Suzanne quickly nodded and Lucy took the phone. Suzanne had been through a lot today. It was only right to help with this unhappy duty.

It was almost two hours later when Lucy, Suzanne, Maggie, and Dana were sitting in Lucy's kitchen, sharing an order of Chinese takeout.

"So Jamie went to stay with a friend?" Dana asked.

"A guy named Kenny that he plays tennis with came to pick him up. I asked him to come here, but I knew he felt awkward about it."

"I can understand that," Maggie said. "It may have been too much for him, seeing all of us tonight. He might need to be with someone who didn't know Gloria that well."

"I'm glad he's not alone tonight," Dana said. "That's the important thing. Suzanne described him as despondent."

"It was so sad. He said he didn't know if he could live without her. Doesn't that just break your heart?" Suzanne sighed and twirled her fork in a pile of lo mein noodles.

Lucy helped herself to a slice of scallion pancake. While she was at Gloria's she'd felt as if she'd never want to eat again. Now she felt suddenly ravenous. Some affirming life force thing kicking in?

"The police said he couldn't stay there," Lucy clarified for her friends. "They're still investigating. He'll probably be able to get back in tomorrow."

"They're acting like it's a crime scene." Maggie sounded surprised. "Did they say why?"

"I asked about that," Suzanne replied. "Walsh said it was routine procedure since Gloria had no known medical problems and she had died alone. He said it was pretty much the medical examiner's call and he was known to do things by the book. Once they get the autopsy back, they'll know the full story."

"I see." Maggie nodded, looking very solemn. She didn't touch her food, but took a sip of hot tea.

Lucy knew how she felt. No one could believe it. It felt as if Gloria might walk in any moment with one of her big, loud "Hi, girls, what's up?" greetings, flaunting some new outfit or a pair of jaw-dropping shoes, Jamie trailing along behind her like a loyal pet.

"Then what?" Dana asked, helping herself to a few more spoonfuls of Szechuan tofu.

"Then he gets the body back and can plan a funeral, or whatever. I wonder if he even knows what she wanted. It's not something most people talk about. Not at her age," Suzanne pointed out.

"She told me a few times. She said she wanted to be cremated," Maggie told them quietly. "And have her ashes spread over George Clooney."

No one laughed out loud. But they couldn't help smiling. The line was just so Gloria. Lucy could hear her say it.

"He'll need some help making plans," Dana pointed out. She put her plate aside and took out her knitting.

Maggie did the same. "We can help him. If he wants us to," she added. "I don't want to seem as if I'm meddling. This is such a hard time for him."

"I mentioned it to him at the house." Lucy picked up a few dishes and brought them to the sink. "He seemed grateful for any advice. He has no idea what to do first."

"There's so much paperwork when someone dies. When Bill died, it was so sudden. He had a will, thank goodness, but there was so much we didn't have in order." Maggie sighed and began casting on stitches with deep plum-colored yarn. She had started her squares for the blanket, Lucy noticed, and had already completed one.

"I wonder about Gloria. All those properties she owns and she has interests in different businesses. I have a feeling it's going to be a lot to unravel," Suzanne said.

Lucy agreed with her. Gloria was never that specific about the details, but her conversations were studded with hints about owning a bit of this and a bit of that. Like iridescent beads twinkling on an evening gown. There was a large cache of real estate, a legacy from George Thurman. But so much more. Lucy was sure that her knitting friends hadn't even seen the tip of the iceberg.

"I can make some coffee, or tea. Would you like to stay here or move into the living room for dessert?" she asked her friends.

"Let's just stay here. It's comfortable." Suzanne also took out her knitting. She'd stopped at home on her way to Lucy's house and picked up a few necessities for her overnight visit, including her knitting bag.

Lucy cleared the plates and the food, then wiped down the table. Her friends didn't seem to care, but she didn't want anyone to find black bean sauce on their project tomorrow.

"Thank goodness Kevin and the kids are away tonight," Suzanne said, measuring her progress against a cardboard template. "I'm so glad I don't have to face them," she admitted. "I'm just too burned-out."

"Get a good night's sleep. You'll feel a little better tomorrow," Dana said.

"If I can sleep," Suzanne replied.

"Suzanne is going to stay here tonight," Lucy told the others.

"That's good. I was wondering. You shouldn't be alone." Maggie had begun knitting and didn't look up.

"This morning I was so relieved to have the house all to myself for the weekend. Now I wish they were all home, driving me crazy," Suzanne confessed.

"What did the police ask you? Did they question you for very long?" Dana asked curiously.

"It felt like a long time. But maybe it really wasn't," Suzanne replied. "They asked me what I was doing at the house

and how I'd gotten in, of course. Then how long I'd known
Gloria and when was the last time I'd spoken to her. How did
she sound, that sort of thing."

"When was that? Yesterday, when she signed your agreement?" Maggie asked, looking up.

"That was the last time I saw her. But I called her late last
night, to see if I could bring the Buellers over. It was about
eleven, I guess. I thought it might be too late to call, but she
always said she was a night owl and since Jamie wasn't home,
I figured it was okay."

"So she must have fallen in the pool sometime after
eleven," Lucy said quietly, trying to piece it all together.
She'd been back here with Matt by then. Not giving Gloria a
thought. The realization was chilling.

"Determining the time of death when someone has
drowned is a little more complicated," Dana told her. "But the
medical examiner has ways of figuring it out . . ." She paused
and Lucy realized that she probably knew more but didn't
want to go into any gruesome details. Not when they were all
picturing Gloria.

"I guess they can tell if she tripped and hit her head, or
something—any sort of accident that made it hard for her to
swim."

Those were all possibilities, Lucy thought.

"Yes, they would see an injury during the autopsy," Dana
replied evenly, without looking up from her knitting. "If she'd
had a heart attack. Or a bit too much to drink and had taken a
bad fall . . . well, it could have happened that way."

"She didn't sound like she'd been drinking when I spoke
to her," Suzanne told them. "She sounded up. Excited about
people coming to see the house so soon. But not tipsy. She'd
already given me the code for the alarm. But it wasn't on when

I got there. She had probably planned to turn it on when she went to bed . . . but never made it."

Lucy placed a pot of coffee on the table along with some cups, milk, and sugar. She didn't have much in the house for dessert but had found a frozen chocolate cake in the freezer— a PMS emergency stash—and had set it out earlier to defrost, so it was just about soft enough to slice.

"We didn't talk for very long. Someone came to the door. I heard the bell and she said she had to go."

"A visitor, at that hour?" Maggie was surprised.

"Maybe she was just getting a takeout delivery?" Dana suggested.

"I saw her in town, at the Main Street Café. She was meeting friends for dinner. You know Gloria. A bird couldn't survive on her calorie intake. I doubt she'd eat dinner out and then order a pizza."

Dana's eyebrows rose behind her reading glasses. "Maybe she had an eating disorder, binging and purging. With Jamie gone, it was the perfect time to indulge."

It was possible, Lucy thought. Gloria was a real perfectionist about her appearance, the ideal candidate for that type of problem.

"Hold on a minute. Before we start slapping a diagnosis on the poor woman, let's just slow down," Maggie cut in. "Gloria is gone. She can't speak in her own defense and we really have no idea why the doorbell rang . . . or if it even was her doorbell you heard, Suzanne. Maybe it was the TV," Maggie posited. "Isn't that possible?"

"I guess so," Suzanne admitted.

"Did she say, 'I have to go. There's someone at the door'?" Lucy asked.

"No, I don't think she did," Suzanne replied, her dark eyes

narrowing as she tried to remember their last conversation. "I guess I just got that impression from the way she told me she had to run. The tone of her voice. I heard a bell and I assumed someone was at the door."

"She may have wanted to end the call for a lot of reasons. We just don't know," Lucy said, agreeing with Maggie.

"I did see two wineglasses in the living room," Suzanne suddenly recalled. "The room was sort of messy when I came in to show the house to the Buellers. I was annoyed that Gloria had forgotten to clean up. Of course, I didn't realize . . ." Her voice trailed off sadly. "Well, maybe she did have a visitor last night. Maybe it wasn't the TV," Suzanne added, glancing at Maggie.

Maggie pursed her lips and looked down at her knitting, gently pulling loose the row of stitches she'd just completed. Lucy was quietly shocked by the sight. She'd rarely seen Maggie take a stray step in her knitting and the blanket square was the most elementary of patterns. She must really be upset, Lucy realized.

"Two empty glasses," Dana repeated. "They may have both been Gloria's," she mused. "You should see our family room after Jack spends a night in there watching TV. There are about ten dirty glasses and dishes lying around."

"Same at my house . . . only worse," Suzanne agreed. "It looks like a catering hall after a wedding."

"Did you tell the police?" Dana asked.

"The detective just wrote everything down. I told him about the wineglasses because he made me go through every single thing I did in the house before we found her. I took them into the kitchen, rinsed them out, and put them in the dishwasher. You don't want buyers looking at a luxury property like that and smelling stale wine, right?"

"What did Detective Walsh say when you told him you washed off the glasses?" Dana asked.

"You know him. He never says much. He sort of scowled. Or maybe that's just his usual expression. The other glass that was outside by the pool was still there when the police came and no one had touched it. I don't think he cared too much, one way or the other. Though the police were pretty careful handling things," Suzanne added.

"I know it wasn't your fault, Suzanne. But if there were any fingerprints to back up the theory that Gloria had a visitor, the evidence went down the drain," Dana replied.

"I guess so. I don't know if it had anything to do with the wineglasses, but Walsh and the medical examiner asked me about Gloria's drinking habits," Suzanne confided. "I didn't know what to say. I felt put on the spot."

"That question is standard procedure when someone dies in an accident. Especially by drowning in their own pool." Dana's husband, Jack, was a former police detective who had left the force years ago to become an attorney. She knew more than most people about the ins and out of police work. "Alcohol use makes all kinds of accidental deaths more likely. And they need to rule out suicide or foul play. They'll check her blood for alcohol and drugs."

"Suicide. Right. They did ask me about her mood the last few days. Why was she selling the house? Did I think she seemed sad or depressed about it. Or if she had sounded depressed when we spoke late last night," Suzanne recalled.

"She seemed fine when I saw her. Did she sound down about selling the house, though?" Lucy asked curiously. "I mean, when you met with her privately. She didn't seem to have any regrets when she told us Thursday night."

"She seemed eager to sell it, I thought," Dana said. "Excited about the idea of getting a new place with Jamie."

"I thought she seemed excited about that decision, too," Maggie agreed. "But that was only natural, since they were newlyweds. She wanted to start off with a clean slate. George Thurman built that house for her, you know. It probably brought back a lot of memories." She sighed and paused to examine her work. "I met her several years after George died," Maggie continued, "and I honestly never expected her to marry again. She was always flitting in and out of relationships. You can just imagine Gloria, ten years younger. She had her pick of men around here. But she never seemed to take any of them seriously. She often told me she didn't see the point in being married. Not anymore. She liked her freedom and she certainly didn't need a man to support her. She didn't see any reason to tie herself down again. I secretly thought she was afraid that most men were only after her money."

"Then Jamie came along and changed her mind about all that." Suzanne sighed and turned her knitted square over to work on the other side.

"Jamie changed everything. I'd never seen her so happy. I mean, really happy," Maggie confessed.

"That's basically what I told the police." Suzanne took a cup of coffee and added a dollop of milk. "That she seemed very upbeat whenever I saw her. As far as her drinking habits went, well . . . I wasn't sure what to say," Suzanne admitted. "Gloria liked to decompress with a martini, or a glass of wine. We all knew that about her. So I did say she drank a little. Maybe more than a little, at times. I'd seen her high-spirited. But she never really overdid it."

"You told the truth. That's all you could do. I'm sure they

asked Jamie the same thing," Lucy told Suzanne. "She really didn't overdo it. She was too worried about all the extra calories."

"He also asked me if she took any medication that I knew of, or had any health problems. High blood pressure, that sort of thing," Suzanne added. "I guess he asked Jamie all those questions, too. I told him she seemed in great shape to me. I'd never heard her mention any physical problems."

"She was very careful about her health. She was in great shape for her age. She really worked at it," Maggie noted, her words edged with regret.

"She did make an effort," Dana agreed. "More than most people. She should have lived a very long life."

"Poor Gloria. Such a waste, such a shame." Maggie was feeling overwhelmed again. She put down her knitting and picked up a tissue from the box Suzanne handed across the table.

"Poor Jamie," Suzanne added. "They didn't have very long together, did they?"

"Not long at all. Jamie is going to need us. He'll be lost without Gloria," Maggie said between sobs.

Lucy felt the same. "He did depend on her. She told me last night that he kept asking her to meet him in Boston, to go to that party. But she didn't want to. She wanted to give him some space. I thought that was very wise of her," Lucy reflected. "But if she had gone, maybe she'd still be alive."

"Jamie said the same thing at the house tonight," Suzanne recalled. "But we can't deal in what-ifs. Life doesn't work that way. I mean, who knows? She could have had a car accident driving into the city and we'd be sitting here saying how could *that* happen." Suzanne sniffed and reached across the table for the tissue box. "The irony of it is that Jamie claims he didn't want his space . . . he just wanted her. . . . Wasn't that so amazingly sweet to say?"

Dana took off her reading glasses and wiped her teary eyes with a tissue. She was also crying again, but very quietly, Lucy realized.

"They were very close. Anyone could see that. Gloria mothered him," Dana said bluntly. "I think she realized it could get on his nerves, sooner or later. Some people might say it wasn't a truly healthy relationship. The age difference and his dependency on her . . . and she obviously needed someone to nurture and even control. But it worked and they seemed very happy together. Happier than most couples I know." Dana shook her head in dismay. "He'll need a lot of time to get his bearings. To go through all the stages of grieving. He's just moved up here, too. We're practically the only friends he has in town."

"Except for some tennis buddies, or guys at the gym," Maggie agreed. "I think Gloria would rest easier, knowing that we're here for him. It's the only thing we can do for her now."

Nobody said a word. Nobody had to. They all knew that Maggie was right.

Poor Gloria was beyond their help now, Lucy thought. But they could still be there for Jamie.

"I know we all feel very sad right now about Gloria. And shocked," Dana added, glancing around at the group. "But I think it's important to remember that she lived a full life. It seemed to me that she achieved a lot of what she'd set out to do in her life and was satisfied with her choices."

"I think that's true." Maggie looked up from her knitting and nodded. "She covered a lot of ground in her short lifetime.

More than most people who live decades longer. I don't think she had many regrets. Or many items left on her long range 'To Do' list. Not like most of us."

"I was thinking the same thing." Suzanne sighed and forced a small smile. "There are so many things I'd still like to do. But I just tell myself, 'Someday. When the kids are older.' Or 'When we have more money.' You know how it is."

"What would you like to do, Suzanne? If you had enough money and enough time?" Dana leaned forward, looking very interested in her answer.

"If I won the lottery or something?" Suzanne said, her tone suddenly brighter. "Gee . . . let's see . . . I'd like to go on a huge trip. I'd like to visit Africa and go on a safari, before all the wild animals disappear. I'd like to go to China and see the Great Wall. I think that would be amazing."

"I'd like to go India and Tibet," Dana confessed. "I'd like to climb the Himalayas and stay in a monastery . . . and take a vow of silence," she added.

She rolled her eyes a bit and Lucy had to smile. She knew Dana loved her job but the poor woman probably did get tired of listening to people talk about their problems day in and day out. Who could blame her?

"I'd like to go India and Tibet. But I'm not sure about that monastery stop. Do they let you knit in a Tibetan monastery?" Maggie asked with a small smile. "You might check that out before you sign on."

"I'll make a note of it," Dana replied. "Knitting can be a very Zen-like practice, though. Don't you think?"

"Oh, for sure," Maggie agreed. "I'm just not sure if it's recognized as such. Officially, I mean."

Dana turned to Lucy. "What's on your long term, 'To Do' list, Lucy? You've been very quiet."

Lucy had not jumped into the conversation, but had definitely been mulling over the question.

"I'd like to travel to some far-off places," she agreed. "But most of my top items are closer to home." She paused. "I'd like to have a child someday," she confided. "That one is still on my list. I think you've all checked it off by now."

Her friends each cast her an understanding, even sympathetic look.

"Don't worry, Lucy. Your turn will come," Suzanne promised.

"I agree. You have plenty of time. You don't need to worry about it," Dana advised.

"If you don't meet Mr. Right, you can always be a single mom. We'll help you," Maggie offered. Everyone else at the table nodded in agreement, looking pleased by the notion. Before Lucy could respond, she added, "Check off 'Have baby.' . . . What else is on the list?"

Lucy paused. "Don't laugh . . . but I've always wanted to play the saxophone. You know, real blues and jazz stuff?"

Nobody laughed but she could see Suzanne struggling. "That would be cool. What else?"

"I'd like to play the piano. And speak another language. I mean, really well. Like Spanish or even Chinese."

"Me, too," Maggie agreed. "But I'd love to learn by living in Spain or Italy for a while. Even for just a summer. That's on my list, too," Maggie agreed.

"I think we should plan a trip. A summer of knitting in Tuscany?" Dana suggested. "Wouldn't that be fabulous?"

"It would be paradise," Maggie seconded the motion. "We could go to Tibet afterward. Sort of an Eat, Pray, Knit tour."

"I'm there," Lucy said, joining the fantasy. "As long as our villa has Internet access."

"That sounds lovely, Dana. And if all of you ever go on this field trip, you have to promise to just hit me over the head, and drag me along. And leave a note for Brian and the kids saying I've been abducted by aliens or something."

"Will they believe that?" Maggie looked amused, but doubtful.

"I hear it all the time." Dana shrugged a slim shoulder. "Do you mean to say . . . it isn't possible?"

Her tone was very serious, but she soon broke into a mischievous smile. A smile that quickly spread around the table. Lucy felt suddenly peaceful inside, connected to her circle of friends. A few minutes ago, they'd been crying. Now they were laughing again. But that was all right. She was sure their friend Gloria wouldn't have minded. She might have even been standing by in spirit, silently approving.

Gloria's passing had been a harsh blow, pulling them all under. But their bonds of friendship and affection for each other were like a little rubber raft that had buoyed them up again, carrying them across this rough water.

It must carry them all for the next few days, Lucy realized. The worst was not over. At least they had each other.

Chapter Five

Gloria's memorial service was planned for Friday, almost a full week after she'd died. The police inquest into her death and the release of her body had taken longer than anyone had expected, definitely longer than Lucy had thought it would.

Finally, there were no surprises. The coroner determined Gloria had died of natural causes, an accidental drowning. A high level of alcohol and drugs found in her blood had most likely resulted in impaired coordination and depth perception, confusion and even blurred vision. Once she accidently fell into the water, her intoxication may have resulted in an inability to swim or lift herself out of the pool, the report theorized.

Detective Walsh had given Jamie this information over the phone. The police and coroner's reports would be available to him at some point in the future, but it was hard to say when. The police gave priority to crime situations and routine paperwork in an accidental death, like Gloria's, was often pushed to the back burner, Walsh had explained.

In the days after Gloria's death, Lucy and her friends had been helping Jamie plan a memorial service and, with the release of Gloria's body, they sprang into action.

Thursday was normally their knitting group night. But it didn't feel right to meet on the eve of Gloria's memorial and they wanted to help Jamie any way they could, even by keeping him company the night before such a trying event.

When they actually got to the house, there wasn't all that much to do, Lucy realized. They converged in the kitchen, storing the various dishes they'd made in the giant, restaurant-quality fridge.

Why did it seem to so often work out that the women who had the least interest in cooking had the best-equipped kitchens? Lucy wondered. There seemed to be some strange imbalance in the universe that tilted in that direction.

Jamie really didn't need all of their home-cooked and home-baked contributions, Lucy knew. A caterer he'd hired had the refreshments covered. But it did make them feel better to add something to the buffet. Or to his freezer, for all the days afterward.

They all gathered around the big farm-style kitchen table, and Suzanne made some herbal tea. Jamie took out the notes he'd made during his conversation with the police. He clearly needed to talk. That was the main thing they could do to help tonight, to just listen, Lucy thought.

"So the police determined that it was definitely an accident? Is that what Walsh said?" Suzanne asked.

"More or less." He looked down at the table, his handsome features transformed by grief and loss. He looked . . . older, Lucy realized. Years older, all of a sudden. He and Gloria wouldn't have seemed so obviously mismatched in age. How ironic, she thought.

Dana had brought her knitting and already taken it out. She looked up at Jamie over her reading glasses. "Were you surprised about the alcohol and painkillers?" she asked quietly. "That's a dangerous combination. You would have thought Gloria knew better."

"She did know better," he said with an edge of anger. "I told her all the time not to fool around with that stuff." He took a steading breath, closing his eyes for a moment. Lucy noticed his hands clasped together on the top of the table, his knuckles turning white.

"So she did that before? Drank and took pills?" Maggie asked quietly.

He nodded, his eyes still closed. "She had these down moods. Sort of a cycle, you could say. It was like, once we were alone and she was offstage, away from everyone, she'd just crash. She was like a helium balloon or something, bouncing around, making everyone so happy. And then all the air rushes out at once and she'd just . . . collapse."

All of her friends looked surprised by this confession. Except Dana, perhaps, who stitched steadily away, Lucy noticed. She didn't show her reactions that easily and probably had some psychological category for this flip side of Gloria's vivacious personality.

"I'm surprised to hear you say that, Jamie," Maggie admitted. "I knew her a long time. I'd never seen that side of her personality."

Jamie shrugged. "She was good at hiding it. She hid it from me pretty well until we were married. Her only flaw," he added. He laughed sadly. "I almost didn't mind, I have to tell you. It made her human. A little less of a goddess."

He did treat her like a goddess, didn't he? Lucy thought. It was still surprising to hear him admit it.

"I knew she liked to drink a little," Maggie admitted. "I never thought it was to excess, though. I mean, so to the point where she'd hurt herself?"

"Not in company. But she would drink alone. In one of her moods. And, of course, that made it even worse," he explained. "That was the reason I kept calling her Friday, asking her to meet me in Boston." His eyes had filled with tears and his voice began to crack. "She'd get into these moods when she was alone. I was worried about her."

"You were right to be worried, it seems," Dana said sadly. "What about the pills? Did she have a problem with prescription painkillers? A lot of people start off taking them for some real injury or after an operation, then they get hooked. Is that what happened?"

Jamie shook his head. "No . . . it wasn't like that. It wasn't that bad. But she did like to take them once in a while when she was in a down mood. I didn't even know she had any in the house. They did find a prescription for pain medication from the dentist in the medicine chest. The same drug that was in her blood. She'd had a root canal a few weeks ago. I guess she just hung on to the stuff."

"I guess so," Maggie said.

"The police said she may have gotten dizzy or even blacked out for a minute," Jamie explained. "Then she fell in the pool and probably panicked."

He swallowed hard and looked down at the table again. The image of poor Gloria, floundering around in the pool, was disturbing to all of them.

It was a lot to think about, a lot to process, Lucy realized. This autopsy had revealed a whole side of Gloria that they'd never seen, not even Maggie. And it wasn't just conjecture on the part of the police. Jamie's words confirmed it.

They had all agreed right away that the house was the only setting up to Gloria's standards and taste. Whatever ambivalence Gloria felt about the place, once she'd married Jamie, he knew it had been her self-designed set and stage. He knew it was the right place to say good-bye to her.

Lucy wondered if Gloria's house was technically his now. He still spoke about the place as if she owned it. She wondered if his name had been added to the deed, or would that be a further complication for him while settling her estate?

The past few days he'd done very little to deal with any such issues, though he had mentioned that a lawyer in town, Martin Lewis, was handling the will and had been named executor. Jamie had clearly not been up to the task of dealing with much else. There was certainly time to sort it all out.

As Lucy helped her friends set up for the gathering, she couldn't help but think about their get-together only one short week ago. Under such different circumstances. Gloria, the perfect hostess, had been so full of life . . . the confidences she'd shared with them. Lucy realized that night she'd begun to feel much closer to Gloria. She thought they all had.

She didn't expect to speak at the service. She hadn't known Gloria long enough to rate that honor. But if she did need to speak, she knew what she would say. Gloria had been a true original. The sort of larger-than-life person you meet once in a great while, and remember forever.

Jamie would certainly never forget her. He seemed stunned, Lucy thought. As if he was sleepwalking. He'd cried himself out the first two or three days and now seemed numb, walking around with a vacant, empty stare.

Sometimes you needed to say the same thing to him

several times before he'd answer. The knitting group talked with him daily. They'd called all the necessary names in Gloria's phone books, they rented folding chairs, even contacted a minister who was willing to say a few words. Gloria had never been much of a churchgoer, but Jamie thought she'd like something officially spiritual at the end.

In keeping with her wishes, Jamie had her remains cremated as soon as the police released the body. He had already set the silver urn on the fireplace mantel, with a simple spray of orchids in a shiny black onyx vase beside it. He did have an artist's eye, Lucy realized.

"That looks perfect," Maggie told him as the group worked on the living room. "What about photographs? Do you have any that you want to display?"

"I gathered some from the study and the bedroom. And some old albums I found in the bookcase. It's all on the dining room table if anybody wants to sift through. I really don't have the heart for it right now. . . . And I'd feel her looking over my shoulder, saying she didn't like any of them," he added. "Gloria always hated the way she looked in pictures. I never understood that. She was so beautiful . . ." He sighed. "I just wish she'd been happier with herself."

Lucy glanced at Maggie, but she couldn't read her reaction. Maggie had been the closest of all them to Gloria. Had she ever glimpsed these insecurities? Lucy had never seen them. Gloria had always projected a total "this is me, love it or leave it" attitude, Lucy thought. But maybe that was just a false front, another facet of the issues Jamie had confided before, her mood swings and drinking?

It hardly seemed the right time to poke that wound. There would be other opportunities to ask Jamie questions, to try to understand what really happened. Gloria had appeared to be an open book, but now it seemed there was a lot they didn't know about her.

"I'll look through the photos," Maggie offered. "I can probably guess which ones she would have wanted to display."

"Want some help?" Lucy offered.

She followed Maggie into the dining room, where Jamie had left several framed photographs and a few thick, dusty albums. Maggie sat at the head of the table and Lucy took a seat to her right so they could look at the pictures together.

"Here's a good one." Maggie picked up a photo that appeared to be a recent shot. Gloria was dressed in a formal, off-the-shoulder black gown with an upswept hairdo and glittering diamond jewelry. She looked like a movie star on the red carpet, one who was enjoying the spotlight. It looked like someone else had been in the picture standing close beside her, but had been cut out, Lucy noticed. All that was left was a portion of a tuxedo-covered shoulder and arm, entwined with Gloria's.

"She definitely would have approved of this one, don't you think?" Maggie held the picture at arm's length to give Lucy a clear view.

"I can't see why not," Lucy agreed. "Looks like she was at some big gala or fund-raiser."

"She gave a lot to charities. And to political campaigns," Maggie added. "If you want to get business done around here, you have to move in those circles."

Lucy didn't know much about "moving and shaking" in Essex County, but she took Maggie's word for it.

They chose some other photos of Gloria from the pile of framed shots. One had been taken on a beach in Rio at sunset, the famous silhouette of Sugar Loaf in the background. Gloria looked like a Brazilian beauty in a pareo skirt with a tropical flower print and a black halter top, her long hair blowing in the breeze.

She looked stunning, Lucy thought, tanned and relaxed. But more than just cosmetically correct, Gloria looked really happy.

"That must have been taken on their honeymoon," Lucy said quietly. "She looks beautiful."

"Truly. From the inside out, too," Maggie agreed. "You can't buy that in a bottle of face cream."

They chose a few more, two that included Jamie. Then Maggie brought the photos into the living room, to see what the others thought. Lucy stayed behind and looked through those that remained.

She found it curious that there were no photographs of Gloria with relatives. Then she remembered Maggie had once told her that Gloria had been raised in foster homes and didn't have any real family connections. A lot like Jamie, she realized. They had both experienced difficult, lonely childhoods and maybe that similarity had also drawn them together.

She pulled over one of the albums and flipped it open. The pictures dated back to the 1980s, judging from the clothes and hairstyles. Most were not very flattering. Gloria flaunted a puffy, layered hairdo and wide-shouldered business suits that made her look like a linebacker for the Patriots.

Interesting to see, though, Lucy thought. She really hadn't aged much, it was amazing. Her face did look different, especially around the lips and eyes, where she'd had the most work done. And her chest, of course. Another gift from George Thurman, she'd once told them.

Maggie returned and looked over her shoulder. "That's George Thurman. I didn't really know him. Just by sight."

The photo showed Gloria and a man who looked a bit older than her. He had dark hair, conservatively cut and sprinkled with gray, and wore large aviator glasses. The photo had obviously been taken at this house some years ago and showed them sitting together under an umbrella table with the swimming pool in the background.

A little girl, about five or six, Lucy guessed, sat on George's lap. She had fair hair and big blue eyes. She wore a pink bathing suit and yellow, puffed-up swim aids on her skinny arms.

"Who's that?" Lucy asked. "I thought Gloria didn't have any children."

"George had a daughter," Maggie told her. "She was about five or six when he died. I'm not sure."

"Oh, I didn't know that. What happened to her?" Lucy asked, glancing at another summer photo of the little family that was on the same page.

"Her mother had primary custody, I think. She just came to visit George and Gloria during the week, or on weekends. George had divorced his first wife to marry Gloria. I believe he gave his ex-wife a good settlement and child support. But it still wasn't an easy situation," Maggie explained.

"I remember Edie saying that."

"Gloria told me once she'd tried to stay in touch with the child after George died, but the mother wouldn't let her. Then George's ex-wife moved out of town, so that was that. Gloria never talked about her."

Maggie sat down again and opened the other album, but quickly paged through.

That seemed likely, Lucy thought. Especially if George's

first wife had been ousted by Gloria. The child's natural mother probably despised Gloria and didn't want to compete for her child's affection with the interloper.

Maggie abruptly flipped her photo album shut. "Nothing good here," she decided. "Nothing she'd want to release for public viewing, I mean."

"I think that's the same story with this book," Lucy replied.

She wasn't as quick to close her album, though. The photos were intriguing and she couldn't turn away so easily from this exclusive glimpse into Gloria's past.

The exercise did stir up more melancholy feelings. Is that all that remained when your life was over? Some pages of yellowed photos? Even for a woman as interesting and vital as Gloria? It wasn't a very comforting thought.

The memorial was scheduled to begin at twelve noon, so that guests who were working could come during their lunch hour.

Lucy had promised to be there early, but had trouble pulling together an appropriately formal, somber outfit. She had a lot of dark clothes, but most items were either too sporty, sexy, or speckled with dog hair.

She finally found a brown linen skirt and oatmeal-colored sweater set, left over from her past life, lurking around office cubicles.

The outfit felt about right, especially with her hair pinned up in a serious-looking knot. I look so responsible, I could interview as a bank teller, Lucy thought as she left the house.

When she turned down Sugar Maple Way, the cars extended down the road for almost as far as she could see. Lucy searched for a spot, parked some distance away, and walked quickly to the house. She entered by the front door and wove her way through the crowd, looking for familiar faces.

She spotted Dana, Suzanne, and Phoebe standing by the glass doors in the living room. Lucy grabbed a glass from a tray offered to her by a passing waiter and joined them.

"Wow, what a turnout," she said.

"And it's not even noon." Dana checked her watch.

"Jamie is still getting flower deliveries. It's starting to look like a greenhouse in here," Suzanne said. Lucy followed her glance and saw a deliveryman carrying in a large arrangement of white roses.

"Where are the flowers we sent?" Phoebe asked.

Phoebe always wore black, so it probably wasn't difficult for her to choose an outfit today. She had removed her nose ring, Lucy noticed, out of respect for Gloria. That was pretty thoughtful.

"That vase of starburst lilies," Dana pointed out. "Maggie added the knitting needles and wool."

"Oh . . . that was really nice." Suzanne started to sniffle and Phoebe handed her a tissue.

There would be plenty more tears shed before the afternoon was over, Lucy knew that was true.

There were many familiar faces from town in the room, local businesspeople who Lucy recognized. Dana's husband, Jack, had come. He stood at the far side of the living room, talking with a man who Lucy recognized, Martin Lewis, the attorney who was the executor of Gloria's estate.

There was another cluster of men in dark, expensive-looking suits standing out on the patio, a group Lucy didn't recognize.

They talked together quietly, checked BlackBerries and

heavy gold watches. They sipped their drinks and gazed out at the pool, looking restless as they waited for the service to begin.

A caption underneath could have read "Time Is Money." And the group didn't look accustomed to wasting either.

"Who do you think those guys are?" Lucy asked her friends, slanting her gaze in the direction of the pack of suits.

"Some business connections. I don't recognize any locals in the group."

"The notorious locals are grazing at the hors d'oeuvre table," Suzanne pointed out. "That's Shirley Carlson in the navy blue suit, she's a village trustee. Karen Wilcox, right next to her? She's a VP at New England Savings and Loan. Those other two guys are somebodies . . . oh right. The smooth-looking guy with the dark hair? Mike Novak. He's a real estate attorney. He's in on a lot of big deals," Suzanne said knowingly.

"I think he represented Gloria from time to time, Dana said. "Jack knows him a little from the club. He's a good golfer."

Dana turned and sipped her drink, wearing a certain expression that signaled to Lucy she probably knew something about Mr. Novak she didn't feel comfortable disclosing. Something more than his impressive handicap.

Between both of their practices, Dana and Jack were privy to loads of confidential information about so many people in town. It seemed that the sight of these local politicians reminded Dana of some juicy tidbit, but one that she didn't wish to share.

Lucy glanced back at Novak, who was now conversing with the bank vice president. Even at this distance she could tell his hair was dyed, with the exception of his sideburns. The gravitas-silver sideburns that might even cost a little extra at the salon, designed to signal wisdom and maturity. He could definitely run for public office with that hairdo, no problem.

"Oh geez, check it out. Gloria Wannabes. A matching set," Phoebe said under her breath. They followed her eye-rolling glance to the living room, where two women strolled in, perfectly groomed and expensively dressed, from their chic, wispy hairdos to the tips of their Manolo Blahniks. They were dripping with jewelry and further accessorized by attractive, much younger men.

"Must be some other club she belonged to?" Suzanne asked the others. "I mean, she had other hobbies besides knitting."

"Right. Those ladies must be local reps from the Cougar Club," Lucy replied.

The women were definitely of a certain type. Similar to Gloria at first glance, Lucy thought.

But not when you really looked close. Not really. Yes, Gloria had availed herself of all the cosmetic advantages, no question. But her good looks glowed with a true inner light. A vibrant spirit and sharp intelligence that shone through the tanning bed complexion.

When you saw Jamie walking beside her, he didn't look like another expensive accessory, a designer handbag, or diamond-studded charm bracelet dangling from her wrist. Not like the male partners of these women.

"Where's Maggie?" Phoebe asked. "I don't think she should miss this."

"Jamie asked Maggie to help in the kitchen. But that was a while ago. They should be around here someplace." Lucy glanced around.

She spotted Jamie outside, near the pool, talking to his tennis partner, Kenny. The guy who had come the night Gloria died and picked Jamie up.

Maggie stood nearby speaking with a man Lucy vaguely recognized. "Who is that with Maggie?" she asked Suzanne.

"Nick Cooper. He just took over the bookstore on Main Street?" she said, trying to jog Lucy's memory.

"And he's been stalking her for weeks," Phoebe supplied. "Though following her to a funeral is a tiny bit twisted."

"He came for Gloria, silly," Dana corrected her. "Gloria was in the bookstore all the time." Lucy knew that was true. Gloria loved to read the latest celebrity tell-alls, diet books, self-improvement tomes, and even thick paperbacks with swirly writing on the cover.

Lucy would see them stashed in her knitting bag like forbidden treats, the kind that often had the words "stormy," "sweet," and "wild" in the title. Usually the same words, just interchanged.

"So this guy Nick is like always dropping by the shop and just sort of stares at Maggie," Phoebe went on. "He's got it bad. And he's old. I mean, who wants to see that?"

Lucy gave her a look. Nick Cooper was not old. He was age appropriate for Maggie. Attractive, too, and they probably had things in common. Both owned shops in town? Both liked to read? Maggie could be intimidating and he seemed . . . intimidated? But even if he did summon up the courage to ask Maggie out, Lucy doubted it would go anywhere.

Maggie had lost her husband, Bill, a little over three years ago and there had been no one since. Not really. Bill had been the love of her life and Maggie didn't expect to meet anyone who would take his place.

She did date from time to time, but it was usually a man who liked her much more than she liked him, and it never went very far. Poor Nicolas Cooper seemed to be falling into that category without even trying.

Maggie left Nick and walked over to the minister. Lucy saw him check his watch, then they both walked over to Jamie. It appeared that the service was about to begin.

"I think the minister is ready to start," Lucy said. "We ought to take our seats."

The four friends headed for the rows of folding chairs that had been set up in the living room, where the big, curving sectional normally stood. Jamie had asked them earlier to sit up front with him. They had helped him so much the last week and they were Gloria's closest friends, he'd said, when they demurred.

"And mine, too," he'd told them.

While Lucy found that hard to believe, it did seem true. He really didn't have anyone else here, besides Kenny, the tennis friend. Not that she'd noticed.

Jamie, Maggie, and the minister came in and the minister took his place at the front of the room. "We're ready to begin the service now, if everyone will please take a seat," the minister said.

Jamie and Maggie sat in the two empty seats at the end of their row. Jamie's expression was stoic as he faced straight ahead. He wore a tan linen sports coat and a black silky shirt underneath with the collar buttoned to the top.

He'd gotten a haircut, Lucy noticed, but he had not shaved since the night Gloria died and his cheeks were covered with a layer of scruffy blond beard that made him look weary and haggard.

There were so many present by now that there weren't enough seats for everyone, even though the caterers had set up over seventy chairs in the living and dining rooms. Lucy had rarely seen such a large turnout at a memorial. And from so many walks of life. She was impressed. Gloria had amazing social skills and could start up a conversation with anybody. She made connections easily, though perhaps close connections were rare.

The minister spoke about Gloria's life and achievements, though it was clear he didn't know her firsthand. Then he invited others at the gathering to come forward.

An old friend named Elaine Curtis came up first. She told some amusing stories of Gloria's high school days in Woburn and how Gloria had persuaded her to move into the city right after they'd graduated. How Gloria had worked in an office all day and went to school at night, to earn her degree.

"What an inspiration she was for me. For everyone who knew her," Elaine said.

Gloria's longtime secretary came up next, Lillian Stahl. She also had nothing but praise for her former boss. Then a very dignified-looking gentleman in an expensive dark suit stepped up to speak. He was bald with a fringe of gray hair and wire-rimmed glasses. He introduced himself as Richard Lamont, a former business partner from the Avalon Group. A friend of both Gloria's and her late husband, George Thurman.

Lucy had noticed him speaking with Mike Novak earlier.

He praised Gloria personally and professionally, as one of the first wave of women executives, and spoke of how she'd bravely paved the way for so many other women in an industry that was such a male-dominated terrain.

"Gloria not only broke through the glass ceiling in this town. Once she got up there, she redecorated," he quipped, making everyone chuckle.

He closed on a more serious note, reminding everyone how Gloria had never forgotten her modest beginnings and always tried to help young people starting out and how she gave so much to the community.

The minister asked if anyone else had any recollections to offer. When no one else came forward, the minister cast Jamie a questioning glance. Lucy wondered if he would speak. He'd been unsure about it. He said he wanted to talk about Gloria but was afraid he couldn't manage it without breaking down.

Jamie finally nodded and slowly rose from his chair. As he stepped to the front of the group, Lucy thought she heard everyone in the room suck in a breath. He stood with his head bowed for a moment, then he looked up. His blue eyes were red rimmed and bloodshot, glassy with tears.

When he finally spoke his words were thick. "I met Gloria less than a year ago. She came into my life and changed everything, with just one beautiful smile. We didn't have much time together. But maybe no one is allowed too much happiness in one lifetime and we had more than our share. Those were the best days of my life and will always be. I know that she touched all of you, too. Because she was like no one else in the world. No one I'll ever know. Nor will you.

"Gloria wouldn't have wanted any crying today. So that's why I'm trying hard not to. She would have wanted a party in her honor, lots of music and good food and wine. She would have wanted you all to enjoy yourselves today, to give her a good sendoff. 'Life is short,' she used to tell me. 'So let's have dessert first.'"

The group laughed and Lucy did, too. But she knew he wasn't just reaching for a comic moment; Gloria did say that, among other pithy credos.

When his audience grew quiet again, Jamie added, "Life is short. So let's not mourn today, but celebrate Gloria's brief but exceptional life. An awesome woman. A perfect wife . . ."

At those words, he finally broke down. Tears spilled from the corners of his eyes, but he didn't seem to notice. "Goodbye, my best friend. My true love and soul mate . . . I will miss you always."

Jamie stood for a moment with his head hanging to his chest. The minister stepped over and helped him back to his seat, where he hunkered down and covered his face with his hands. Maggie was sitting closest to him and patted his back for a moment.

The minister closed the service with a brief prayer. When it was over, people stood up from their chairs and stared around, looking dazed. Then they began to walk over to Jamie to offer their condolences. Many were on lunch breaks and had to leave, Lucy knew.

Jamie had spoken more eloquently than she'd ever heard him before—or expected he could. If Lucy had ever doubted his feelings, she did believe now that he truly loved Gloria and her death had irrevocably altered him.

He might someday return to his sunny, boyish persona, she thought, but not too far underneath you would find a withdrawn, stony layer, hardened forever by this stunning loss.

Chapter Six

After the memorial Lucy went back to work, lasted a few hours at the computer, then spent most of the night knitting.

She'd been working steadily on her blanket squares, the perfect project for the rattling days after Gloria's death. She'd chosen blue yarn and had two down, with six to go. While she clicked away at the simple stocking stitch, she couldn't help but consider what she might work on next.

She wanted to make something for Matt, but wondered if it was too soon in the relationship. They'd only been going out three months. There seemed to be dating rules for everything—how soon to call, when to pay for dinner, when to sleep together . . . Was there some guideline for handmade gifts? It did seem like a big step in the relationship.

A sweater was the obvious choice. At the rate she knitted, if she started in June it *might* be done by the time the cold weather hit. Things were going well, but you never could predict what would happen. They might not even be going out by the time she finished. How depressing would that be?

No, she just wasn't ready for it.

Not that she didn't have sweater-size feelings for him. But he wasn't completely untangled from his marriage, and they both needed to take things slowly and carefully. Tiptoeing a bit, you could call it. Which is what gave her the idea to start with socks.

Phoebe was the queen of sock projects and her long and very happy relationship with Josh had been nourished entirely by her gifts to him of strikingly original footwear. But they were still socks. Not full-length overcoats, or knitted sports car covers, or cable-stitched two-man tents.

Socks were the way to go, Lucy coached herself as she headed down Main Street the next morning, tugging Tink away from an abandoned pizza crust and many other less appetizing finds on the Saturday morning sidewalk. As soon as she finished her blanket squares, she'd start with Matt's feet and work her way . . . up.

No one had mentioned getting together for a recap of Gloria's service, but as Lucy strolled up the path toward the Black Sheep at about half past nine, she had a feeling her friends would congregate there this morning.

The shop didn't officially open until 11:00 on Saturday, but when she tied Tink's leash to the porch rail, she noticed Suzanne's huge SUV parked across the street and saw Dana heading up the walk with her red travel mug in hand, her knitting bag slung over her shoulder.

"I had a feeling I would see you here," Dana greeted her.

"I'm whipping through my squares. I need some yarn."

"I had a little break between appointments to hang out

and visit." Dana opened the door and let Lucy go in first. "Not that we need an excuse. We did miss our meeting on Thursday. Maybe we're all suffering knitting group withdrawal."

Lucy thought that might be true, especially after losing Gloria. It made her feel needier.

Even though they had all been at Gloria's house to help Jamie prepare for the service and then attended it en mass, that wasn't quite the same thing as their weekly get-together.

"We're back here," Maggie called from the back of the shop. "Suzanne beat you both," she added.

"I can't stay long," Suzanne said, taking a big sip from her coffee. "I'm running an open house. I still have to put up more signs. It's not even my listing, I just got stuck helping out. Not that I have any hot properties to push."

Not with Gloria's house taken off the table, Lucy thought.

"I wonder if Jamie will still want to sell," she said instead.

"I was wondering the same thing, believe me. But it really seemed too rude and insensitive to ask. Even for me," Suzanne admitted.

She liked to characterize herself as some tough-talking real estate babe, but Lucy knew Suzanne had no truly hard edges to speak of.

"Maybe he'll bring it up before you have to," Maggie said. She took out a project from her knitting bag, not one of the blanket squares, Lucy noticed. But Maggie was such a fast, skillful knitter, she could work on three projects simultaneously and still finish her seven squares with time to spare.

The project she'd taken out appeared to be almost done. Quite a pretty little camisole top knit with fine, silky pink yarn. Lucy guessed Maggie was making it for her daughter, who was in college and doing a summer internship at a TV station up in Portland.

Maybe she should skip Matt's socks and try a camisole. He'd probably like that even better.

"That's really pretty," Lucy said, admiring Maggie's work. "Is it for Julie?"

Maggie nodded. "She e-mailed me a rush order. I need to pop it in the mail on Monday."

"Lucky girl to have a mother who can just whip this stuff out. Is the pattern hard?"

"Easy as pie," Maggie promised, though she did say that about most projects. Then she turned to Suzanne, continuing their conversation about the house. "I wonder if Jamie's name is on the deed. Or if the property has to go through probate," she added, switching back to Suzanne's topic of conversation.

"Oh geez . . . I didn't even think of that. They haven't been married very long. Maybe they didn't have time to take care of all that legal stuff. Just my luck." Suzanne sighed. "How long will that take?"

"It depends," Dana replied. She had reached the top of the back section of the yellow vest and was just about done. "Gloria probably left a will, but her estate might be complicated. It could take a few months."

"Something tells me I need to go to plan B for the ortho-dontist bills."

"That might be a good idea," Maggie agreed.

They heard Phoebe coming down the back stairway that led from her apartment into the storeroom. It sounded as if someone was with her, then Lucy realized she was just talking on the phone.

She appeared in the doorway, her cell phone pressed to her ear. "I don't know yet," Lucy heard her say. "I'll call you back." Then she shut the phone and stuck it in the pocket of her ragged denim shorts.

"Maggie? Do you need me here all day?" she asked, hanging on the doorway.

"I'm not sure. Why do you ask?" Maggie replied evenly.

"My friend Crystal is driving down to Cranes Beach. It's so great out. Do you really think we're going to be busy?"

Maggie glanced at her assistant over the edge of her glasses. "People knit all year long, Phoebe. Not just in the winter," she reminded her. "But I guess you can have part of the day off. How about if you go to the beach now and come back by two? If it's really a slow day, maybe I'll go home and do some gardening and you can close up."

"Deal," Phoebe replied. She disappeared into the storeroom, humming happily.

"You're a nice boss," Suzanne complained. "I don't think Mary Alice would let me skip work and go to the beach today," she added, talking about the broker at Premier Properties.

Maggie shrugged. "Life is short, Suzanne. Maybe you should just jump the fence and go."

"Now you sound like Gloria," Lucy told her.

"Yes, I know." Maggie sighed, binding off a row with a yarn-threaded needle. "Seems she was right."

Lucy felt the conversation edging back to Gloria, but before anyone brought up the memorial service the bell above the shop door announced a new visitor. Jamie walked in.

He wore dark glasses that covered a good part of his face. Lucy could still see that he looked drawn and ashen. He hadn't been getting much sleep, he'd told them. It was catching up with him.

"Jamie . . . come in. I didn't expect to see you today," Maggie said, greeting him warmly. "You must be exhausted."

"Never felt so tired in my life." He dropped into a chair next to Suzanne and let out a deep sigh. "I couldn't sleep and I didn't feel like hanging around the house . . ."

It felt so empty, Lucy guessed, especially after the crowd that filled it yesterday. Now that all the anticipation of the memorial was over, he must be feeling Gloria's absence even more keenly.

"I brought you something." He opened a recyclable grocery tote and took out three bakery boxes, then set them on the table. "Just some muffins and cake left over from yesterday. I thought you could put it out for the customers, you know, on the tea table."

Maggie often had a table set up in the afternoon with coffee, tea, and pastry. In the summertime, she offered cold drinks like lemonade and iced tea. Another reason her customers loved visiting the shop and usually stayed longer than they'd expected to.

"Why wait for customers? You could put it out right now," Suzanne hinted broadly. "All I had this morning was a tiny bowl of bran bits. Tasted like garden mulch soaked in skim milk."

"Help yourself, please . . ." Maggie set some napkins on the table, then reached over and flipped open the lids on the boxes. A sweet, buttery scent quickly filled the air. "Oh, this stuff looks good. Thank you, Jamie. You didn't have to bother."

"It would have only gone to waste." He sighed and sat back in his seat. "I had to come into town anyway, to see Martin Lewis, the attorney handling Gloria's estate. He's the executor. He wants to talk to me about the will and settling the estate. It's all pretty . . . overwhelming," he admitted.

"It must be," Suzanne sympathized, picking out a muffin

and placing it on a paper napkin. Lucy could tell she was itching to ask about the house, but didn't want to seem ghoulish.

"Was there any insurance?" Maggie asked. She didn't seem to feel any such inhibitions, Lucy noticed.

Jamie shrugged. "Gloria didn't believe in it. She told me once that she'd never planned to get married again and she didn't have any children, so she didn't see the point. She had planned to leave all her money to charity . . . until we got married, I mean."

Sounded like there was a will. Lucy wondered if Gloria had put Jamie's name was on it. She hoped so. She didn't know much about how these things worked, but that would probably make it easier for him and faster for the estate to be settled.

"I can see her reasoning," Maggie replied.

"It doesn't matter. I would have felt terrible getting money like that, because she died," he confided in a quiet voice. "I mean . . . I never cared about what she had."

"We know that, Jamie," Dana assured him. But Lucy knew what Dana was also thinking: There were plenty of people in town who believed Jamie to be the complete opposite, that he had only married Gloria for her money and had unexpectedly lucked out with her unfortunate accident.

Edie Steiber, for one, was probably gloating and spreading that spin on the story right now, Lucy thought.

"I know sometimes, when a spouse passes away and the finances are all in a tangle, the survivor is really stuck until probate is completed," Dana began in a concerned tone. "Are you okay, Jamie? Do you have enough to live on right now?"

"There's a bank account with my name on it and some credit cards. I'll be fine. For now, anyway."

"That's good to hear." Dana sounded relieved and turned her attention back to her knitting. "I hope it goes smoothly."

"If you need anything, anything at all, you must let us know," Maggie made him promise. "At least she had a will . . . and how was that left? Had she changed it since you married?"

Lucy thought that question was a bit forward of Maggie, but she really wasn't being nosy, just concerned. As they all were.

"Yes, she changed it when we came to live up here. This lawyer I'm going to see today, he said I'm the sole beneficiary."

"What about the house? Is that part of the estate now?" Suzanne asked.

"I'm not sure. Gloria put my name on the deed . . . so I guess it's not?" He shrugged again. "She really had a thing about it. She dragged me down to some lawyer's office as soon as we came up here from Florida. I mean, I didn't really care one way or the other if I owned the house with her."

"She wanted to look out for you," Dana said. "It was the responsible thing to do."

As Lucy expected, Suzanne saw her opening and jumped in.

"I know it's too soon to decide," Suzanne began slowly, "but Gloria did sign an agreement with my firm. It would probably be best if we had something in writing from you to take the property off the market. I mean, if you *don't* want to sell it anymore," she quietly clarified.

Lucy didn't bother to glance under the table, but she would have bet five bucks Suzanne had her fingers crossed.

"Oh, I still want to sell it," he told her, sounding definite about something for the first time this morning. "I'm just not sure how that will work now; if I have to wait or whatever. This lawyer I'm meeting will probably tell me, right?"

"I'm sure he will," Suzanne promised him.

"That's one thing I do know. It's hard to be there without her. I've even thought of moving into a hotel or something. But I don't want to waste the money," he confided. "I just miss her so much. Everything reminds me of her. It's very . . . hard."

"The next few weeks, and even months, are going to be very difficult for you," Maggie warned him. "I went through it, too. I know how it feels. Just take it one day at a time. One hour at a time. Sooner or later, you'll come out the other side."

Jamie nodded as he looked down at his hands. "I still can't believe it. That's the problem. I keep expecting her to walk in a room. Or I go outside and think that she'll be there, sitting by the pool on her chaise longue, knitting or reading a magazine. Sometimes I feel as if she's right next to me. In the middle of the night. I feel like I can just reach out and touch her . . ."

He shook his head, as if to shake out the disturbing images. Then he leaned forward, covering his face with his hands.

The Black Sheep knitters sat silently. They exchanged glances, but Lucy could see that no one knew what to tell him. Not even Dana.

"I'm just wiped out," he confessed, his face still covered. "It's like some big wave crashed over me and slammed me down, and I can't get up again. I can't even get out of bed in the morning," he confessed. "How am I going to take care of all this legal stuff? How am I going to have a show? I don't think I can do it. I don't know when I'll be able to paint again. Never, maybe . . ." he said bleakly.

"Jamie . . . slow down. Take a breath," Dana consoled him. She reached out and rested a hand on his broad shoulder. "I'm sure you feel overwhelmed. That's only natural. But you can't make any big decisions right now. It's much too soon. You have time to figure these things out. Just give it time."

"Please don't give up on your show, Jamie," Maggie implored him. "Gloria wanted that so much for you. Dana's right. Don't even think about it right now. You're in no state to make that decision."

"Maybe I can help you with questions about the property and all that," Suzanne offered.

Jamie swallowed hard and finally lifted his head up again. He took a deep shaky breath. "Thanks, guys. You're the best. I mean it."

Lucy's heart went out to him. He was really suffering. She wished there was something more they could do, but she felt so helpless to ease his pain. She knew that all her friends felt the same.

The bell above the shop door sounded. Lucy turned and saw a young woman walk in. She didn't seem to be a typical customer, dressed in an even edgier Goth girl style than Phoebe wore. Her outfit was solid black, cargo pants on the bottom and a T-shirt with the armholes cut off. A camouflage-print backpack was slung over one boney shoulder and her thin white arms provided a pale backdrop for several inky tattoos.

Even her long straight hair had been dyed a shade Lucy would call Deep Space Black, a ragged cut with dark eyes peeping out from under spiky bangs. A black cotton bandanna, imprinted with tiny pink skulls, was wrapped around her head like a headband.

She entered slowly and waved when she reached the middle of the shop, swinging her pack around and holding it protectively to her chest. "Is . . . a . . . Phoebe around?" she asked shyly.

"Oh, you must be her ride to the beach," Maggie answered.

The girl smiled, looking relieved. "Right. I'm Crystal? Her friend?"

Question talker, Lucy realized. People who end practically every statement on a questioning note? Teenagers often talked that way, she'd noticed. Crystal was a bit past her teens, about Phoebe's age, in her early twenties, Lucy would guess, but could remain a question talker for life.

"I think Phoebe went back upstairs to get her things. Have a seat, I'll call her." Maggie picked up the receiver from her portable phone, which she had on the table, and dialed the number of the apartment above.

The girl walked to the table with a purposeful stride, her eyes cast down. She hung her pack on the back of a seat near Dana and sat, still staring down, her shoulders hunched, as if trying to make herself invisible.

"Hi, Crystal." Dana leaned toward her, making an effort to be friendly. "Are you a knitter?"

Crystal shook her head. "Phoebe says she'll teach me? She does make some cool stuff."

"Come back sometime. We'll teach you. It's very easy once you get the hang of it," Maggie encouraged her.

Crystal replied with a head bob. "Sounds good. Maybe I will."

"How do you know Phoebe?" Suzanne asked. "Do you go to school with her?"

Crystal offered another quick head bob. "We were in a class together spring semester? Modern poetry?"

Crystal seemed reluctant to make eye contact with anyone, her gaze fixed now on the tabletop. Lucy saw her glance dart to Jamie for an instant, but he seemed unaware of her, or anyone in the room, for that matter.

Jamie had been staring vacantly into space all this time, and most likely hadn't heard a word of Crystal's interview. Lost in his thoughts about Gloria and all the complications he faced in the wake of her death.

He suddenly checked his watch and rose from his chair. "I'd better go. I'm late for my appointment. Thanks again for listening." His gaze swept around the table, touching each of them. "I appreciate it. Really."

"Don't be silly. Come here anytime. We're always around. And call if you're feeling down and want some company. Or just need to talk," Maggie reminded him.

"I will," Jamie promised. "I'll see you later," he said, then headed to the door.

After he left, the group was very quiet again. Crystal picked up a stray knitting needle and tapped it on the table, keeping time with some inner beat. Lucy noticed the toe of her shredded black Reebok joining in.

She had a lot of anxious energy, it seemed. No wonder she was so thin.

"That was our friend Jamie," Dana explained as she began to cast on for the back of Jack's vest. "He just lost his wife. She was a good friend of ours. She used to knit with us."

"Too bad. That's sad." Crystal stopped tapping and nodded again.

Before the conversation could go any further, Phoebe

appeared in the doorway and noisily strolled in on her rubber flip-flops. She was hardly visible under a voluminous white T-shirt, which Lucy guessed belonged to her boyfriend, Josh, and could have done double duty as a minidress. A lumpy-looking knapsack a lot like Crystals was slung over her shoulder.

"I'm here. I couldn't find my sunblock. Sorry."

"No problem. I was just hanging with your friends."

"Yes, Crystal has just been hanging with us," Maggie echoed, sounding as if she were trying to speak a foreign language but had mangled the accent miserably. "Crystal wants to learn how to knit. You ought to bring her back sometime, when there's a beginner's class or a knitting group night."

"Sure, if she wants. They didn't freak you out too much, did they?" Phoebe asked blandly.

Lucy knew Phoebe was just being her sarcastic little self. But Crystal didn't seem to have the same sense of irony and took the question very seriously.

"Um . . . no. They're pretty cool?" Goth Girl replied.

Whoa, Crystal thinks we're pretty cool!? Did anyone else hear that? Lucy wanted to ask her friends.

But she decided to wait until the two girls were out of earshot.

"Catch you later," Phoebe said, waving as she left for her personal beach day.

"Two o'clock, please, Phoebe. That was our deal. We might be able to have summer hours more often, if this works out," Maggie called after her. Sort of a promise and a warning intertwined, Lucy thought.

"I guess I'd better go, too," Suzanne said. "It's after ten."

She rose and straightened a sleeveless hot pink top bordered by white and yellow flowers that had been appliquéd. She wore it over a white skirt. Lucy remembered when she'd knit the top last winter and fussed as she worked on the flower trim, when it seemed as if summer would never come again. Well, here it was. Suzanne was prepared, looking very stylish and professional.

"That was a lucky break for Jamie, that Gloria had put his name on the deed and changed her will," Lucy said.

"Lucky for me, too," Suzanne admitted. "If the house was part of the estate, who knows when he'd be free to sell it. Even if he wanted to."

"It takes several months for an estate to go through probate. Even when the situation is straightforward," Dana told them, gathering up her project. "It sounds like Gloria's might be more complicated. But with the house in his name and his name on the will, it shouldn't be too bad."

Maggie's expression held a thoughtful look. "That was very responsible of Gloria to take care of those details right away. I know she was a good businesswoman, but she could be scattered in a lot of ways, too. Or just didn't think the rules applied to her. Like she was invulnerable, so why worry about a will? Jamie makes it sound as if she was very concerned that he be taken care of if anything happened to her. Do you think . . . ?" Maggie shook her head. "I don't know what I'm saying . . . just forget about it."

Maggie's aborted line of logic had caught Lucy's interest. "Go on, what were you going to say, Maggie? Do you think Gloria had some sort of premonition about her accident?"

"The thought did come to mind," Maggie admitted. "People do have these intuitive feelings about their . . . demise.

And what he said the other night, about her dark moods. That worried me, too," she admitted.

Dana had packed up her knitting, but remained at the table. "That was troubling. I had to wonder if it was really an accident. Wasn't that what he was hinting at?"

"Suicide, you mean," Maggie said quietly. "It just seems unthinkable if you knew her. But it seems we didn't know her nearly as well as we thought, from what Jamie disclosed the other night."

"I wasn't thinking suicide," Suzanne piped up. "I kept thinking about those empty wineglasses. And the knock on the door while I was on the phone with her. Someone came to visit that night. Maybe she expected them. Maybe that's the real reason she didn't go to Boston to meet Jamie. She had . . . an appointment."

"On a Friday night, after eleven o'clock, while her husband is out of town? An appointment? Or maybe . . . a date?" Lucy's question hung in the air a moment.

Dana cast a serious look Lucy's way, confirming that she agreed.

Maggie looked surprised and even alarmed at the direction the conversation had taken.

"Oh, dear . . . all this speculation is getting a little wild, don't you think?" Maggie laughed nervously and abruptly left her seat.

She quickly walked to a cupboard and randomly pulled out drawers, looking for something. Signaling the end of the conversation, Lucy felt.

Dana stood up and picked up her purse and knitting bag, preparing to go.

"Wild talk, okay. Maybe. But I have to confess, now that

the initial shock has worn off, the entire story of the accident doesn't sit well with me," Suzanne insisted. "We all knew Gloria. Don't you feel there's something about it that doesn't add up?" she asked finally. "Something that doesn't really . . . ring true?"

Lucy couldn't put her finger on it. But once Suzanne had voiced her unease aloud, she realized that she felt the same way, too.

Chapter Seven

Before Lucy could voice her agreement, the bell above the shop door sounded. Two women walked in side by side, almost identically dressed in crisp cotton shorts, tank tops and thick-soled sandals, suitable for chasing children across playgrounds or pushing jogging strollers. Each carried a knitting tote hooked over one arm, their eyes glowing with a certain elated look Lucy recognized. Mothers of young children who had managed to escape the house on a Saturday morning.

Their conversation, easily overheard, confirmed Lucy's guess. "And she knows my kids aren't allowed to eat anything with white sugar, chocolate, or corn syrup. But at Nana's house, anything goes. You should have seen them. They were bouncing off the walls."

"My mother-in-law is *exactly* the same. She does it just to push my buttons," the other woman replied.

"Hi there . . . I'll be right with you," Maggie called out politely. "Time for the knitting at the sandbox group. Not that I'm ready yet," she murmured to her friends.

Suzanne, Dana, and Lucy quickly got out of Maggie's way so she could start her workday. They exchanged good-byes and headed out the door; Suzanne to her open house, Dana to her patients, and Lucy back to the cottage with Tink.

But it seemed far too nice a day to head straight back home, where—like it or not—housework and real work waited. The laundry had piled shoulder high and puffs of dog hair floated around her living room like rolling balls of sagebrush.

Despite the call of such irksome duties—or maybe, because of it—Lucy took the long way home, heading down Main Street to the harbor and the village green. She preferred her house neater and cleaner, but when she was on a deadline she just had to let everything go, and the last few days so much time and thought had been taken up with Gloria's accident and memorial service, she'd barely had time to do any work at all.

She passed the Schooner, which still looked busy with breakfast customers, though it was well past 10:00. She wondered how Edie felt about Gloria now. Any remorse at all for wishing the deceased woman ill? Or did she still think Gloria was a fool who'd gotten just what she deserved?

No doubt, Edie would stop in at the Black Sheep sooner or later, to share her opinion with Maggie. Lucy hoped she wouldn't be there to hear Edie expound on that subject again and was glad Edie had not come by this morning, while Jamie was there.

The conversation had taken a wild turn once Jamie had gone, though, Lucy reflected. Dana had dropped a bombshell and there had been little chance for anyone to respond.

But Dana's observation had definitely struck a nerve in

Lucy. Though the police investigation had seemed thorough, for those who really knew Gloria, something really didn't add up.

Gloria had seemed so upbeat and cheerful at the Main Street Café that Friday night. And Suzanne reported the same attitude during their phone call. Had she really taken such a drastic turn soon after?

Sucking up so much wine and painkillers that she'd totally lost control and had been unable to save herself?

And what had spurred such a sudden U-turn in her emotions?

Had she heard bad news . . . maybe from that mysterious visitor?

Or did the mysterious visitor have something to do with her accident?

Maybe she'd fought with Jamie over the phone and he felt too guilty now to admit it.

Lucy's thoughts were spinning. There was just no way of knowing. And what could they do about it now?

While her friends might agree that all these questions were valid, there was nothing substantial in her suspicions. Or Dana's. Just a feeling they all had. Except for the doorbell Suzanne claims she heard over the phone and the wineglasses. But the police had either covered those points in their inquest or thought they were unimportant.

Too bad there was no way to see the police report. Jamie had been told it wouldn't be available for weeks, maybe longer. He'd seemed satisfied with conclusions and explanations of the police and coroner. Was it right of any of them to start questioning and stirring things up?

Lucy couldn't say. She couldn't even say if she was

imagining things or not. Maybe, when somebody close died as suddenly as Gloria had, it was only natural to seek definitive explanations. To seek closure.

Maybe there were no definitive explanations here and never would be. That was hard to accept, but it seemed they would have to.

She and Tink had reached the village green. A light breeze kicked up a few waves in the harbor. Boats were moored, one right next to the other, so many this time of year it looked like the mall parking lot at the holidays.

While Lucy was lost in thought about Gloria's sad end, Tink was quietly stalking a huge, slow-waddling goose. Geese were a big problem on the green, but no one could figure out how to get rid of them. As the big dog made her move, Lucy was rudely jerked back into reality.

"Good try, pal," she told Tink once she'd recovered her balance. "Dream big."

Matt had his daughter, Dara, this weekend, so Lucy had Saturday night and Sunday free. He wasn't quite ready to introduce Lucy to his little girl, who looked charming from her photos. Lucy loved kids and was very close to her two nieces, Regina and Sophie, who were around the same age as Dara. But she understood. It was a big step and might even make waves with his almost ex-wife, which was the last thing she wanted right now.

She did miss him, but it was just as well. She needed some time alone this weekend to catch up. Aside from housework, she had to catch up on her real work. And her knitting.

She'd lost a lot of ground in both territories the last few days with Gloria's death and memorial service. If she'd managed to make it to the computer at all, it would have been too difficult to concentrate. Knitting, of course, was always a balm to her troubled mind and soul. But she'd been too tired and distracted to make much progress on that front, either.

On Sunday morning she sat down to work but found herself answering e-mail, then wandering around the Internet. She'd seen Gloria's obituary in the *Plum Harbor Times* the day after her death. Today, for some reason, she decided to take another look. She'd been so upset last week, she'd just skimmed it, with hardly any information registering.

The article came up quickly. The story of Gloria's drowning had made the front page of the newspaper and her obituary had also been placed prominently, not pushed to the back pages with the rest.

The text ran along a flattering head shot, an official PR photo that Gloria must have sent the newspaper at one time or another. "Gloria Sterling—Real Estate Investor, Recognized for Charity Work, Dead at Age 51" the headline read.

Did they have to put her age in boldfaced type? The irony of it, considering the great efforts Gloria had made to hide that number. Lucy scrolled down the page, skipping over the description of Gloria's watery demise and her formative years, growing up in foster homes in Woburn, a somewhat depressed suburb of Boston. "Soon after graduating high school, Ms. Sterling relocated to Boston's metropolitan center and took classes at night at a business school, while working as an administrative assistant in an accounting firm . . ."

The article spared a single line to her first husband, Bob Cranston, a union that had lasted only three years. Gloria had once referred to Bob as her "starter marriage." The article then chronicled her rise to the top of the corporate food chain.

"While working as a junior accountant at Clive & Thurman, a commercial realty firm, Ms. Sterling met and married her second husband, George Thurman. They were married for ten years, until Mr. Thurman succumbed to lung cancer a year after his diagnosis.

"The Thurmans were very active in the commercial real estate market of Plum Harbor and the surrounding area. They were also prominent political donors and fund-raisers for many charities, and founding partners of the Avalon Group, developing the Stoney Harbor Outlet Mall, Harbor Corporate Park, and many other improvements to the community."

Did an outlet mall qualify as an improvement to the community? Maybe to some people it did. Lucy wasn't sure about that one.

"Ms. Sterling sold her interest in the Avalon Group nearly two years ago," the article reported, "but continued to invest in local building projects and deal in commercial properties.

"In 2008 she received the prestigious Women Who Make a Difference Award from the Three Village Chamber of Commerce for her generous donations and fund-raising efforts on behalf of the Lung Cancer Foundation and New England Women-for-Women, a college scholarship fund and mentoring program for young women from low-income families in New England."

Wow, Gloria was a busy bee, wasn't she? Lucy had no idea. But she wasn't surprised.

The next quote, from a former business partner, Richard Lamont, summed Gloria up perfectly: "Gloria Sterling was formidable. She was an iron French-manicured fist in a velvet glove, part of a generation that paved the way for female executives. She made me sit up and pay attention, I'll tell you that much." Lucy recalled Richard Lamont had spoken at the Memorial Services and said practically the same thing about Gloria.

Finally, there was some mention of Jamie toward the very bottom.

"Ms. Sterling often spent winter months at her home in Boca Raton, Florida, where she met and married her third husband, James Barnett, last December. After honeymooning in Brazil and Argentina, the couple returned to Plum Harbor in late March and took up residence in Ms. Sterling's home in The Landing.

" 'Gloria was an amazing person. She could do anything she set her mind to,' Mr Barnett, an artist, said of his late wife. 'She was always an inspiration to me.'

"Ms. Sterling had no children. A memorial service will be held at her home on Friday at twelve noon. Her husband asks for donations to the charities noted above in lieu of flowers."

Lucy printed out the article, though she wasn't sure why she wanted to save it. She never saved stuff like that. But this was different. This was Gloria.

Before closing her computer she randomly typed the words "Avalon Group" in the search engine. She knew Gloria had been involved in some heavy-duty business deals, but that was before she'd ever really met her.

A zillion listings instantly appeared. Seems it was a popular name, picked up for everything from information technology firms to Christian rock groups. Lucy found a few listings about the land development group in Plum Harbor, mostly PR announcements about their plans for various building projects.

One article title did catch her eye. It dated back to last November. "DEC Clears Proposed Site of Sea Breeze Colony."

Lucy pulled it up and read it through. It seemed that a parcel of land owned by Gloria's former partners, and slated as a development of three- and four-bedroom homes on half-acre plots, had been declared by the Department of Environmental Conservation unbuildable, due to pollution from a dry-cleaning plant that had once occupied the spot.

It other words, Avalon was trying to build on a teeming, toxic waste dump, and the government blew the whistle on them.

The land had been ordered for cleanup, but nobody wanted to cover the cost. The county was responsible, but these days the budget had higher priorities. If the Avalon Group wanted to wait for the bureaucrats to clean up the mess, they'd be waiting a long time, Lucy guessed. But the developers didn't want to pick up the check, either, so a ping-pong match ensued. One that seemed destined for the court system with the building project stalled indefinitely.

But the article reported that, "A recent study by the DEC determined a thick layer of clay under the top soil provides an adequate barrier from possibly harmful toxins. Therefore, the land has been reclassified as fit for use."

A lucky break for Gloria's former partners. Their valuable contributions to the community continued.

Lucy checked the date of the article, wondering if the houses had ever gone up. She had no idea how long a building project like that would take. The article was pretty recent and there had been a drastic slowdown in building lately. She assumed the current economic setbacks had slowed this project down, too.

But she didn't want to waste more time checking on that. What did it matter? She was just about to end her procrastination break and open her files of real work, *The Big Book of Things That Flap, Swoop, and Fly*, when a familiar name popped up in the very last lines of the story.

"Attorney Michael Novak, representing the Avalon Group, stated that his firm 'has always been, and continues to be, committed to the safety and well-being of Essex County residents and we are satisfied with the agency's latest findings.'"

Michael Novak. Lucy remembered him. He'd been at Gloria's service, a smooth-looking attorney hanging out with local power brokers. He'd registered on Dana's antenna, Lucy recalled. Dana had said he'd done some work for Gloria.

Still, Lucy had a feeling there might be something more to that story. She decided to print out the article and show it to her friends. And persuade Dana to spill the beans about Mr. Novak.

Lucy worked until the early evening, ate a quick bite, then took Tink for a walk on the beach just before it grew dark.

When she got home, she decided not to work overtime tonight on the children's book design, and settled down with her knitting. A quick cruise with the remote yielded nothing worth watching on TV. Not even a good classic movie, which was just as well. She really didn't feel like having any distraction right now and enjoyed the simple, repetitive stitch of the blanket squares, which grew with such quick, satisfying progress.

She'd already finished three squares since the group had started. Maggie had been right. Sometimes a simple, mindless project was just what you needed to flush out the toxins in the knitting lobe of your brain. Even better, the effort was going for a good cause, keeping someone in need warm this winter.

She was casting on for a new square when the phone

rang. She let the message machine pick up, then heard Matt's voice. She hurried to pick up before he'd barely said hello.

"I'm here for you. Just screening," she admitted.

"So relieved to hear I rate."

"You always rate with me," she assured him. "How was your weekend? How is Dara doing?"

"She's great. We had a good time. We went biking at a new park, and went over to the Children's Museum in Boston."

"Oh, I know that one. I took my nieces there last winter. The bubble exhibit was my favorite."

"Me, too. I loved standing in a giant bubble. What an experience. Dara loved the whole place. She didn't want to leave."

Lucy laughed. "Well, you have to take her back again sometime."

Did that sound too much like, "And I could tag along? Maybe it's time for me to meet Dara?" Lucy hoped not. That really had not been her intention. At least, she didn't think so.

"I've just been working a lot this weekend," she reported. "I had to catch up. I lost time last week with . . . you know, Gloria."

"Sure. How's it going?" he asked in quieter tone. "How are you feeling now?"

"I'm okay, I guess. Jamie is a real mess. He stopped at the shop yesterday morning. He's really having a rough time."

"I'll bet. I can't imagine what he's going through," Matt said sympathetically.

"He has to settle the estate now, too. Gloria had a lot going on. It's going to take a while to figure it all out."

"Money causes complications," Matt said simply. "But he should end up pretty well set when it's all over, don't you think?"

"Oh, sure. No question." Lucy sighed. "But I do think it's unfair that so many people in town think he married Gloria for her money. I don't think it was that at all. I think he really loved her. You just had to see them together. Or the way he mourns her. It was the real deal."

Matt was quiet for a moment. "I believe you. I don't think an age difference matters. If it works, it works," he said simply.

Did Matt think they worked? Lucy wondered. Or was the jury still out on that question?

"So what are you knitting lately?" he asked, changing the subject. "Anything interesting?"

Matt knew how to knit a little, too. Dara had gotten a craft kit for her birthday last year and he was such a good dad, he'd learned with her. But she couldn't say he was really into it. Yet . . .

"I was trying to make you a sweater," she admitted. "But I gave up."

He laughed. "Well, at least you tried."

"The knitting group is working together on a charity project—we're making blankets for Warm Up America. They distribute the donations to homeless shelters and hospices. Places where people need warmth and comfort."

"That's a really nice project. If it's simple enough, maybe I could make one with Dara."

"It's really easy. Maybe we could all make one together," Lucy offered, hoping she wasn't being too pushy now. "I am going to knit something for you, right after this project," she promised. "I was thinking socks would be good for a start."

"Is that a hint? Do I have cold feet?"

"Sometimes," she admitted. "I thought I'd start with socks, and work my way up."

He didn't answer for a minute. "Good plan . . . which reminds me, I really called to see if it was too late to come over. Feel like some company?"

Lucy had to smile. "Wow, that was smooth."

"Is that a yes or a no?" he asked with a laugh.

"That's a yes. Just give me a minute to straighten up."

"Okay . . . but just a minute." He sounded eager to see her, as if he had really missed her. Lucy had missed him, too, truth be told.

She hung up the phone and put her knitting aside. She was glad she'd spent a little time yesterday cleaning the cottage and had changed the sheets on the bed.

"Your pal Matt is coming over," she told Tink.

Tink stared up at her, wagging her tail wildly, her tongue hanging down to her chest.

"That is sort of my feeling about it, too," Lucy admitted to her canine confidante. "But drooling is not attractive. Men say they like it, but they really don't, hon. Trust me on this."

Chapter Eight

*L*ucy woke to the sound of rain on the roof and window-panes. She realized it was still very early. The bedroom was practically dark and the alarm clock wouldn't go off for hours. How nice, she thought. She snuggled even deeper under the quilt, circled by Matt's arms and warm body, thinking how pleasant rain could be on a summer morning.

Then she remembered it was Monday and they both had to get up and start the week. Tink must have heard the bed-springs creak, her canine ears on superalert. Lucy heard the dog trot quickly down the hallway and then enter the bed-room, where she promptly pounced in her daily wake-up-call manner.

Matt pulled Lucy closer and murmured into her hair.

"You shouldn't let her jump up on the bed like that. You have to train her better."

"Thanks for the advice, Doc. Any charge for that?"

"Let's see," he said, rolling her over. "Give me a minute. I'll think of something."

• • •

By the time her alarm clock finally sounded, Matt was gone and Lucy was forced to start the day. The rain continued steadily, preventing a long walk with the dog into town.

Lucy called Maggie in the afternoon, but they were interrupted by the UPS man delivering a shipment of hand-dyed wool that Maggie had been waiting for.

"That reminds me, I'm flying along with my blanket squares. I definitely need more blue yarn."

"Come by tomorrow, I'll have it ready," Maggie promised. "I think Jamie's going to stop in around lunchtime. I called him yesterday, to see how it's going with Martin Lewis and all that. He wasn't around, but he just left a message."

"I'll come at noon then. I'd like to see him, too."

Lucy did want to see Jamie and also wondered how the appointment had gone. She hoped he didn't have to wait too long to settle Gloria's estate. He'd said there was a bank account and credit cards, but what if the process dragged on? How long could those resources last? She wondered what he'd do.

Get a job, like the rest of us? a little voice replied.

She didn't know why, but that option for Jamie seemed off the table—right now, anyway. He'd have to put his artwork aside if it came to that and that would be a real shame, she thought.

Lucy woke early on Tuesday and got a few hours, of work done before she headed into town at noon. Monday's rainy skies had cleared and she blinked at the bright sunlight as she emerged from the cottage's cool interior.

It was a funny thing about her aunt Laura's old cottage. It

always felt cool in the summer, with a breeze wafting through from the front door to the back porch, and no need for air-conditioning, maybe because the neighborhood was only blocks from the beach. But it was also snug and warm in the winter; good insulation and a wood-burning stove helped. The old-fashioned design was amazingly compact and energy saving, and Lucy felt herself right on track with the less-is-more trend.

When she arrived at the knitting shop, she found a few customers milling around inside, examining yarn and paging through pattern books. Maggie had the shop arranged so that her customers felt comfortable knitting and socializing all day, or just having some alone time, in a comfortable environment. Like a Starbucks but with loads of yarn and needles, Lucy sometimes thought.

She saw Phoebe helping an older woman at the back of the shop, consulting a pattern book as they examined some skeins of light blue yarn.

Maggie was at the other side of the store in a nook where she kept her spinning wheel. She wasn't spinning herself, but showing someone else how to do it. A pale yellow fleece sat on the spindle and a thin fiber strand extended out to the wheel.

"There you go . . . very nice. Just keep an even tension, not to loose or too taut. You don't want to snap it," she encouraged her student.

She looked up and noticed Lucy, then quickly came over. "Good, you're here. Let's go out to the porch," Maggie suggested. "I need a break."

Lucy went outside again and Maggie followed, scooping up a few balls of wool from the counter in the middle of the store.

"Here's your yarn. I even rolled it for you." Lucy had already taken a seat in a wicker chair and Maggie handed down several balls of blue yarn.

"Wow, what service. What a nice shop. I ought to come back here sometime."

"We aim to please," Maggie assured her, taking the seat nearby. "There's Jamie, I was wondering what happened to him."

Lucy looked up and saw Jamie's shiny black BMW convertible pull up to a space in front of the Black Sheep. A sweet ride, truly deluxe. Was it in his name or Gloria's? Did he own it outright or still need to make big payments? So much to worry about now that he hadn't given a thought to when Gloria was alive, she realized.

He hopped out and came up on the porch. He was carrying two big shopping bags and set them down in front of Maggie.

"I brought you something. Some of Gloria's wool and needles and all that. I thought she would want you to have them," he added.

Gloria was a dedicated knitter and had money to spend on any yarn that struck her fancy, so Lucy suspected she had a giant stash tucked away somewhere. Jamie just hadn't come across it yet. But these two bags, brimming with goodies, were a generous sample.

She peaked in a shopping bag and spotted the fine tangerine yarn from Gloria's last project, the mist lace scarf. It made her sad to recognize it.

"Don't you want to keep some, Jamie?" Maggie asked with concern. "Not now, but someday, you might want to start knitting again."

A serious expression dropped over his face. "Maybe . . . but

I'd rather just go out and buy new stuff. It would remind me too much of her to use any of this. You take it. Give it to someone who can't afford supplies or something."

"Oh, don't worry. It will go to good use," Maggie assured him. "We're making a blanket for a charity. We'll probably make a few before the winter and I might even hold a workshop for the cause. I can use some of Gloria's yarn for that. I think she'd have liked the idea."

"Yes, she would have." He nodded in agreement and sat down on a wicker chair across from them.

"So, how did it go with that attorney the other day? Martin Lewis?"

Jamie shook his head, looking disturbed. "Not well. Not what I expected, anyway."

"Oh, what do you mean? Isn't the will clear?" Lucy asked.

"The will is clear. No problems there. But Gloria's investments and all these properties . . . it's a big mess. He hasn't even gotten very far into it yet, but it doesn't look good. She put a lot of money into real estate the last few years and the lawyer said when the bubble burst, her fortune took a big hit," Jamie reported honestly.

"That is bad news," Maggie said. "She certainly never let on to me that anything was amiss with her business interests."

"Me, either. And I was her husband," Jamie reminded them. "How did she keep this from me?" he sounded very sad, almost angry. "She should have trusted me. She should have confided her problems. She should have let me help her." He looked up again, his big blue eyes sweeping over them.

"Yes, she should have," Lucy replied quietly. "But maybe she didn't want to . . . to worry you. You were busy with your own work and trying to get a start with your painting. I know she really wanted you to focus on that."

He stared at her a moment and then let out a long sigh. "That probably was part of it. She was too . . . protective or something. She didn't think I could handle the truth, I guess . . ."

Or maybe worried that if her much younger husband knew she didn't have a fortune, their hot romance would suddenly cool? Even Gloria must have had her insecurities about the relationship.

"Gloria was like that. Very independent. She never wanted anyone to see any weakness in her," Maggie said quickly. "It wasn't just you, Jamie."

"Yes, I guess so. She hated to look weak or needy. But she just held all that worry inside and . . . maybe that's why she got so upset that last night. And ended up having the accident."

Maggie sighed. "Poor Gloria. I hope that isn't how it came about. I hate to think of her feeling so alone and troubled. When she had all of us to turn to."

Jamie shook his head sadly. "Me, too."

It was big news. Lucy didn't know what to say.

"So, what happens now?" she asked him finally. "Do you just wait and see how the estate sorts itself out?"

"Sounds like there's not much I can do. Mr. Lewis told me that it usually takes around three months. But Gloria's estate is more complicated so it will be longer. He needs to make sure that anybody who thinks they have a claim has enough time to come forward. It's the law or something. I'm not really sure, but this whole process is watched over by the court."

"Right, I knew that. Even if you have a valid will, the court makes sure debts and taxes are settled first. Like the funeral costs and medical bills. That money goes out before any beneficiaries can receive an inheritance," Maggie explained. "The heirs are actually getting what's left over, no matter what the will says they are due."

She had gone through the process when her husband died and appeared to remember it well.

"That's right. Though it sounded a lot more complicated when he explained it to me." Jamie's tone was flat. Disappointed? Surprised? Lucy couldn't quite pin it. Just plain drained. He was emotionally exhausted. Anybody would be.

He sighed again and rubbed his hands across his eyes. "I don't know . . . he was going on so long with all these legal terms. I didn't understand half of it."

Lucy glanced at Maggie. Jamie wasn't at all business-minded. She was sure the conversation with Martin Lewis about the probate process had sounded like a foreign language to him. But most people, unfamiliar with the process, would find it confusing. It wasn't just Jamie.

"So you don't have any idea what the liabilities are," Maggie clarified.

"Nope . . . I don't even know what she owned, all the real estate around town. Mr. Lewis is making an inventory of the estate. He'll show it to me when it's done, of course. But that will take a while, too. I'm sort of in limbo right now."

"Maybe Suzanne could help you," Lucy suggested. "You should give her a call."

"That's a good idea. I've gone through piles of papers at home, but I can't figure out half of it."

"What about the house? Is that part of the estate?" Maggie rose and picked up the watering can. She walked to the nearest window box and began deadheading the petunias.

"The house is in my name. Mr. Lewis says that's clear."

"Oh, that's good to hear." Maggie glanced at him over her shoulder. "One less thing to worry about."

"I guess." He paused and let out a long breath. He stared out at the street, his jaw set. Lucy sensed there was something else troubling Jamie, even more than he'd told them.

"Is there something worrying you about the house, Jamie? Did you decide not to sell it after all?"

He turned to her, then shook his head. "No, I need to sell it. There's no question now."

Lucy felt he was trying to say that he had even more reason now than just his grief over Gloria.

"You mean, to pay back Gloria's debts?" Lucy asked, feeling puzzled.

"Yeah, but not the ones Lewis is figuring out." He took another deep breath. "I had this . . . this visit from these guys Sunday night."

Maggie left the window box and quickly returned. "What kind of guys? What are you talking about?"

"Big guys. With thick necks . . . and gold jewelry? The kind you see in the movies?" he said with a shaky laugh. Jamie was not a small man. If he was calling some other guys big in such an awed tone, they must have been total hulks.

"What did they want?" Lucy prodded him.

"Gloria owes somebody lots of money. They didn't say who. I assume it's their boss. They want it . . . and they don't want to wait for the estate to go through probate."

"Oh." Maggie's expression fell. It didn't sound good to Lucy, either. "She took some sort of . . . shady loan?"

Jamie nodded bleakly. "They didn't spell it out for me, but that's what it boils down to. A private loan. From private people who like to be paid back quickly. With interest. Lots of it."

"But you can't pay them back. Not right now," Lucy insisted.

"That's what I said. But they didn't like that answer." Jamie held up his right hand, which was covered by white first-aid tape that wrapped around the base of his thumb and wrist.

"Somehow they know that I like my hands in working order. This huge guy, twice my size at least, he grabbed my wrist and nearly twisted my hand off. He bent my thumb back so far, I thought he was going to break it off."

Maggie gasped and covered her mouth with her hand. She quickly stepped closer to Jamie and lifted his hand so she could get a better look.

"Let me see," she insisted. Lucy saw that the skin under the tape had taken on a dark purplish tone. "Did you go to the emergency room for an X-ray? It might be broken."

"You have to tell the police, Jamie," Lucy said before he could answer.

He sighed and took his hand back. "I don't think so. It won't help. It might even make it worse." Lucy had a feeling they had threatened him, but he didn't want to admit it. "What if the information gets out? I don't want to have Gloria's name smeared in the papers, linked with something like that. I'd feel terrible if that happened."

"What are you going to do?" Lucy felt alarmed. People like that would come back. The next time, it would be even worse.

He looked perplexed, overwhelmed. She felt so sorry for him. First Gloria dies so suddenly. Then he finds out her business affairs are a complete mess . . . and now thick-necked collection types are harassing him, practically breaking his bones to make their point.

"I don't know . . . I told them I really and truly didn't have any money right now. I could sell my car, but that wouldn't even cover it. I have to sell the house. Or take a loan against it. Or just wait until the estate comes through probate."

"What did they say?" Maggie asked quietly, sitting in the wicker chair next to him again.

"They said I'd better figure it out. Fast. Then they finally went away."

Maggie shook her head. "Jamie . . . I really think you need to tell the police. This could get dangerous."

"No police. I don't want the police involved. They warned me. That will only make it worse. Gloria made a mistake dealing with these people. But she must have felt desperate. Pushed to the edge. I'll just have to muddle along and handle them the best I can."

Lucy glanced at Maggie. She felt the same, but there didn't seem to be any way to change his mind.

Jamie stood up, ready to go. Maggie stood up, too, and walked him to the porch steps.

"Why don't you stop by Thursday night? Just to say hello if you like. We'll all be here for the meeting."

"Oh right." He nodded and slipped on his sunglasses. He still hadn't shaved and his beard had grown in quite thick. He looked good in a beard, Lucy thought. More arty, maybe? "Okay, maybe I will."

Maggie and Lucy said good-bye and watched Jamie walk down to the street to his car. Just as he left, they spotted Dana strolling down Main Street toward the shop. Dana paused to wave to Jamie as he pulled away in the black convertible. He lifted his hand and waved back.

"Hi, guys. Sorry I missed Jamie, was he here long?" she asked cheerfully. She sat in the seat he'd just vacated. She'd brought her lunch in a white paper bag and her knitting tote, Lucy noticed, and set them on a little wicker table between the chairs.

When Maggie and Lucy didn't answer right away, she gave them curious, appraising stares.

"Something the matter? You both look upset."

"We are upset," Maggie replied. "Jamie just stopped by. He had a lot of news about Gloria's estate. Things aren't going well for him."

She sprinkled the flower box with one hand, gently separating the plants with her other so that the water reached the soil.

"Not at all," Lucy echoed, thinking of Jamie's bandaged hand.

They quickly filled Dana in on the news, including the visit from the thick-necked thugs. Dana frowned but didn't say a word. Lucy saw her eyes grow even wider at the end of the story.

"That's awful. And he won't go to the police?"

"He says he doesn't want anyone to find out that Gloria had been dealing with that element. It would tarnish her name."

"Oh dear . . . there was a lot about Gloria we didn't know." Dana had already spread out her lunch, but had only nibbled at the neat rows of sushi rolls. She sighed and took out her knitting. "She was very secretive. Very compartmentalized, wasn't she?"

Lucy was tempted to agree . . . then realized she didn't really know what Dana meant.

"Able to separate out different parts of her life," Dana

explained. "Which everyone does, to some degree. It's a very useful tool and most successful people do that very well. But some people go too far."

Lucy considered Dana's assessment. "Well, she did have all this debt, but acted like she was still rich. But maybe she thought of it as a temporary setback and had a plan to catch up. She was resourceful."

"That's possible, too. I think a lot of independent businesspeople survive sometimes by their wits and by keeping a positive outlook," Dana said. "They tough it out. Not even allowing the possibility of defeat to enter the picture," Dana continued. "A lot of the time, they do get through it."

"Don't you remember what she said when we were talking about facing hard times in life?" Lucy reminded her friends. "Gloria said, 'Just pick up your skirts and plough on.' I had a feeling that she had some specific situation in mind, something going on in her life right now."

"I did, too," Maggie admitted. "But she had faced so many challenges, she might have been thinking of something in the past, too."

That was true. Lucy thought about Gloria's life history, outlined in the obituary and the article she'd read Sunday about the Avalon Group and their dealings with the Department of Environmental Conservation.

"Dana, who is Michael Novak?" she asked, abruptly changing the subject.

Dana had carefully exchanged her knitting needles for a set of chopsticks and was picking up a bite of tuna roll with cucumber. "He's an attorney in town who did some work for Gloria. He belongs to our club and plays a lot of golf. He was at the memorial service, remember?"

"I remember. But . . . who *is* he? Is he a nice guy? Were he and Gloria friends? Were they enemies?"

"Why do you ask?" Her eyes were wide, as if she'd hit an unexpected dab of wasabi.

But it wasn't wasabi, Lucy could tell. "Spill it, Dana. I can always tell when you answer a question with a question that something is up."

Dana smiled nervously and took a big swallow. "Okay, you got me."

Then she leaned forward and looked around to see who else was on the porch. They were alone, but she still spoke in a hushed voice.

"I really shouldn't be telling you this. Gloria told me in the strictest confidence. But it wasn't in a therapy session or anything like that . . ."

Lucy was relieved to hear that. Dana honored her client confidentially with the strictest code of ethics.

"But . . . what?" she prodded her.

"I suppose since she's passed away and we were all friends, it's all right to tell you . . ." She paused and took a breath. "Gloria had an affair with Michael Novak. A very long one. I think it may have even started while George Thurman was still alive. Maybe when he got sick, toward the end."

Lucy sat back, feeling shocked. Maggie looked surprised, too. She apparently didn't know this about Gloria, even though she'd been the closest to her.

"How did you learn about this relationship?" she asked Dana. "Did Jack tell you?"

Dana shook her head. "Gloria told me. Not too long ago, either. We were all just getting friendly at the knitting shop. I guess she thought, since I was a psychologist, I could give her some advice. So she asked me out for coffee one day when we met in the Book Review."

"And she told you about Michael Novak?" Lucy asked. Dana just nodded.

"She wanted advice about the relationship? Does that mean she was still seeing him after she married Jamie?" Maggie asked, sounding totally flustered now.

"No, she'd broken it off totally before she went to Florida. It was very painful for her. They'd been on and off for years. A lot of fighting and making up. But Novak would never leave his wife. So Gloria went down to Florida to get some distance, a change of scene. That's the reason she stayed down there so long on that last trip. And then she met Jamie."

"And it was a whirlwind romance and they return to town married." Lucy filled in the ending of the story, unable to stop herself.

"Exactly," Dana said, selecting her last bite of maki roll. "Wasn't Michael Novak surprised."

"Right . . . most people bring back a box of oranges," Maggie said drily, quoting Edie Steiber.

"Like a typical man, once Gloria was unavailable, Mike Novak suddenly decided he couldn't live without her," Dana continued. "Suddenly, he could get a divorce and he wouldn't accept that it was over. He tried to convince Gloria that she'd just married Jamie on the rebound. Or simply to get back at him. A totally egocentric interpretation," she added with a laugh.

"Did she?" Maggie asked, sounding as if she didn't know up from down anymore.

"Of course not. She really loved Jamie. I'm sure of that," Dana said calmly. "She just didn't know how to shake loose of

Mike. They'd been through a lot together. And he was pressuring her, trying to confuse her."

"What did you tell her?" Lucy asked.

"I told her not to let Mike get into her head again and muddy the waters in her new marriage. It's easy for an old lover—especially with a volatile history like she and Mike had—to play with your emotions. To make you question if you made the right choice. But she knew she had made the right choice with Jamie and she finally told Mike it was absolutely over and he had to let go."

"Did he?" Lucy persisted. "I mean, did she ever tell you that?"

"We never spoke of it again," Dana told them. "She came to me for counseling more or less, even though it wasn't formal therapy. I never thought it was right to ask her about it, unless she brought it up first. Do you think something more happened between them?" she asked Lucy curiously.

"I don't know. But I know what Suzanne would say if she was here right now."

"What would that be?" Maggie asked, her brow creased in a deep frown.

"She'd say, 'Who came to see Gloria the night she died . . . and what about those two wineglasses, huh?'"

Chapter Nine

*L*ucy was right. That's exactly what Suzanne did say after her friends filled her in on the story Thursday night, when they gathered for their weekly meeting.

It was Maggie's turn to host, and they met at the shop at seven o'clock. Phoebe had a class but planned on joining them later. A wave of warm, muggy weather had followed Monday's showers and they decided to sit out on the porch to catch a breeze off the harbor.

There was a round wrought-iron table just left of the front door with several chairs around it and Maggie had set out the dinner she'd made for them, a Greek salad with grilled chicken. Paired with crisp pinot grigrio, a dish of hummus, and some pita bread crisps, it was a perfect light supper on a summer night.

Though it was still light out at 7:00, Maggie had set out several candles and glass lanterns. There was also an antique light fixture hanging over the table, so there would be enough light to knit. Maggie hadn't turned that lamp on yet, preferring to have the group enjoy their dinner in the twilight.

"Wow, my brain is still reeling." Suzanne sat back, staring at Maggie and Dana as they finished filling her in. Maggie related Jamie's various travails with the estate and the thugs who had nearly broke his thumb. Dana told her about Gloria's relationship with Mike Novak. "I sure missed a lot eating lunch at my desk on Tuesday."

"That will teach you," Lucy told her.

"I've learned my lesson, believe me." Suzanne looked around at the others. "Let's have a quick show of hands. Who thinks Gloria's late-night visitor—and probably the last person to see her alive on this earth—was her old flame, the sly-looking, silver-sideburned attorney?"

Suzanne raised her hand. Lucy did, too.

Dana said, "I abstain."

Maggie said, "I vote . . . we just don't know."

"Too bad I washed those wineglasses." Suzanne sighed. "Fingerprints would have nailed it, even for the police in this town. Who knows if the police even took fingerprints around the house? I mean, they thought it was an accident."

"Well . . . the only way to find that out is to either wait for the report or ask Detective Walsh. Who wants to call him?" Dana challenged her friends.

"Not me. I've had enough of that man for a lifetime." Maggie waved off the suggestion, sitting back in her chair.

Lucy could understand her reaction to the mere mention of the deadpan detective's name. All of Maggie's friends could.

He'd practically arrested Maggie for the murder of Amanda Goran, a rival knitting shop owner who'd been found dead in her shop back in early March. Of course, Maggie had not been the killer, but once Detective Walsh had zeroed in, he did seem to have tunnel vision.

Was that the problem here? Once he'd decided that Gloria had died of natural causes he'd overlooked crucial evidence?

And where exactly was this line of logic going?

"Wait . . . what are we saying here?" Lucy asked her friends.

"Do you really think Mike Novak may have been involved in Gloria's death?"

The words "he killed her" or even "pushed into the pool" still seemed too extreme to say out loud.

Her friends didn't answer, they just exchanged quick glances. Suzanne dipped a pita crisp into the bowl of hummus. "Despite what Jamie said about her dark moods, she just sounded too normal to me that night on the telephone to end up full of wine and pills, floating facedown in a pool a few hours later. I don't know if I think Mike Novak pushed her in. Or they fought and it was an accident . . ."

"Or they had some sort of emotional confrontation that got Gloria so upset that she self-medicated and did have an accident?" Dana offered. "But I think Suzanne is right. There must have been some catalyst. Some important confrontation with somebody. Or some bad news she learned that night that sent her into such a tailspin. Something is missing in this story."

"I agree." Maggie's low, serious voice drifted out of the shadows. "Was Mike Novak the visitor? He sounds like a good candidate. But that's all I can say. It may have been news about her finances. Or something to do with that bad loan she was involved with. It seems there was so much we didn't know about Gloria that there may be other situations and other people in her life that could have been part of that fateful night." Maggie sighed and shook her head. "I will say that something happened. Something important. It might mean there was foul play, or even suicide. And her death was not just a random, unfortunate accident."

"And it wasn't her own fault for dying because she got herself intoxicated," Suzanne added sadly. "Which is what a lot of people must think. Even if they won't say it out loud."

That was true, Lucy realized. A classic case of blaming the victim. Perhaps the police were less inclined to ferret out some wrongdoing because Gloria's blood report showed that she was drunk and full of pills. The thinking might be "Well, too bad, but it was her own fault."

"What should we do now?" Lucy asked her friends. "I know we don't like Walsh, but . . ."

"We can't go to Walsh on our own," Dana cut in. "That's up to Jamie. He's her husband. It wouldn't be appropriate for us to jump in. We're not even related."

"Yes, you're right," Lucy said. "It wouldn't be appropriate at all."

"We need to tell him what we think. That there are some elements of this story that just don't add up and he ought to ask the police to investigate again," Suzanne recapped for all of them. "But what do we say about Novak? That's a sticky bun . . ."

"Is it ever," Dana sighed. She put her dish on a side table and wiped her hands on a napkin, then took out her knitting. "Jamie might know about Mike. Gloria may have told him. You know, the way couples tell each other about their past relationships? It was over. She had no reason to hide it."

"Maybe she did. And maybe she didn't," Suzanne offered.

"I'm not sure that she was so open with him," Lucy agreed with Suzanne. "Look at how many secrets she kept about her business and her finances. You said it yourself. Gloria compartmentalized? I think she kept Mike Novak in a very separate, secret compartment."

Dana had her knitting needles in hand and starting casting on a golden yellow square. "Very good, Lucy. You're a quick study."

"Gloria was always trying to protect Jamie," Maggie offered. "She didn't want him to worry about money. Or she just didn't trust him to understand the pressure she was under, the way you shield a child from serious matters. She wouldn't have wanted him to worry about this, either, is my guess."

"Oh, I don't know. Maybe she didn't tell him about the money because she was afraid he would leave her," Suzanne said bluntly. "Even Gloria wasn't immune to some insecurities."

"That could have been part of it." Lucy had already thought of that.

"Getting back to Mike," Maggie cut in, "I'm not sure she would have told Jamie about that relationship. She'd broken off with Mike before she went down to Florida. But that affair sounds to me like it was a simmering volcano. I think she would have been afraid that Jamie might have felt threatened. Or jealous. She wanted him to concentrate on his painting and for them to live a carefree life together. Why bring Mike into the picture? He would have been the snake in the garden. He would have just sullied it. The truth about Mike was . . . too real."

Maggie's explanation made sense. It did seem as if Gloria was trying to recapture a lost Eden with Jamie.

Maggie had finished her salad and also had her knitting out, working on a plum-colored square that was about halfway completed. Her needles moved swiftly, like a knife cutting through butter, Lucy thought. Maggie could easily do an entire blanket on her own, but it was more fun to pool their work together.

"She did insulate him from the usual worries married couples share," Dana agreed. "She did create an ideal little world for them."

Suzanne bit her lip. "It was sweet. I don't think she told him about that nasty Mike. No, I don't think he knows."

"We're sort of stuck," Maggie decided. "We have to assume he doesn't know. And we can't tell him. He's had enough shock these last two weeks. He doesn't need this bag of trash tossed on top, tarnishing his good memories."

"I agree." Suzanne picked out a juicy calamata olive from the leftovers on her plate and popped it in her mouth. "How much can the poor guy take? But we should tell him something. I mean, he really must get the police involved again."

"Yes, he should go back to the police," Dana agreed. "We can tell him that we've been thinking about the person who came to the door that night, and about the wineglasses, and it all seemed more suspicious to us. Did the police really look into the possibility of foul play?" Dana practiced. "How does that sound?"

"It sounds good," Lucy told her. "After that shakedown from those two hoods, he might be more inclined to think in that direction."

"Yes, he might. That must have been scary." Suzanne wiped her fingers with a napkin and pushed her dish aside. "Do you think he's coming by tonight? Because I did a property search for him on the Internet and the results came back. I wanted to give it to him."

"Property search? What was that?" Dana asked curiously.

Maggie rose and piled their plates to take them inside. "He's gone through Gloria's papers, but still can't tell how much property she owns."

"Won't the executor of her estate tell him that?" Lucy asked.

"Well, not exactly." Dana turned and handed Maggie a few more dishes. "The inventory of her assets is part of the estate and Martin Lewis has to pull all that information together, verify it, and then have all the property appraised. He can show Jamie his list. But I don't know at what state, or how long it will take before he does that."

"But Jamie can probably find it out on his own and get some idea of what she had, is that what you're saying?" Lucy asked.

"It was very easy to do," Suzanne cut in. "I didn't even need to look through any files. I just did a Lexus search on the 'Net. All the real estate transactions are public record. You just type in some information and the records come back in twenty-four hours."

Suzanne reached into her knitting bag and pulled out a file folder. "It's all in here . . . reads like a telephone book of Plum Harbor. She owned quite a nice piece of the pie."

"I think when she sold her share of the Avalon Group she invested most of the proceeds in real estate," Maggie recalled. "Of course, the market was booming then. But she probably bought in at exactly the wrong time."

Maggie went inside with the tray of dishes. Lucy rose to stretch her legs. "Can I see that printout?" she asked Suzanne, knowing she was being nosy. "I'm just curious," she admitted.

"Sure, take a look." Suzanne handed her the folder.

Lucy opened it and scanned the first sheet. The listing of the property was long, with dates and information about the various transactions. She hardly knew what she was reading, but skimmed the pages anyway. She recognized some of the street names, but some were unknown to her. Not all of the property was in Plum Harbor, of course. The names of the individuals or corporations who had owned the property prior to Gloria were also listed.

One name jumped out at the bottom of page three: Michael Novak. A property that he owned had been transferred to Gloria for the sum of . . . one dollar?

Wait . . . there was another one, Lucy realized, noticing another similar transaction on the same page.

Lucy's head popped up. Suzanne and Dana were both knitting and didn't spare her a glance. She felt like she was suddenly vibrating. She'd felt she might have just stumbled on something significant . . . but she had no idea what it meant.

Before she could say a word, sounding the alarm, she heard heavy steps coming up the porch. She glanced over to see Jamie. She forced a smile and quickly closed the folder, then slid it across the table, back to Suzanne.

"Hi, Jamie, we were wondering if you were going to drop by," Dana greeted him. "How are you doing?"

He shrugged and jammed his hands in the front pockets of his jeans. "The same, I guess . . ."

"Yes, I'm sure," Dana said sympathetically. "Come, sit down." She pulled out a chair for him. "We've been working on a project for a charity," she explained. "We're all knitting squares in different colors, then we'll put them together and make a blanket."

Jamie picked up one of the plum-colored squares that

Maggie had completed and left out on the table. "Nice and soft," he said, fingering the wool. "This will make a great blanket."

"That's what we're hoping," Maggie explained. She came outside again, carrying a tray with coffee, cups, and a large tart filled with fresh peaches.

"Hmm, did you make that, Maggie?" Suzanne asked.

"Yes, I did. I sort of had a craving for it. Peaches aren't really in season, but I mixed some ripe ones up with blueberries. Cooking's just like knitting. Sometimes you have to improvise," she added.

"Good things can happen by accident," Jamie agreed.

Maggie cut the tart and gave everyone a slice with a scoop of vanilla ice cream on the side.

"This is delicious. I love fresh peaches, they're the best," Suzanne oozed.

Lucy was enjoying her tart just as much, but preferred to savor it in silence. Everyone was quiet, she noticed, all mulling over the same question right now—how were they going to tell Jamie about their suspicions and encourage him to talk to the police again?

"I have that information you wanted, Jamie," Suzanne said. She handed him over the file. "All the property records, addresses, dates of transfer. It's all there."

Jamie flipped open the folder. "Wow . . . thanks. How did you pull this together so quickly?"

"I'd like to take a lot of credit, but it was actually very simple. There's a special search site. I didn't do much at all."

"I really appreciate it," he said sincerely. "I didn't have a clue about where to start."

"It wasn't any trouble. I can go over it sometime if you

want. I'm familiar with most of those areas and what the houses are worth."

"Oh good . . . that would help, too," he said, taking a big bite of tart.

"When do you meet with Martin Lewis again?" Maggie asked.

"I'm not sure. He said he would call and keep me posted." Pretty vague, Lucy thought. This was going to be a long process. Poor Jamie. He really didn't have a clue, did he?

It grew quiet again. Lucy glanced around, wondering who was going to start. Or would they chicken out?

She looked at Maggie, but Maggie averted her glance and focused on her tart. Suzanne sipped her coffee, then met Lucy's gaze . . . and discreetly shook her head.

Lucy looked at Dana, but she was staring at Jamie. Dana sat back and took a breath, a deep, centering breath, and Lucy guessed that Dana was about to jump in.

"We were all talking about Gloria before you came, Jamie. Especially about the night she died," Dana began slowly.

Jamie sat up and put his fork down. "Really . . . what about it?"

"We have some concerns about the way the police investigated. We don't think they did a very thorough job. It's hard to explain," she said, pausing to gather her thoughts.

Yes, it is. Especially if you have to leave out Mike Novak. Very hard to explain without that card on the table, Lucy thought.

"We're still troubled by the question of who came to visit her that night," Dana added.

Jamie looked confused. Lucy wondered if he even remembered what Dana was talking about.

"When I spoke to her on the phone about showing the house that Saturday, the doorbell rang and she said she had to go," Suzanne reminded him.

"Oh . . . right." He looked like he remembered now. "You told the police about that, right?"

"Yes, I did. But I don't think they did a very good job of following up. Did they ever tell you who it was?" Suzanne asked him.

Jamie shook his head. "No . . . they didn't. But I didn't really think too much about it. I mean, maybe she got takeout or something."

"That would have been pretty easy to trace," Dana pointed out.

"And I saw her at the Main Street Café that night. I don't think Gloria would have had two dinners. She barely ate one," Lucy added.

He sighed and sat back. Lucy felt bad for overwhelming him when he already had so much on his mind.

"You know, people were coming back at all hours of the night, with papers for her to sign, dropping things off, picking things up. I just didn't think much of it, to tell you the truth."

It sounded to Lucy like he thought they were just getting into some hysterical female speculation. Making a big deal out of nothing. Were they? she wondered.

Dana picked up her knitting again and examined the progress. "And the two wineglasses Suzanne saw," she continued. This was a slippery slope, Lucy thought. But she trusted Dana to navigate it. "That would also indicate that someone came to visit. Someone that she knew, don't you think?"

When Jamie didn't answer right away, Suzanne said, "The

last few days we've found out a lot about Gloria we weren't aware of. Doesn't that also make you wonder?"

Jamie looked about to reply. Then he stopped himself and took a breath.

"I hear what you're saying. I do," he said finally. He sighed. "I guess I just don't want to think about that night too closely. The way she died . . ." He paused again. "But maybe you're right, I don't know. Maybe the police didn't do a good job of figuring out how this happened. I probably should go back and talk to them again. I will," he promised. "Because I'll tell you this, if someone purposely set out to hurt her . . . or even scare her," he added, holding up his bandaged wrist, "I'm going to kill them with my bare hands."

"Oh Jamie . . . we're so sorry we upset you." Maggie's voice oozed with sympathy.

"I'm sorry, Jamie. But we thought it was important enough to bring to your attention," Dana added.

"Maybe we are imagining something. I hope so," Suzanne backtracked. "But there are a lot of loose ends in this story. You might feel better down the road if you're not left wondering."

"That's true. I'm not thinking clearly right now. Once this all settles, I might want more closure."

It sounded to Lucy as if they had persuaded him. She wondered now how the police—more specifically Detective Walsh—would respond.

They heard voices on the walk. Lucy looked over to see Phoebe and her friend Crystal coming toward the shop.

"Phoebe's finally here. Oh, she brought her friend," Maggie noticed.

Phoebe and Crystal came up on the porch and everyone said hello. It suddenly seemed a little crowded with the two young women leaning on the porch rail. There weren't any empty seats left at the table and they hadn't thought to bring any over from the other side of the porch.

Jamie stood up and slipped the folder Suzanne had given him under his arm.

"I've got to go. Thanks for the dessert, Maggie. It hit the spot."

"Glad you could stop in. Are you sure you're okay?" Maggie added quietly.

"I'm fine. Really." He forced a small smile. "She was your friend, too. I know you're all concerned."

"Yes, we are," Dana said. "That's what this is all about."

Jamie seemed to understand and had taken no offense, Lucy thought. She did feel sorry for upsetting him again, though. But it couldn't be helped.

He gave a quick good-bye around the table and left.

Phoebe dragged a chair over from the other side of the porch and Crystal took the one Jamie had left empty.

"Did you guys have any dinner?" Maggie asked them. "I think there's some Greek salad left."

Phoebe made a face. "How about some pie. It looks really good."

"It's a peach tart. And it isn't dinner . . . is it?" Maggie replied.

"It has fruit. That's healthy." Phoebe held out a plate. "Some ice cream on the side would be nice. Thank you."

Maggie gave her a look, then dished out the tart. "Same for you, Crystal?"

"Yes, please," Crystal said politely.

Their meal reminded Lucy of one of Gloria's favorite sayings: Life is short, eat dessert first.

But she didn't want to share that story again. Her friends

had been bogged down enough in their memories and grief.

As the young women ate their peach tart, Maggie settled back in her seat and picked up her knitting. "So Crystal, would you like to learn how to knit tonight? We're into a very simple project, perfect for beginners."

Crystal shrugged a boney shoulder. "Sure, I'll try it. I'm not exactly Miss Coordination."

"It's not that hard. Not any harder than using chopsticks," Phoebe pointed out, "and you can use two hands so it's probably easier."

Maggie dug into her knitting bag and pulled out an extra pair of needles and a printed sheet made up with the Black Sheep knitting shop logo on top that showed the very basics for a beginning knitter—how to hold the needles, cast on, and perform the knit and purl stitches. It was really *Sesame Street* stuff every beginner needed to master.

Maggie seemed to have the handouts stashed in every purse and tote, always ready to give them out to anyone who showed the slightest interest in learning how to knit. She was sort of a Johnny Appleseed of knitting, Lucy thought, wandering around, spreading the seeds for future knitters.

"Let's see, what yarn should I give you?" Maggie asked herself aloud as she peered into a basket that now sat in the middle of the table. "We're making squares for a blanket. Blue, plum, and gold. We wanted two people on each color . . . but we lost one of our . . . of our knitters," she said simply, meaning Gloria, who had intended to work on the blanket with them. Right after she finished her scarf.

"We could use another person working in plum." Maggie picked up a ball of plum-colored yarn and showed it to the new recruit.

"Okay. Cool." Crystal stretched out a length of the yarn and looked it over. She appeared to like it, despite her spare style of expressing herself.

"Good. It definitely helps if you like the yarn you're working with. Especially on your first project," Maggie encouraged her.

Little did Crystal know that once you got hooked on knitting you would not merely "like the yarn you were working with," but become obsessed with the stuff, craving it, longing for it, fascinated by yarn as if you were under a spell. You'd see a skein of yarn somewhere and feel you just had to have it . . . or die.

Different colors and textures, thickness and weight. Ribbon yarn, cashmere, hand-spun, and hand-dyed colors. The sight of yarn would do something to your brain and you would lose control, mindlessly carrying skeins to the cash register, whether you knew what you wanted to do with that yarn or not. You would sock these coveted treasures away for future use, then go out and buy more. Every true knitter's guilty pleasure. And that's how you acquired your stash.

This poor child did not have any idea of what was potentially ahead for her, starting with this innocent, simple lesson.

Maggie showed her how to cast on and demonstrated the simple stocking stitch for the square. "When you get to the end of the row, you'll need to turn it over and start on the other side. I'll show you," Maggie promised.

Phoebe had also finished with her dessert/dinner and pulled her knitting out of her knapsack, tucked her long legs under her, and set to work on her square. She was working with the same color as Lucy, a rich shade of dark blue.

The group knit steadily without talking for a few minutes.

Since the project was so simple, no one had to start fretting about a goof-up, or stop to rip out stitches, or ask Maggie to make it right. Crystal seemed to get the hang of it quickly.

Then Maggie said, "Jamie gave me a lot of Gloria's yarn. I was thinking, since she wasn't able to help with the blanket but wanted to, it would be nice to include a square in her honor. We do need one extra one in the center."

Dana stopped working and put her knitting down. "Maggie, that's a lovely idea. So thoughtful of you."

"Oh well . . . I miss her," Maggie admitted. "It would help me feel a little better to honor her memory in some small way."

"Me, too," Lucy agreed. "How about a square in the center with a star? I'd always thought of her as sort of a star in the group. Someone special who sits in."

She had thought of Gloria that way, though sincerely hoped no one would ask her to knit a square with a star, which was a bit beyond her abilities right now. There would be something in the center, but it might look more like a wriggling starfish when she was done with it.

"A star . . . I like that idea." Suzanne looked up and smiled.

"She was a star," Maggie agreed. "A shooting star that lit up the sky for a brief time. A rare sight."

She swallowed hard and Lucy hoped her suggestion wouldn't make Maggie cry again.

"I like it, too," Dana said, "but you'll have to make that one for us, Maggie. A shooting star is a bit beyond any of our modest skills."

"Oh, you're all very good. You're just lazy. You rush too much," Maggie chided them. "And you skip the gauge, which catches up to you. Save time up front, waste time later."

Lucy hated to knit a gauge for a pattern, a small sample

piece that tested the number of stitches you would need per inch, which could vary from the pattern due to the tension of your own stitches, the needles, and the thickness of yarn used. Good, methodical knitters like Maggie knit gauges . . . the rest of them, Lucy included, just charged ahead and called for backup when they messed things up.

"All right, I'll do it. I can work out a pattern on some graph paper later. If Lucy makes a sketch."

"Sure, I'd love to." She'd made the suggestion, so that made sense.

"Then we can decide together how I should use the colors," Maggie proposed.

"This dark blue yarn for the background would be awesome." Phoebe held up one of her squares. "That's like the night sky, with the star zipping across in the gold yarn?"

"And some purple and cream trails?" Dana added. "Or is that too much?"

"Not at all. We want to make it special." Maggie took the blue square from Phoebe and held it out, trying to envision a star graphic knitted into it. "Maybe I can add another accent color and wander out of our palette just a bit."

"Oh wait . . . let's use some of Gloria's wool, if she has the right colors . . ." Maggie got up from her chair and walked over to another table on the porch, where she had left the two shopping bags Jamie had brought over.

She carried over a bag and started digging through it. "I think I found some of the plum. Oh, what's this?" She pulled out a sheet of paper. "The pattern for the Mist Lace Scarf," she said in a melancholy tone. She lifted her head and sighed. "The scarf that fell in the water with her. Jamie says he disposed of it, along with the clothes she had on that night. It must have been ruined in the chlorine anyway, but . . . it seems like a shame that her last project was lost."

"That is a shame. She was almost done with it, I think," Dana recalled.

"Does anybody want this?" Maggie asked, holding out the pattern instructions. "It's such a beautiful stitch."

Dana leaned forward and took the sheet. "I'd like to try it sometime. Maybe in black for evening wear." Her voice trailed off as she looked over the pattern, then turned it over. "Look at this. Looks like some sort of list . . ."

Dana brought the sheet closer to the light. Lucy leaned over her shoulder to see it, too.

"It's a list of addresses," Dana told the others. She looked up. "It looks like Gloria's handwriting."

Lucy took the sheet next. She didn't know Gloria's handwriting, but she did recognize two addresses on the list. Both had been on the printout Suzanne had made for Jamie: the same properties that had been transferred from Mike Novak for the sum of one dollar.

She felt her mouth grow dry. She wanted to tell her friends about this suspicious coincidence . . . but didn't think this was a good time.

Lucy swallowed hard and passed the sheet of paper to Suzanne, who waited to see it. "Yes, it's a list of addresses. Might be properties that Gloria owned and was thinking of selling," Lucy said lightly.

Suzanne looked the list over quickly. "Good guess. I see the address of the condo and the commercial building on here that she wanted to put on the market." Suzanne looked over at Maggie. "We should give this to Jamie. It might be nothing, just notes to herself. But it might be something."

"Yes, it might be important," Maggie agreed. "I'll call him and tell him I found it."

Maggie folded the sheet and tucked it in her pocket.

Lucy tried to concentrate on her knitting, but squirmed in her chair. She was bursting to tell her friends the small but perhaps significant bits she'd noticed tonight, about the deed transfers and the overlap with this list.

It might be important. It might be another signal, pointing to Mike Novak and his possible presence at the house the night Gloria died.

Had they made that list together? Or had Gloria made it in preparation for his visit? Lucy was starting to get the feeling that all the pieces were on the table, but she still couldn't see where things fit, or what this all added up to.

"Hey, I have an idea," Suzanne said suddenly. "Let's line up all the squares we've made so far and see how it looks. I think that would be some good positive reinforcement."

Spoken like a true mom, Lucy thought.

"It will be fun to see our progress." Dana liked the idea, too, and began rummaging through her knitting bag for her squares. "I think I brought all my squares with me."

"I've made three so far," Lucy told her friends as she also searched through her knitting tote.

"I've only made one." Phoebe held up her contribution. "But we should put them together and see what we've got."

"All right, if that's what you want to do. Let's go inside and put them out on the big table," Maggie suggested. "There's not enough room out here."

They grabbed their knitting bags, then trooped inside to the table at the back of the shop. Everyone put down her squares and Maggie found the blanket pattern in her cupboard and brought it over.

"Okay, here's how it will go . . ." She moved the colored squares around like pieces on a game board, finally lining them up in a pattern. Of course, it was incomplete, but Lucy could get the idea.

Lucy put a piece of paper in the middle with a quick sketch of a star. "That's Gloria's square," she said.

They walked around the table, appraising the arrangement from different angles. "It's going to look good," Dana decided. "We made nice choices with the colors."

"Not bad," Suzanne agreed. "What color should we use to stitch it together?"

"Dark blue," Lucy suggested.

"I like the plum," Phoebe said.

"Oh no . . . gold would be the best," Dana overruled them.

Maggie laughed. "Guess we'll have a vote when we get there. But it is good to step back and get the big picture. To think *outside* the knitted square."

Yes, it was good to think outside the square, Lucy agreed.

Their project was still missing a lot of pieces, but it was easy to visualize the complete blanket from the squares that were there.

If only the story of Gloria's final hours was as easy to visualize from the bits and pieces they knew so far.

Chapter Ten

The knitting group adjourned a few minutes before 11:00. The blanket preview was a big success and gave them all a motivating boost.

But Lucy had no chance to share with her friends the odd items she'd noticed—the curious transactions between Mike Novak and Gloria on Suzanne's property search list and the identical properties appearing on the handwritten list on the back of the mist lace scarf pattern.

When she got home that night, she was too tired to send them a group e-mail, and the idea of doing that seemed a little obsessive. At least Dana would think so.

She did think that Maggie should make a copy of the notes on the back of the pattern before giving the original to Jamie. Why she should do this, Lucy wasn't quite sure. In case the Black Sheep knitters came across more disturbing coincidences that somehow connected to the list?

The police would be looking into this entire situation soon, she reminded herself, *if* Jamie could persuade them.

She recalled how stubborn and inflexible Detective Walsh had been when Maggie had been dealing with him.

But this is different, Lucy reminded herself. Jamie was the bereaved husband of a woman who'd died under strange and shocking, if not downright suspicious, circumstances. The police ought to listen to him and take another look, if only to humor him.

On Friday morning, Lucy had to buckle down and focus on her work. The art director for *The Big Book of Things That Flap, Swoop, and Fly* wanted to see the first three chapters by Monday. Never mind that it was not the schedule Lucy had been given at the start. There were unforseen reasons for the rush, beyond anyone's control, and she couldn't complain too much or they wouldn't hire her again. Simple as that.

This new deadline was going to cut into her time with Matt this weekend. Unfortunate since he was free, didn't have Dara, and might be able to borrow a friend's sailboat.

Just my flipping luck . . .

Lucy hit a key on her computer and opened a new file. A giant pair of webbed feet filled her oversized monitor. While the image made her smile, all she could think was, I'd hate to knit socks for those babies, never mind Matt's big feet.

She still had several more blue squares to complete for the blanket and couldn't start Matt's promised socks for some time. She wondered if Phoebe's friend really wanted to take part in the project or had only been trying to be polite last night. Crystal did not look like the "trying to be polite" type, that was for sure, but you never know. Would the Goth girl even finish the square she'd started?

Lucy had seen plenty of people attracted to knitting and

very excited about it at first, then lose interest and fall by the wayside. Sometimes this was because they never got the rhythm of working the needles or didn't spend enough time knitting to reach that deep, meditative level—knitting in the zone.

Lucy didn't have a handle on Crystal yet. The girl was so quiet. It was hard to get a sense of her beyond her appearance. And appearances could be misleading. Take Gloria, for instance. Her larger-than-life personality had been off-putting at first, but she'd turned out to be quite a deep and thoughtful person.

Phoebe wouldn't be friends with a complete airhead, Lucy reasoned, so her new girlfriend must have more to her than tattoos and a skull-emblazoned wardrobe.

But if Crystal turned out to be Gloria's replacement in their group, which was possible if she kept knitting, that would be a pretty ironic choice by the hand of fate. Lucy couldn't imagine two women who were more opposite, at least as they appeared on the surface.

Lucy worked through the day and made good progress. If she worked a bit after dinner and kept up the pace tomorrow, maybe she could sneak out for a sail with Matt after all. Gloria's sudden passing had served as a reminder that life could be frighteningly brief. Given a chance to take a sunset sail with a man she was crazy about, should she really stay home, staring at a computer screen full of webbed feet?

On Saturday morning, Lucy woke early and took Tink for a long walk into town. The dog had been sadly neglected on Friday and they both needed the exercise. One major drawback of working on a deadline was the LBS factor—lower body spread. When she was working hard, she had little time or energy for any activity beyond dog walks. By the time a project was done, Lucy could feel—or imagined very vividly—her thighs and butt spreading out like a thick slice of melted cheese, oozing over the edges of her desk chair.

Maybe life was too short to worry about flabby thighs, too, Lucy thought. Still, she urged the dog from a slow pace into a light jog down the last hill to Main Street.

When she walked into the knitting shop, she found Maggie alone, sitting on the love seat in an alcove at the front of the shop. Her yarn swift was clamped to the small table in front of the couch and she was rolling a ball of yarn. The *Plum Harbor Times* was spread out across the table beside a cup of coffee.

"You're out early for a Saturday," she greeted Lucy.

"A big chunk of a project is suddenly due Monday. I just wanted to get some fresh air before I chain myself to my desk."

Lucy headed back to the storeroom and poured herself a cup of coffee.

"That sounds pretty miserable," Maggie called after her. "It should be nice weather, too," she added as Lucy returned to her cozy spot.

"So I hear. Thanks for the reminder." Lucy smiled at her. She sat down and sipped her coffee. "Did Jamie come back yet to get that list on the scarf pattern?" she asked.

"He picked it up yesterday afternoon. He didn't think it was anything important. But he said he was going to give it to Martin Lewis, in case it helps the inventory."

"Oh, that could be," Lucy replied. "You didn't happen to make a copy, did you?"

Maggie shook her head no . . . then looked up. "Wait, I did make a copy. Dana said she wanted to try the pattern and I wasn't sure where Gloria had found it. Did you want to try making the scarf, too?"

"I wasn't thinking of the scarf. I meant the list."

"The list? Oh, I'm not sure if I copied the back of the page. I don't think there were any pattern instructions there. What did you want with that?"

"I don't know. With all the speculation about what may have happened at Gloria's the night she died, I thought it might come in handy at some point. Jamie ought to tell the police about it," Lucy added.

"That's true. He said he called Detective Walsh and they spoke about our suspicions. Walsh promised to review his report and one from the corner's office again. But Jamie felt he might have just been humoring him."

"I don't think the police will do anything," Lucy said flatly. "Look at it from their perspective. They're overloaded with cases, violent crimes with obvious victims and obvious criminals. They were able to investigate this situation quickly, file a report, and decided that she died of natural causes. They're not going to go out of their way to make more work for themselves, generating a murder investigation, when there are plenty of other crimes to solve with lots of obvious in-your-face evidence."

"Do you really think Gloria was murdered?" Maggie abruptly stopped rolling the yarn but the swift kept spinning.

"Did I say 'murder'?" Lucy shook her head. "Oh . . . I don't know. But it could have been. Considering Gloria's condition at the time, she could have been pushed into the pool and easily have drowned without any obvious signs of a struggle."

Maggie straightened out the yarn and prepared to start again. "I thought of that, too," she admitted. "Well, I thought of it and kept pushing it out of my mind. I kept telling myself that the police examined the house and examined her, and they would have come to that conclusion if there was any foul play."

"Right. Just like they figured out who killed Amanda Goran so quickly."

Maggie glanced at her over the edge of her glasses. "No comment."

"They may not even know about Gloria's relationship with Mike Novak. We didn't tell Jamie, so he didn't add that to his list of things worth looking into again."

"I know. But if they start investigating the situation again, they might discover that link on their own," Maggie pointed out.

"You didn't know and you were a good friend of hers. It could remain hidden. I guess we could tell Walsh. But I hate to go around Jamie's back."

"Me, too. I don't think any of us want to do that," Maggie insisted. "Look, we did our part. Jamie took our advice and prodded them. Let's see what the police do. Maybe they'll figure that angle out when they take a second look."

Lucy didn't have much hope the police would make a sincere effort, but Maggie seemed to. She guessed it made sense to wait a bit before going directly to Detective Walsh and telling all that they knew.

"There was something more I noticed last night," Lucy confided. "Beyond the mystery visitor and the wineglasses."

"And Gloria's relationship with Mike Novak," Maggie added.

"Well, it's related to that," Lucy told her. "I was looking at the real estate records Suzanne printed out for Jamie. I noticed that there were two properties listed that had been owned by Mike Novak and transferred to Gloria recently, for the sum of one dollar."

"Oh . . . that is strange." Maggie frowned. "Thought I have heard of people transferring deeds that way. Sometimes, within a family. It makes it official, but they don't have to pay any taxes, or something like that."

"Yes, the tiny sum makes it official," Lucy knew. "But why would he be giving her these expensive properties? The dates were pretty recent, too—within the last year."

"Before or after she went to Florida?" Maggie asked. She had almost finished rolling the wool and the swift was spinning quickly.

"Definitely before. The dates were last year." Lucy remembered that much.

"That was before she'd broken up with him," Maggie recalled. "Maybe the property was a gift of some kind?"

"Or repayment for a loan," Lucy realized. "But there was something else. That list on the back of the pattern . . . I saw at least one of the properties Mike Novak transferred to her on that list, too."

"Oh . . . that is an interesting coincidence." The skein had come to an end and the last strand flew off the swift and sent it spinning like a lawn ornament on a windy day.

"Interesting, yes. But what does it mean?" Lucy tossed her head in frustration.

She heard Tink give a bark. She looked over at the bay window and saw the dog up on her front paws again, looking in.

"Does she want you for some reason?" Lucy could tell by Maggie's tone that she was afraid Tink might have an accident on her lovely porch, ruining the ambience.

Lucy stood up. "I don't think so. She just had a long

walk . . . oh, it's those silly stuffed sheep you have in the window again. They're driving her mad."

Maggie laughed. "I'll get her one for Christmas."

"She'd chew it to shreds in about ten seconds. Major vet bill."

"You get a discount there," Maggie said lightly. "How's that going, by the way?"

"It's going great." Lucy noticed a new issue of a knitting magazine she hadn't seen before and picked it up from the table. A not-so-subtle diversion from the conversation.

It was going great. She and Matt had a great time together and he *was* just . . . great. It was his relationship with his Almost Ex-Wife that struck a sour note, at least in Lucy's thoughts. But Lucy didn't want to get into that this morning.

"How's Nick Cooper?" she prodded Maggie. "I saw you talking to him at the memorial service. Phoebe told me he likes to drop in to say hello."

Maggie's cheeks grew pink, Lucy thought. Or maybe that was just a trick of the light in the shop.

"Phoebe talks too much. But he does drop in," Maggie admitted. "He came by yesterday, in fact. With two tickets to a performance of chamber music at the library."

"You're going out with him?" Lucy wasn't quite sure that's what Maggie meant.

Maggie nodded and turned her attention back to the yarn swift. "Uh-huh. Tonight."

"Why didn't you tell me?"

"I'm telling you now, aren't I?" Maggie shrugged. "I guess I got tired of putting him off. Maybe Dana's right. I might like him more than I think. I just don't like the idea of liking anybody . . . if you know what I mean."

Lucy had heard Dana give Maggie that analysis, but never thought Maggie really heard the advice.

"Just relax and try to enjoy yourself. It's only a date."

"Oh dear . . . that's what everyone says. Why does that advice make me feel like I'm going to the dentist?"

Maggie stood up and detached the swift from the table.

Lucy stood up, too. She had to smile at Maggie's dismay. Her friend was really forcing herself to go through with this. She must have taken pity on the poor guy. But Lucy hoped it would turn out fine and Maggie would have a much better time than she expected.

On Sunday afternoon Lucy did manage to escape her office and went out with Matt on a small sailboat he'd borrowed from a friend.

Neither of them were experienced sailors, but somehow that made it more fun. Together, they knew enough to maneuver the boat in and out of the harbor without mishap and glided along the open water without luffing the sails, riding up on rocks, or totally capsizing.

Outside the harbor, with blue water and sky as far as the eye could see, Lucy did feel distant from everything. her work pressures and the cupboard of troubling thoughts she carried around in her head, including the torpid pace of Matt's divorce. Even questions about Gloria's death seemed far away, like the tiny buildings on the shore. Having Matt close all day was a perfect distraction and she always felt happy and calm around him.

Matt had to be up very early on Monday to perform several surgeries, so he decided it was best if he didn't stay over. Lucy would have liked him to, but it was just as well.

She used the extra hours at night and in the early morning to complete her work and sent the files off by e-mail to her client before lunchtime.

As she cleaned up her office and picked up around the house, she wondered about Maggie's date with Nick Cooper. She hadn't heard from Maggie yesterday and didn't know if that was a good sign or a bad one.

Lucy was sifting through a pile of newspaper, trying to figure out what belonged in the recycle bin, when she stopped to read an article in the *Plum Harbor Times*. The news item was placed fairly deep in the issue, back on page five. But the headline quickly caught her eye.

"DEC Officials Apprehended for Alleged Fraudulent Reporting." The article went on to describe how a local official of the Department of Environmental Conservation had been investigated for accepting bribes from large corporations in exchange for false reports on toxic land issues and cleanups.

She swiftly read through the paragraphs, coming to a riveting phrase: " . . . and land development firms have been named in the court documents filed yesterday, such as the Avalon Group, in regard to the Sea Breeze Colony, which is still under construction."

The Avalon Group, again. This time, she noticed, there was no statement from the Avalon spokesman, attorney Michael Novak, pledging the firm's commitment to the health and safety of Essex County residents.

There was no mention of him at all. And yet, Lucy had a creepy feeling that somehow this late-breaking news blast did fit in the picture somewhere.

She wasn't sure when the paper was from and quickly checked the date on the top of the page. Friday, June 19.

She'd been so busy the last few days, she hadn't kept up much with the news. Thank goodness she hadn't thrown it out.

She ripped out the page, then went to her computer and found the other article she'd seen, the one that talked about the Sea Breeze housing development and the land contamination there. She printed it out and saved it with the scrap of newspaper.

Did this mean that the Avalon Group had bribed the government's environmental engineers to deliver a favorable report on their toxic building site? Which meant that the entire project had to be torn down. What a loss. And in today's economy, too.

A pretty big hit, Lucy thought, even for a group with deep pockets. A pretty big secret to keep, too.

Was it a secret worth killing somebody over?

Lucy quickly pushed the thought aside. It was hard enough to think of poor Gloria dying by accident. Imagining her scared and terrorized was too much.

Lucy checked the clock on the stove. It was nearly 3:00. She decided to jump in the shower and then show Maggie these articles. It was too complicated to explain it over the phone. The shop would be quiet at this hour and they could talk without too many interruptions.

It was too hot outside to walk, so Lucy drove her Jeep the short distance into town, the news articles tucked into her knitting bag. What would Maggie think of this twist, she wondered? What was there to think? Imagine if that development had gone up and nobody learned about the bogus report? Lives would have been in danger, Lucy thought.

Some people had no conscience. Lucy was relieved when she figured out that Gloria had sold her share of the firm well before their involvement in the Sea Breeze project, relieved and satisfied. Gloria had been aggressive in business, that was for sure, but their former friend wasn't ruthless. She would never have acted so unethically. Lucy was sure of it.

Lucy parked and walked up to the shop. It was well past lunch hour and she knew she wouldn't find her pals, Suzanne and Dana, brown-bagging it on the porch. But she did find Jamie, sitting with Maggie in a pair of fan-back wicker chairs.

Maggie was busily knitting; it looked like the square with the shooting star for the center of the blanket. Jamie sat nearby, both sipping from tall glasses of iced tea.

Lucy forced a smile, but secretly felt disappointed. She didn't want to talk about the newspaper articles she'd found in front of him. That conversation would definitely include Mike Novak and she needed to consult with her friends on the best way to handle this latest hot potato that had been tossed her way.

Lucy hoped Jamie wouldn't stay too long and she could wait him out.

"Hello, Lucy. Did you finish that blue yarn already?" Maggie asked her cheerfully.

"Yes, I'm zipping along. I was in town so I thought I'd grab more yarn." Blue yarn for her blanket squares was far from the reason for her visit, but seemed like a good excuse right now.

Lucy sat down in a wicker chair near Jamie. A group of women on the other end of the porch sat at the wrought-iron table, knitting together, but she didn't think they could overhear the conversation.

"How are you doing, Jamie?" Lucy looked him over. She could tell his worries and grief weighed heavily.

"Hanging in there," he replied, forcing a brief smile.

"Any word back from the police?" Lucy asked. "Do you think they'll reopen the case?"

"Oh, I don't know. Maybe it's too early to say. But I did call again this morning, just to give that detective a nudge—"

"Walsh, you mean." Maggie filled in the blank for him. "I'd like to give him a nudge. I'd like to give him a poke with one of these." She held up one of her knitting needles and grinned slyly.

A slight smile hovered on Jamie's mouth, but he soon looked serious again. "I don't think they're going to do anything more. I don't think they're taking much interest."

"That's too bad," Lucy said sincerely. If the police didn't follow up, she and her friends might feel obliged to step forward and offer their suspicions and what they'd put together so far. But could they go around Jamie's back to do that? It didn't seem right.

"I'm not surprised," Maggie said. "The police are a little dense in this town."

"I've been thinking, Jamie, if the police won't take a second look at Gloria's accident, you could always hire a private investigator. I'll bet Dana's husband can give you a good recommendation." Lucy hoped her tone was persuasive but not too pushy.

"That's an excellent idea." Maggie put her knitting down and looked over at Jamie. "A friend of Jack's might give you a break on the charges, too."

"If they find new information"—which we would contribute, too, Lucy silently added—"you could bring it to the police and they'd have to follow through."

Jamie rubbed his bearded chin. "That is a good idea. Then we'd all know for sure if anything else happened that night, besides poor Gloria just . . . losing control and taking a bad fall."

"It would give you some closure," Maggie advised him. "And us, as well."

"I'll give the police another day or two. If they put me off with more excuses, I'll hire somebody," he agreed. "I think we'll all feel better getting to the bottom of it."

Lucy was relieved to hear him say that, though she wasn't sure that the real answers to these questions were going to make anybody feel better. Most likely, they'd feel a lot worse.

"Well, that's settled, then." Maggie took a sip from her glass. "Would you like some iced tea, Lucy? It's over on the table. By the way, I didn't expect to see you today; weren't you in lockdown mode, trying to meet some deadline?"

Lucy rose and poured herself a glass of tea. "I got the work in this morning, just under the wire."

"Good for you." Maggie nodded at her.

"Good for you, Lucy. It's nice to hear someone's work is going well." Jamie spoke quietly, his tone edged with self-contempt.

"Jamie . . . you can't expect yourself to be painting right now. It's totally understandable if you need to take a break."

"That's what I've been telling myself." He swallowed hard and stared down at his hands. "But sometimes I think if I could work, it would make me feel better. It would be some distraction from missing Gloria so much, and everything else that's going on."

Lucy felt sorry for him. She knew what he meant. Sometimes work was the perfect escape. It seemed an extra cruel twist that along with losing Gloria, his painting had been taken away from him, too.

"I understand," Maggie said quietly. She reached out and briefly touched his shoulder. "You should try to work, then. How do you feel about the gallery show? Have you thought any more about it?"

"I can't do it," he said bluntly. "I have to be straight with the guy who owns the gallery. I just keep putting it off."

Maggie's expression fell. Lucy felt concerned, too. "Maybe it can be postponed," she suggested. "Gloria wouldn't have wanted you to miss this opportunity, Jamie."

"She was so proud of your talent. She had so much confidence in you," Maggie reminded him. "She was sure you'd be a great success. This show was going to be the start."

"That's just it. I can't do it without her. She was my center, my base. I was never able to _bare_ down and really focus before I met her. She gave me that," he told them. "And now, without her, I'm just flying off in all directions again. I don't know where to start."

He'd lost his confidence without Gloria. It was as simple as that, Lucy realized. Making art—real art—was sort of a high-wire act without a net. The artist had to have a clear head and strong focus and the utmost confidence that they would not tumble. Jamie had felt that kind of confidence for a short time, but had lost it now.

"You're letting the negative voices in your head get control, Jamie. 'If a candle will doubt, it will go out,'" Maggie said quietly.

He grinned sadly. "Who said that?"

"Emily Dickinson."

"Her heroine," Lucy added. Maggie glanced over, but didn't correct her.

"I've seen your work," Maggie said. "You have talent. Plenty of it. But talent isn't enough. I think you might regret it if you miss this chance to move forward with your career," she said honestly. "I think you should go back in the studio and try to work through it. Try to remember all the encouragement Gloria gave you. She's still there, you know. Watching and cheering you on."

Jamie's eyes glazed over. He nodded without saying anything. He rubbed his face with his hands and took a deep breath.

"I think you could help, Maggie," he said, turning toward her.

"Me? What can I do?"

"I'd like to do your portrait. Would you sit for me?" he asked in a quiet, almost shy voice.

Maggie leaned back and laughed nervously. "There are plenty of women around here who'd make far better models, Jamie. In case you haven't noticed."

"No . . . you're the one. Will you do it? It would help me, honestly," he added.

Lucy waited to see what Maggie would finally say. She had started fiddling around with her knitting again, but Lucy could tell Maggie was stalling.

"Oh well . . . if you really want me to. I guess it would be okay." She glanced up quickly at him, then back at the dark blue square she had just begun. "You know I'm not very good at sitting still for long periods of time. I mean, unless I'm occupied in some way . . ."

"She means, unless she's knitting," Lucy translated for him.

Maggie was in fact one of the most indefatigable people Lucy had ever met. She was like a honey bee, always buzzing around in some productive task.

"I'll do a portrait of you knitting, then," Jamie offered. "That would be perfect. You could sit right here, or inside the shop."

"Oh . . . well, that could be fun." Maggie seemed to warm up to the idea once knitting needles were included. "Let me think about it. I like both those ideas."

"Great. I'm glad you'll do it." He gave her a grateful look, then stood up and picked up his car keys and sunglasses from the wicker side table.

Lucy smiled as she said good-bye but was secretly pleased to see him go. She was dying to show Maggie the news article she'd found. She opened her knitting bag and fished around for it.

She'd just found it when Phoebe strolled out of the shop with her friend Crystal. "I straightened out all the stock in the back of the store and unpacked the delivery. Do you think I could leave a little early today, Maggie?"

Maggie glanced at her watch. "Is it nearly five already? Okay, you can go. It *is* pretty slow this afternoon."

"Must be the hot weather," Lucy said. "Most people just want to stay inside, in their air-conditioning."

"Most people do," Phoebe agreed, sounding grouchy.

Maggie sighed. "Phoebe wants me to turn the air higher. But it's a big expense and with people walking in and out all day, it makes it worse. It's not very good for the environment. I'd just as soon get another overhead fan."

Phoebe put her hands to her head, as if the wind from a huge fan was going to blow her away. "No, not another fan. Please, no . . . it's like working in a wind storm."

"Why don't you and Crystal have some iced tea?" Maggie soothed her irrate helper. "There's a big pitcher of it, right over there," she offered, "and some cookies."

The young women looked at each other, then silently agreed to try the tea and cookies. They filled their glasses and sat at the wrought-iron table at the other side of the porch, which was now empty.

"You'd think since she's so young, she'd be more

green-minded," Maggie said with a sigh. "You can't have summer without hot weather. I don't understand why people complain so much about it."

"Neither do I," Lucy said. She was not a huge fan of air-conditioning either. But maybe that was because she'd been raised in Massachusetts and shivered through so many frigid winters, she appreciated summer weather when it finally came.

"Do you want that blue yarn? I have more inside." Maggie put her work aside, about to get up and get it.

"I didn't really stop by for yarn," Lucy confessed. "I wanted to show you something." She took out the articles and handed them over to Maggie. "Something I didn't want to talk about in front of Jamie."

"Oh . . . what's this?" Maggie asked curiously as Lucy handed over the articles.

"I was throwing out some newspapers this morning and saw that article. It mentions Gloria's old firm, the Avalon Group."

Maggie pushed her reading glasses higher on her nose and read the scrap of newspaper with interest. "I must have missed this. When did it appear?"

"In Friday's paper. I missed it, too. But a few days ago, I was sitting at the computer and goofing off, and I found this article, too. Also about the Avalon Group and that pollution situation at the Sea Breeze Colony site."

She gave Maggie the first article she'd found, the one that mentioned Mike Novak, then waited while Maggie read it. Phoebe and Crystal had their heads close together, drinking iced tea and munching cookies. They glanced over a few times, then started laughing at something.

Lucy couldn't imagine what was so amusing, but was sure it wasn't flattering.

"Well . . . that's interesting." Maggie handed the articles back to her. "Mike Novak again. His name keeps popping up, doesn't it?"

"Yes, it does. We're not imagining that." Lucy stuffed the papers in her purse and sat back. "I checked the dates. Gloria had already sold out her share to her partners when Avalon started the Sea Breeze project last spring, so she wasn't any part of that bribery situation."

"I noticed that timing, too," Maggie said. "But she was still involved with Mike. Dana said she didn't break it off until last fall, before she went down to Florida."

"Maybe she knew and he gave her the property in exchange for her silence," Lucy speculated. "Though I hate to think of her doing something like that."

"I hate to think that of her, either. If those houses had ever gone up, people could have gotten sick. They could have died."

"Gloria was a tough businesswoman, but she had a good heart. Look at all the work she did for charities," Lucy reminded her friend. "I don't think she knew anything about it. Novak could have kept it from her."

"He could have." Maggie nodded, looking soothed by Lucy's words.

"It is a pretty creepy coincidence that her former business partners get into this major jam, and Gloria drowned just a few days before the story came out."

Maggie's expression darkened. She looked very troubled. "It is creepy, isn't it?"

Chapter Eleven

"What should we do?" Maggie asked Lucy.

"I don't know . . . I don't know what we can do."

Lucy truly didn't have a clue. The choices that came to mind seemed either improbable or inappropriate. The whole situation made her feel frustrated and confused. There seemed to be any number of creepy coincidences piling up, but none of them connected. None of it fell into any sort of pattern.

Lucy rose from her seat and walked to the porch rail. She gazed out at Main Street, quiet and empty at this time of the day. A woman with a long, swinging ponytail pushed a double stroller down the sidewalk. A man jogged down the street in the opposite direction, huffing and puffing, his T-shirt dark with sweat. It was shaping up to be a very sultry summer night.

"I guess I'll go now, Maggie. It's after five," Phoebe called from the other side of the porch.

"Oh . . . okay, Phoebe. You have a good evening. Do you have a class or something tonight?"

"We're just hanging out downtown. I'm going to run

up and get my purse. Be right back," Phoebe said to Crystal.

Her friend nodded and sat on the porch steps, hugging her knees. Despite the heat, she wore layers of spandex tops today, a yellow camisole under a gray one and a black one—of course—over that. The colorful sets of spaghetti straps tangled on her shoulders, as seemed to be the style these days.

The trifecta of camis wasn't quite long enough to reach the top of her dark green cargo shorts. Lucy noticed a belly button ring that looked pretty painful and a tattoo on the back of her shoulder that had not been visible before—a skull with a heart and a rose, and the word "bad"—or did it say "sad"?— written underneath, in tortured, swirly script.

Crystal sensed that Lucy was studying her and yanked down the shirts.

"Hey, how's it going?" She turned to Lucy and smiled self-consciously.

"Okay, Crystal. How are you? Still knitting?"

"Hey, I'm on it. One stitch at a time and all that." She glanced at Lucy again, her dark gaze sliding out from under long straight bangs.

"She's doing fine," Maggie said. "She showed me her progress and we fixed a few glitches."

Phoebe came out again, her big purse hooked over her arm, her skinny wrist covered with colorful, plastic bangles. "Okay, let's go. I don't care where we eat, as long as there's plenty of air."

Phoebe turned and gave Maggie an accusing stare.

Maggie laughed and waved good-bye to them. Lucy did the same.

"She's so grouchy today. I think she had a fight with Josh, but she won't say," Maggie reported after they'd gone.

"She does seem to be spending a lot of time with Crystal. Maybe Goth Girl isn't a good influence," Lucy ventured.

"Oh, she's okay. I had plenty of students who looked worse than that and were really great kids underneath the costumes." Maggie paused. "Is it the body art that puts you off? I know it bothers some people. But I have one myself," she confessed with a sly smile.

"You have a tattoo?" Lucy didn't mean to sound so shocked. "You never told me that."

"You never asked." Maggie shrugged.

True, but mainly because the question had never even occurred to her. Who would have imagined it? Now that the inky truth was out of the bag, Lucy was curious.

"What does it look like?"

"It's small . . . a small hummingbird, actually. And I'm not going to give you any more details, or tell you where," she added tartly, guessing Lucy's next question.

"Now I *really* want to know," Lucy admitted with a laugh.

"Have you ever thought about getting one?" Maggie asked, cleverly diverting attention from herself, Lucy realized.

"I have. Mainly when I'm at the beach . . . or see a picture of Angelina Jolie in an evening gown."

"She seems to pull it off easily. Though I wonder how well that look will wear by the time she's my age." Maggie laughed, then glanced back at Lucy. "What kind would you get? Any tigers or dragons, like Angie?"

"Oh . . . I don't know. Is this a personality quiz or something?" Lucy laughed at Maggie's serious expression. "Let's see . . . something small and discreet. A yin/yang symbol, maybe. On my ankle."

Maggie looked surprised. "You've given this a lot more

thought than you let on, Lucy. I'm surprised you haven't followed through yet."

"Now that I know your secret, I'm inspired. I'll have to
check with Matt first," she added.

Maggie shook her head in disapproval. "Body art is not
about pleasing your partner. It's about pleasing yourself. It's
about . . . empowerment. It's a very primitive practice, mark-
ing yourself with ink drawings. Ask Angelina. Or Crystal."

"Maybe I will. And I didn't mean to sound judgmental
about Crystal," she added. "I barely know her. Phoebe seems
to like her a lot."

"Yes, she does. And we know that Phoebe, despite her own
fashion choices, is an excellent judge of character."

Maggie wasn't being sarcastic, either. Phoebe did have a
good—albeit magenta-streaked—head on her shoulders.

"I'd better go, too. Tink needs her dinner."

Maggie shook her head and smiled. "You talk about that
dog as if she were your only child. You know that, don't you?"

"And there's a problem with that?"

"No problem. She's probably good practice for you." Before Lucy could come up with a snappy answer, Maggie said,
"We can't go to the police with any of this. It's all sort of flimsy
and I still don't think we should go behind Jamie's back."

"And if we try to explain any of it to him, we'll have to
include the affair between Gloria and Mike Novak," Lucy finished for her. "And we can't do that, either."

"It would be difficult. What if he starts to think that she
didn't really end it? It could be so hurtful to him." Maggie
stood up and placed some dirty glasses on a tray. "He's not
ready to deal with a bombshell like that right now. I think we
just have to wait."

Lucy agreed, though she found it interesting that now Maggie was protecting Jamie from the harsh realities, just like Gloria once did. Maybe he was just the type of man women liked to take care of. Older women, especially.

"Either the police will take an interest again," Maggie added, as she carried the tray to the door, "or Jamie will hire the private investigator. That's the place we can unload all these disturbing bits and pieces, don't you think?"

"Possibly," Lucy said. "And a PI may not even need to tell Jamie about the affair. But he—or she—could use the information to find out more."

"That's what I'm hoping."

Lucy moved forward to open the door for Maggie.

"Now, stop snooping around the Internet, please?" Maggie implored her. "I think we've learned enough disturbing secrets about Gloria."

Lucy had to agree with that, too. Maybe it was time to put this all aside and get on with her life.

"So, how was your date with Nick Cooper?" Lucy asked.

"Okay, I guess." Maggie shrugged. "He's very nice, but I don't think we'll get together again."

"That bad, huh?"

"It wasn't bad," Maggie said quickly. "He's a good conversationalist. We have a lot in common." Her voice trailed off again. Then she shook her head. "But, not for me. Not right now, anyway."

"At least you gave it a try," Lucy replied.

As a wise man once said, "It don't mean a thing if it ain't got that swing." Nick Cooper didn't seem to have it. Not for Maggie, anyway.

They said good night and Lucy headed home, looking

forward to a sunset stroll and harassing some seagulls with Tink.

Lucy kept her promise to Maggie and didn't troll the 'Net Monday night for more ragged pieces to the "Avalon–Mike Novak–Gloria Sterling" puzzle. She did send an e-mail to Dana and Suzanne, and filled them in about the overlapping information she'd noticed on the list of properties and the list on the back of the knitting pattern.

"Did you see that, too, Suzanne?" she asked her, wondering.

She also sent links to the two articles she'd found on the 'Net about Avalon, and told them what she and Maggie had decided.

Suzanne was often on the computer late at night, after her kids had gone to bed, answering e-mails and shopping. It was a dangerous time to have a credit card within reach, she often told her friends, especially if she went anywhere near a site that sold yarn.

Lucy saw replies from both of them right away and opened Dana's first:

Lucy—This is getting complicated. If the police won't follow up, we should wait to tell the private investigator. Jack can give Jamie a name or two.

Namaste,

Dana

Dana was really into yoga these days and signed her e-mails that way now. Lucy wrote back a short note, saying she'd told Jamie to call Jack for a recommendation and hoped he reached out soon.

Suzanne's note was a little more feisty and chatty, as Lucy had expected. Her e-mails were always longer than Dana's and careened crazily into a million others topics, the way Suzanne talked after a few cups of coffee. But the missives always made for amusing reading.

Dear Sleuthy-Lucy (my new nickname for you, don't you love it?)

Never had a chance to look over the list. Printed it out at the office right before I ran over to Maggie's. But I'll take a look tomorrow.

WOW, Gloria got some bargain. I knew she was a sharp cookie but . . . that first property is worth real dough. I think the other is the condo she wanted to sell. What could this mean? I think we need to take a meeting with Counselor Novak and get to the bottom of it. Why wait for some private investigator. Who knows if Jamie will ever hire one?

Let's just ask the guy point blank—what the heck was going on? I know he won't spill the whole story, but as I've learned from the real estate biz, you can usually tell if there's really water in the basement by the kind of excuses people make up about the puddles. I think we should go for it. When, where, and how?

XOXO Suzanne

Lucy stared at the message. Was Suzanne serious? Sometimes it was hard to tell. Could they confront Mike Novak and ask him questions about Gloria? Things could get pretty nasty.

Before her imagination could wander too far, another message popped up from Dana.

Sue and Lu—On second thought, I'm with Suzanne. I think we ought to confront him. We're all former friends of Gloria, right?

To answer Suzanne's questions: Where? The Harbor Club. He tees off just about every morning in the summer at 5:30 and takes a fast nine holes before going into the office. (Jack is equally obsessed and has mentioned meeting up with Novak out there at the crack of dawn.)

How? We go to the club around 7:00 for an early breakfast on the patio. He has to pass us walking off the course.

When? Tomorrow morning. The fair weather is going to hold up a few more days and we won't be rained out.

Get back to me on this ASAP—

Namaste, my dear ones.

Dana

p.s. Should we invite Maggie?

Whoa, this plan was in motion. Just as Lucy began to type a reply, she heard a little *ping* as Suzanne's message flew in her box first.

L & D—

I'm in, ladies. Meet you at ground zero at 6:45. Any dress code required? Or should I just go undercover in my tennis togs?

S.

Lucy quickly typed back her message:

Dear Daring Dana & Snoopy Sue—

You have tennis togs? I'm impressed. I'll try to find a little madras golf skirt, or maybe one with tiny whales printed all over it.

See you there.

Lucy

p.s. I think it's too late to pull Maggie in. She might try to talk us out of it.

After a moment, another note came from Dana:

L & S—

O.K. It's a plan. I'll give Maggie a call, but I agree, I don't think she'll want to take part. See you guys at the club, 6:45. Lucy, skip the whales, but bring your knitting, just in case he decides to shoot 18 :)

XOX

D.

It was a challenge to get out of bed in time to shower, feed and walk the dog, and dress appropriately for breakfast at the Harbor Club . . . and arrive there by 6:45 the next morning.

Bleary-eyed, Lucy drove toward The Landing, where the club was located, wondering why she'd even bothered going to bed the night before. And what the heck were they going to say to Mike Novak if they did indeed encounter him?

The Harbor Club occupied the former grand estate of some Gilded Age tycoon who had made his fortune in canned clams. The mansion was a replica of a famous British manor house, the main building an imposing brick structure with a slate roof, several chimneys, and long white columns across the classic façade.

Lucy could practically hear the sound track of one of her favorite costume dramas, a Jane Austen novel brought to the big screen, as she drove in and pulled up to the round drive-way at the entrance.

She expected to see Mr. Darcy in his waistcoat and high riding boots sprinting out to meet her. Instead, a young His-panic man neatly dressed in a blue windbreaker and black pants hopped down the front steps and quickly pulled open the door of her battered white Jeep.

Do you tip the valet now or later? Lucy was never sure. He efficiently handed her a car check, jumped behind the wheel, and drove off before she had time to figure it out.

Luckily she had remembered to grab her purse and

knitting bag from the front seat. She took a breath and walked up the steps to the club's lobby.

While she gazed around at the faux Regency-era décor, Dana appeared from behind a huge silk flower arrangement. "Good going, Lucy. Suzanne is already at the table."

Lucy followed Dana through the club's lobby and a dining room, then out to a sunny patio that was shaded by a wooden trellis that supported a thick leafy awning of wisteria.

"Wow, this is beautiful," Lucy said, admiring the setting, tables covered in crisp, white table linens and the view of the golf course, which was a supernatural green, covered with dew, some mist still rising as the day grew warmer.

"It is pretty out here. We don't use the place enough, though. Jack mainly entertains here for business. I'm just not the clubby type," Dana said quietly as she took her seat.

It was true. Dana was not the clubby type and Lucy often forgot she and Jack were members here.

"I love that wisteria," Suzanne said, gazing overhead. "I wish I could get mine to grow like that. I wonder what they feed it."

"Paté? Caviar? Filet mignon?" Lucy ventured.

Dana ignored her. "The vines are over one hundred and fifty years old, planted when the house was built. Some of the members complain that the leaves fall in their food, and cocktails, and they want it chopped down. Replaced by a motorized, green canvas thingy . . . can you believe it?" Dana shook her head in dismay and snapped open her napkin.

It *was* hard to believe, but sounded about right, when Lucy considered her impression of places like this.

Dana glanced at her watch. "We'd better order. It's almost seven. I checked with the starter. Novak's definitely out there and he could be coming off soon."

Dana had taken a seat with a clear view of the golf course and the area near a little outbuilding where golf carts scooted in and out.

There were more golf carts zipping over the gentle peaks and valleys of the course than Lucy had expected. And more golfers out there, too. But she and her friends were the only group on the patio, except for a very old, very well-dressed couple sitting in a far corner. They reminded Lucy of pictures she'd seen of the Duke and Duchess of Windsor.

Lucy picked up her menu, golden script printed on white stock. A list of gourmet breakfast choices, including eggs Benedict and a heart-healthy version, as well as brioche French toast.

No prices, of course. Membership had its privileges.

Her stomach rumbled with nerves or maybe it was just still sleeping. Either way, she wasn't sure she could eat a thing.

"I think I'll just have coffee and a blueberry scone," she said, putting the card aside.

"I'll have the crêpes with berry medley, orange zest, and crème fraîche," Suzanne announced cheerfully. "Sure beats those Stop N Shop toaster pancakes we fix at home."

Dana ordered the yogurt and granola with a cup of warm water and lemon. She claimed the tart day starter cleaned out the liver.

Lucy gave her a look, then asked for more coffee. She'd prefer to live with a dirty liver, if that was the remedy.

"So, now what do we do?" Suzanne asked. She seemed nervous. Lucy felt the same. Was this a huge mistake?

"You know, we could always just have a nice breakfast and do some knitting . . . and then go on about our day," Lucy suggested.

"You mean, chicken out?" Suzanne asked, sipping her ice water.

"I mean . . . socialize. You know, Dana, I don't know why you've never asked us to have breakfast here before. It's a real treat."

"I should have," Dana agreed. "But we didn't come here this morning to hang out like club ladies." She looked at each of them, urging solidarity with her calm, centered gaze. "Just leave it to me. I know what to say."

Lucy looked at Suzanne, who shrugged. "Okay, you're in charge," Suzanne replied. "We'll just jump in with backup, as necessary."

The waitress had brought their orders and placed the dishes down in front of them. Suzanne approached her crêpes with due respect.

"Right, just follow my lead," Dana instructed. "I think it will go fine."

No one said a word more about it. They ate breakfast, then took out their knitting and waited. Each time a golf cart rolled up to the little gatehouse and the brightly dressed golfers emptied out, Lucy's pulse quickened. But so far, she had not recognized Mike Novak in any of the groups.

Dana was watching, too, from her seat that faced the course. She suddenly leaned closer to Suzanne and Lucy, her blue eyes wide with alarm. "That's him . . . he's coming off the course. I see him in that cart that's parking."

Suzanne sat back and took a deep breath. She reached over and squeezed Lucy's hand, then dropped a knitting needle, which rattled on the cement floor and rolled under the table.

"Just stay calm everyone . . ." Dana reached into the pocket of her white hoodie, pulled out a lip gloss, and swiped a bit over her mouth. "How do I look?" she asked her friends.

"Great," Suzanne whispered back, "go get 'em."

Dana smiled widely and sat back in her chair. Lucy saw her stare out toward the course, then give a big wave, her glowing smile ratcheting up a few more watts.

"Mike . . . Mike Novak? Why, hello . . . how are you?" she cooed as he approached their table.

Lucy glanced up at him for an instant, then down at her knitting again, stitching away at another blue square. She almost didn't recognize the notorious attorney in his golfing outfit, pale blue slacks, and black polo shirt with a ubiquitous embroidered emblem on the pocket.

He wore a black baseball-style cap that said "Pebble Beach" across the peak and pulled it off, exposing his distinctively dyed hair. The graviatas sideburns were even phonier looking close up.

He stared down at Dana curiously as she leaned back in her chair to get a better look at him. He was tall and lean, quite good looking, Lucy thought. She could understand Gloria's attraction. He was also a more appropriate choice for her in age and experience than Jamie. But there's always the X factor and sometimes what looks good on paper just doesn't translate to real life.

"Dana Haeger," Dana reminded him. "Jack's wife. Is Jack out there? He's just been obsessed lately. Trying to break eighty," she confided, rolling her eyes. "How was your game? Did it go well?" she rattled on.

"Not too bad. I had two birdies on the back nine." Lucy wasn't sure what that meant, but pitied the poor birds nonetheless.

"Good for you. Better to finish on a good note, don't you think?"

"I guess so," he agreed, looking at her curiously now.

"Listen, I saw you and Beth at Gloria Sterling's memorial service. I'm so sorry I didn't get a chance to say hello," she apologized in a more intimate tone.

"Oh . . . that's all right. Awful news about Gloria." An appropriately somber expression fell over his features. "What a tragedy."

"Yes, it was." Dana nodded, looking sad. "Why don't you sit down and have a cup of coffee with us?" she said quickly.

The table was set for four and an empty chair stood beside her. She gestured at it and offered another inviting smile.

"Oh . . . I don't know." He smiled briefly, then checked his watch. A Rolex, Lucy noticed. Not a knockoff from a stall at the mall, either. "I'd love to . . . but I really have to get into the office. This early morning golf game is my secret weakness."

Don't be so modest, Mike, Lucy nearly said aloud. A guy like you has plenty of secret weaknesses, I'll bet.

"Just for a minute?" Dana wheedled him. Lucy was fairly shocked. She'd never seen Dana go into coquette mode before. She was pretty good.

"We're all old friends of Gloria's, you know," she added, glancing at Suzanne and Lucy. "We just want to talk to you a minute. About her. It won't take long."

"Gloria?" Now she'd snagged his interest. He was tugging off his black golf glove, but it was stuck. "What about her?" he asked pointedly.

"Well, let's see . . ." Dana paused and pursed her glossy lips. "We know you had a long, close . . . relationship with her. And we know you gave her some property recently. Transferred a deed, or two." Dana stopped and waited to see his reaction.

He stared at her bug-eyed. Then his gaze narrowed.

"Who told you that?"

Dana shrugged. "It's public record. You can find it pretty easily on the Internet."

Of course he knew that. What he was really asking was, "Why were you looking?"

He stared down at all of them. Then, with his mouth set in a harsh line, he took the seat between Dana and Lucy. He yanked his chair in closer to the table and it made a scraping sound, like nails on a chalkboard. He was a big man and Lucy could practically feel the heat radiating off his body.

"So . . . what's this all about? Just get it out on the table. I don't have all day," he reminded her.

"Neither do we," she assured him. "Let's start with the property. Why did you transfer those deeds to Gloria? We know she didn't pay you anything."

He shrugged. Lucy could see he thought they were no match for him. "How do you know we didn't exchange any money? Maybe we just wanted to hide the transaction, avoid the taxes."

"Possibly. Though it is illegal and you're an officer of the court. You could get disbarred if anyone discovered it."

He didn't answer that, but held her in a steady gaze.

"I was repaying Gloria for a loan she'd given me. I didn't have the cash, but she was willing to accept the title to the property. Like Monopoly, you know?"

His tone had turned a bit condescending, Lucy thought. Or maybe he was trying to strike a humorous note?

Dana didn't look like she was buying it, but it was plausible. "I guess you'd have some letter or agreement, to back that up?" Dana asked him.

He nearly laughed at her. "Who's asking?"

"How about the police? We hear from her husband they

might be investigating her death again. They may have been mistaken, calling it natural causes so quickly."

Touché, Dana, Lucy thought.

"And now, some very curious information about her life is coming forward. Gloria had a lot of secrets, you know?" she asked.

Yeah, he knew. He was one of them.

Mike Novak looked angry now; his tanned face had turned into a scowling mask. The kind people bring back as souvenirs from exotic locales.

"Gloria and I had a long, complicated relationship," he said bluntly. "I don't know what she told you about it. But we ended it last year. She wanted me to leave my family and I wouldn't do it. Even for her. Except for settling that loan, I didn't have much contact with her since she got back from Florida with . . . with that South Beach idiot boy she married."

Now that was a lie. Dana knew he'd been practically stalking Gloria, trying to persuade her to come back to him. Maybe he thought he could undermine the version she'd told her friends, now that she was gone and couldn't refute him.

"You didn't try to see her or call her in all that time?" Dana asked. "That's not what she told me."

"Once or twice, in regard to the loan, maybe," he backtracked, gazing out at the golf course again.

Dana followed with a combination punch. "Did she know Avalon bribed the DEC to report that the Sea Breeze site was safe to build on? Is that why you gave her the property?"

And when did you stop beating your wife, Mike? Lucy silently added.

His head snapped up again. "You know I can't discuss Avalon. That's privileged information."

"Oh . . . right," Dana said meekly. Of course she knew, she was an attorney's wife. She'd just wanted to rattle his cage a little.

"So where were you the night Gloria fell into her swimming pool?" Suzanne suddenly asked him. "You didn't happen to drop by her house to chat about the those loans? Or reminisce about old times?"

He leaned forward angrily, his bright white teeth bared like a snarling dog. "I was right here, the entire day," he said in a low harsh voice, one finger tapping the tabletop. "I played twenty-seven holes, ate dinner with some friends, and then got sucked into a card game that didn't break up until two a.m." He turned to Dana. "Not that I owe you women any explanation. I don't even know why I'm talking to you . . ."

Lucy decided it was her turn to jump in and deflect his attention from Dana. "Sounds like you're a real family man, Mike. I can see why it didn't work out with Gloria."

He glared at her, then stood up, nearly knocking his chair backward. He picked up his golf cap and glove.

"I think you ladies ought to go back to the nail salon and stop meddling where you don't belong. You don't know what you're doing and you could hurt a lot of innocent people, wandering around town, spreading this kind of malicious . . . slander."

He tugged his hat back on and grabbed his golf cart.

"It's slander. I won't sit still for it," he added, a not-so-subtle warning that he knew how to file a lawsuit and didn't mind filling out the paperwork.

"I catch your meaning, Mike," Dana said lightly. "Luckily I know a good lawyer."

"Yes, lucky for you. Tell Jack I'd rather meet him on the golf course than in a courtroom. But if I have to, I will."

Head hunkered down, shoulders set, he stomped off, dragging his clubs. The cleats on his golf shoes made a racket on the stone floor.

They all sat perfectly still for a long moment. "Just breathe," Dana murmured. "In through the nose . . . out through the mouth. Slow and steady," she coached them.

Lucy did as she was advised. She even closed her eyes for a moment. Facing down a shady attorney first thing in the day was very draining. Maybe she should take a yoga class today.

"Dana, you were masterful," Suzanne said. "No offense, but I didn't think you had it in you. The way you handled that guy? I was blown away."

"Why, thank you. I rather enjoyed it. I do deal with a lot of sociopaths. I know how they operate."

"Well, what do you think?" Suzanne asked her and then looked at Lucy.

"I think he could be lying about the property transfers. But sounds like he has an airtight alibi for the night Gloria died. Maybe he wasn't her mysterious visitor after all?"

Dana sounded genuinely disappointed to realize that theory had been taken off the table. Lucy was, too.

"I guess not," Suzanne agreed. She sounded puzzled. "But if it wasn't him, who could it have been? I think we're back to square one."

Lucy didn't like hearing that, but she had to agree. They had ventured to the dark side to face down the fearsome golfing cyborg, Mike Novak. But they hadn't ended up any closer to filling in the blanks in this saga.

Maybe Maggie had been right to discourage the adventure. Maybe it wasn't their place to try to solve this conundrum. Maybe it was all just as it appeared—Gloria had fallen in the water and drowned by accident and there was no great mystery to it.

Maybe it was best left now to the police or a private investigator working for Jamie, and they had followed their slim thread of suspicions and quasi-incriminating facts as far as they would stretch.

Chapter Twelve

*L*ucy was actually relieved that the knitting group wasn't meeting until Friday night. After Tuesday's showdown with Mike Novak in the hushed, luxurious environs of the Harbor Club, she needed a break from talk about Gloria, and even from her dear friends.

Suzanne, who was hosting the meeting at her house, had e-mailed everyone on Tuesday night about a sudden change in her schedule. Thursday was her mother-in-law's birthday and she'd been called into action.

Kevin invited her here for a barbeque. Without even asking me, by the way. Nice, right? Think I'll try that Ragin' Cajun Arsenic Marinade I found online the other day. As Emeril says, "Kick it up a notch." :)

While Suzanne was cooking up revenge fantasies Thursday night, Lucy was cooking for Matt. They usually ate out, so making him dinner was sort of an event . . . and made her a little nervous. She decided to make something simple, so she wouldn't be jumping up and checking the food every five seconds.

Suzanne had served them a pasta dish earlier in the spring, with roasted asparagus, artichoke hearts, and pesto sauce. Lucy decided to try it, figuring she could fix it ahead. A big salad, some bread, and dessert from the bakery would fill out the rest of the menu and leave her time to take her third shower of the day. It was still hot out and not the greatest night for cooking. The steam from the pasta pot had provided a minifacial, which saved time on her primping-for-the-boyfriend routine.

Matt arrived right on time, with a bottle of cold white wine, a bunch of sunflowers, and a gigantic chewy bone for Tink. The hostess gift for the dog bode well. He obviously planned on staying over and wanted Tink fully occupied.

They ate outside, on the little brick back patio behind the cottage where Lucy had placed an umbrella table. It was a perfect summer evening, the air smelled sweet and flowery and the light from the sinking sun cast the yard in long golden shadows.

The garden looked lush, with all kinds of perennials and huge flowering bushes in bloom. Lucy didn't know the names of half of them. She hadn't taken much interest in the property so far, beyond mowing the lawn and raking leaves. But Maggie was an avid gardener and had been teaching her about different plants, what grew best where. Lucy could see herself getting into it. She'd always liked to dig in the dirt as a kid.

"This pasta is great. You're a woman of many talents, Lucy," Matt said.

"Suzanne's recipe. It's really easy," she confessed.

She sipped her wine. Matt was a fairly good cook himself, not some single guy surviving on Chinese takeout and sub sandwiches, so his compliment was even more meaningful.

She was secretly glad he liked it. Had the Almost-Ex cooked much? He hadn't mentioned it.

It was still light out after dinner. They decided to take a walk down to the beach with Tink. Matt took her hand as they reached the water's edge.

"You seem distracted tonight. Anything going on?" he asked. "Worried about work?"

"Work is fine. The art director liked the chapters I handed in. They called yesterday."

"That's good."

She glanced at him. She usually didn't share all the gossipy goings-on from her knitting group, maybe because they hadn't been seeing each other all that long. Maybe because a lot of it was so silly, hardly necessary to pass on. But this business with Gloria did weigh on her mind and she wanted to let Matt in on it. Wasn't that what you were supposed to do in a good relationship?

"There is something I've been thinking about a lot. Something that has to do with Gloria," she began.

"Gloria? What about her?" Matt had let Tink loose. He tossed a stick and then sat in the sand, waiting for her return. He might be sitting there a long time, Lucy thought. She folded her long cotton skirt under her and sat down next to him.

While Tink played fetch, she filled Matt in on the suspicions she and her friends had about Gloria's death. All the loose ends that didn't quite tie up, not nearly as neatly as the police and coroner had determined.

She also told him about their confrontation with Mike

Novak, though she edited the story a bit, making it sound as if it had been an accidental meeting and they had not been lying in wait to pounce on him and as if the conversation had been much more reasonable.

He still looked troubled. Very troubled.

"I understand what you're saying, Lucy. And I agree, the questions do sound valid and this guy Novak sounds pretty shady. But you shouldn't be messing with this stuff." He sounded almost angry with her. Concerned, she realized. "This is for the police to figure out. I thought you learned your lesson with that loony tune Cara Newhouse."

Matt was talking about the night Lucy had suddenly figured out who had murdered yarn shop owner Amanda Goran. It had not been Maggie, of course. But it wasn't Amanda's estranged husband, either, whom the police had brought into custody.

The culprit had turned out to be an old student of Maggie's, who had tried to frame her. By the time Lucy realized it—on her way home from her first date with Matt—Amanda's killer had Maggie in her sights, too, and Lucy accidentally had walked in on the confrontation.

"A memorable evening. Our first date, too," she reminded him.

"Right. And those lovely memories will forever be eclipsed by recollections of hours in the police station, giving sworn statements."

Lucy had to laugh. It was almost true. She leaned closer and kissed him on the ear. "You've made a big impression since. Believe me."

"That's nice to hear . . ." He squeezed her hand. "Let's go home. I'd like to impress you some more."

Matt stood and offered Lucy a hand up, then he whistled once and called the dog.

Miraculously, Tink galloped back, then stood wagging her tail, awaiting further instructions. Lucy had expected to be chasing her down the beach, waving dog biscuits for half an hour, her usual method of getting Tink's attention.

She was relieved. Who wanted to ruin the mood with that routine?

"Good dog, Tink." She leaned down and quickly clipped her leash. "You are a very good dog tonight . . . yes, you are."

Matt hung around a little longer on Friday morning than he usually did on a weekday. Lucy made breakfast, toasted pieces of French bread left over from the night before, butter, good jam—which she got at Christmastime from friends and never knew what to do with—fresh strawberries, and coffee. They sat at the table outside again, the birds chirping in the branches and Tink lying under the table, catching all the toast crumbs. They read the newspaper together, exchanging sections, like a regular couple.

Nice, Lucy thought. But scary.

He had just left for his office when the phone rang. Lucy went inside to pick it up, or at least screen the message. She wondered who would be calling her this early. Her sister, Ellen, possibly, who had probably already cleaned her huge house, put in a load of laundry, and started dinner. She was disgustingly organized.

But it was not Ellen, Lucy realized once she heard a voice speaking. It was Maggie.

"Hey, Mag. What's up?" Lucy answered cheerfully.

"Are you walking the dog into town this morning?"

Maggie's tone was even, but tense. As if she were struggling to remain calm.

"Probably. I just have to jump in the shower. I'm getting a late start."

"Oh." She was quiet for a moment. "Well, if you do come this way, stop by. I want to show you something."

This sounded important, despite Maggie's low-key manner.

"What do you need to show me?"

"I can't explain over the phone," she said impatiently. "Just come. You'll see." Then she hung up.

The spare but intriguing message got Lucy motivated. She took a quick shower, yanked on shorts and a T-shirt, and pulled her wet hair back in a ponytail.

Tink was used to going out earlier and did a little hysterical dance of need by the back door, which made it even more challenging to secure the leash.

"Where is the Dog Whisperer when you really need him?" Lucy grumbled as Tink tugged her out the door. Once outside, Tink was happy to race into town. She thought Lucy's double-time pace was a new game.

They reached Maggie's shop in half the usual time, and after Lucy tied the leash on the porch and filled Tink's portable bowl, she went straight inside.

"I'm here," Lucy announced herself. "What's going on?"

"Come in the storeroom. I'll show you," Maggie called from the back.

Lucy walked back to the storeroom. Maggie was at the sink, washing her hands. Lucy saw streams of red running into the sink, as if Maggie had just been dyeing something.

"There, on the table," Maggie said, slanting her head.

Lucy walked over to the small table in the center of the

room. It looked like a dead animal laid out on a black plastic trash bag.

It was stabbed through several times with long knitting needles and streaked with bright red blood.

"Oh geez . . . what is that?" Lucy jumped back and covered her mouth with her hand.

"Looks like a voodoo doll, doesn't it?" Maggie asked, almost laughing. Was she in shock? Lucy wondered.

"Where did you find it? Is it a raccoon or something?"

Maggie stepped over from the sink, drying her hands on a paper towel. "No, thank goodness, I wouldn't have gone near one of those, dead or alive. Look closer, Lucy, don't you recognize it? I think your dog would."

Lucy allowed herself a longer look. Then she felt awfully stupid. "Oh . . . for goodness sake. It's just one of those stuffed sheep from the front window. . . . But who in the world did that to it? And where did you find it?" she repeated. "Did someone get in here last night?"

"I thought that at first, too. But there are still three sheep in the window. Someone must have gone out of their way and bought this one, to make a point. I found it outside the front door, dangling from a piece of yarn that was hooked onto the porch ceiling."

"Didn't something like that happen in a movie with Michael Douglas and Glenn Close?"

"That was a pet rabbit. Boiled in a pot," Maggie reminded her.

"Not too far off. This was definitely the work of a bunny boiler, I'll tell you that much."

Now that she knew it was not, nor had ever been, a living creature, Lucy felt better. Free to poke the mutilated sheep with her finger.

"Watch it, that red stuff is horribly sticky. But it did wash off my hands, thank goodness."

"Is it paint?" Lucy checked a dot of the stuff stuck to her fingertip.

"I don't think so. It's probably ketchup mixed with something oily. It smells like ketchup. I didn't taste it, though," Maggie added.

"Let the police taste it," Lucy suggested.

When Maggie didn't answer right away, she said, "You've called them . . . didn't you?"

"I called you. Then I thought about calling them. But . . . I'm not sure what to do."

Before Lucy could argue with her, she turned and picked up a piece of paper from the counter. A simple sheet torn from a spiral notebook, frizzed edges and all.

"There was a note, too."

"Yes, I see," Lucy murmured as she scanned the sheet. It was written in block letters with thick black marker.

BLACK SHEEP—STAY OUT OF IT.
OR YOU'LL BE SORRY.

She put the note back on the table. "We shouldn't have even touched it," Lucy said, remembering how Suzanne had messed up the fingerprints on the wineglasses.

Maggie laughed. "Lucy, come on. This was a silly prank. Childish, really. You're taking it much too seriously."

It did seem childish. Who could have done it? Lucy's first guess had been Mike Novak. But a mangled stuffed animal did not seem his style. A certified letter, announcing a lawsuit—that would be more his style.

Still, Lucy was astounded by the stunt. "Doesn't it bother you that someone went to so much trouble to try to scare you? To scare all of us? Where did you buy those things anyway, at the toy store in town? We could go over there and ask if they'd sold any recently . . ."

"Lucy . . . let's not, okay?" Maggie's tone was half-imploring, half-warning.

Lucy knew what she was driving at. But if she didn't want to look into this herself, why not call the police? Maggie grabbed two mugs and the pot of coffee and walked out into the shop and over to the big table. Lucy followed her.

"It does disturb me a little," Maggie admitted. "But I don't want to get involved with the police again. I'd have to visit Detective Walsh and be grilled about all our speculations about Gloria. And who we spoke to about it and when. Not to mention that ill-advised encounter with Mike Novak on Tuesday. Even though I didn't take part, I'll be tarred with the same brush, you know."

Maggie cast Lucy a look. She had not approved of the idea and felt she'd been proven right when they reported their misadventure.

Lucy could see her point. Maggie had been traumatized by her last involvement with Walsh and the local police department. Lucy wasn't surprised that she wanted to avoid them, and admitting that, once again, she and her friends were poking their noses—and knitting needles—where they didn't belong.

"Before you know it, Walsh will start accusing me of pushing Gloria into the swimming pool," Maggie added tartly.

A wild exaggeration, but Lucy didn't even try to contradict.

214 / Anne Canadeo

"All right. It's your call. Another lead for Jamie's PI. If he ever hires one."

"Oh, he did. He didn't wait for a firm reply from the police about reopening the investigation. He just went ahead. Jamie said he was going to meet with the man today."

That news was welcome. "I guess the investigator will want to speak with us."

"Yes, definitely . . . you can ask Jamie all about it. Here he is."

Maggie looked at the front of the shop and Lucy did, too. Jamie had just walked in, a large sketch pad tucked under one arm.

"I'm going to sit for the portrait this morning," Maggie explained. "Just to get the spot and the pose right. Phoebe should be here in time. She was at Josh's place last night," she added, glancing at her watch.

Lucy was glad to hear that Phoebe hadn't been in her apartment upstairs when the sheep vandal had struck, even though the culprit had apparently stayed outside.

Jamie had walked to the back of the store and greeted them. "Ready to be immortalized?" he joked with Maggie.

"Is anyone ever ready?" She smiled and shrugged.

She hadn't dressed in any special way this morning, Lucy noticed, though perhaps had given a bit more attention to her curly brown hair and added a tiny bit more makeup than usual. But she was having her portrait painted. That qualified for some special primping, didn't it?

"Listen, Jamie, before we start, I need to tell you something. I was greeted by a very odd package at the front door when I came to the shop this morning," she began.

He sat down at the table and listened to the story without interrupting. His smooth features darkened with worry. He insisted on going into the storeroom and seeing the desecrated toy sheep, which Maggie had wrapped in a plastic bag and left beside a trash pail.

"That's awful. You need to tell the police," he insisted.

"She doesn't want to get involved," Lucy cut in. "She has her reasons."

Jamie looked confused. "I'll tell them. I have no idea if they're going to investigate Gloria's death again. They won't give me a straight answer. But maybe this will make them sit up and take notice."

"Maybe," Lucy offered. "What about your private investigator?"

"Yes, when is he coming on the scene?" Maggie asked.

"He's coming to town later today. He wants to meet with all of you, hear what you have to say. Do you think we could work that out somehow?"

"We're going to be at Suzanne's house tonight for a knitting group meeting. I'm sure she wouldn't mind if he stopped by. If that wasn't too late," Lucy added. "We usually start at seven."

"That should work out. He said he might need to stay over in town one night, to look into everything thoroughly. I'm going to call him later and I'll let you know," Jamie promised.

"It will be a relief to hand off our concerns to a professional," Maggie confided. "A great relief," she added.

"For me, too," Jamie said. "I guess at first I preferred to believe that poor Gloria died by accident. I just didn't want to think of her being frightened. Or that someone purposely set out to hurt her." His voice grew shaky and Lucy thought he might be tearing up. "But we have to find out what really happened. I have to do that for her, at least. I can't live with myself if I don't."

Lucy reached down and patted his shoulder. "You *will* find out, Jamie. I know you will."

Lucy glanced at Maggie over Jamie's head. Maggie gazed at him with sympathy. "You'll be coming to Suzanne's with the investigator, Jamie, won't you?"

"I wanted to come. But he prefers to talk to people alone. He says he gets more candid interviews that way."

"That makes sense." Lucy knew for a fact that there were a few things they had to tell the PI they had purposely kept from Jamie.

"Why don't we get started?" Maggie changed the subject in a brighter tone. "I was thinking I could sit in the front room on the love seat. Or maybe out on the porch, on the far side with the morning glory lattice in the background?"

Jamie seemed lost in his thoughts for a moment, but snapped back to real time. "Outside sounds good. The light should be excellent."

"That's what I thought, too." Maggie led the way and they headed out.

Just as Lucy walked out onto the porch she saw Phoebe strolling up the walk. They said hello, but Phoebe seemed most interested in greeting Tink.

"Hey, doggie. How's my little Tinker Bell?" A charming name for the large shaggy hound, Lucy thought. "You must be hot in that fur coat, huh, baby?"

The panting dog sat obediently, grateful for the attention. Phoebe glanced over at Jamie and Maggie, who were already moving around the fan-back wicker chairs at the far corner of the porch.

"Jamie is going to paint Maggie's portrait," Lucy explained. "He's just making sketches today to start."

Phoebe looked over at them again. "If it comes out good, she should hang it in the shop."

"That's a good idea," Lucy agreed, especially if she was portrayed holding her knitting.

"Could someone run inside and get my knitting bag?" Maggie asked, as if reading Lucy's mind. "I think I left it in the storeroom."

"I'll go," Lucy said. "I think you're in charge of the shop this morning," she told Phoebe.

"Under control," Phoebe promised as she slipped inside behind Lucy. Lucy found the bag quickly, then noticed a basket with skeins of yarn for the blanket squares. She guessed that everyone would need more yarn tonight, running low the same way she was on their designated color. She brought the basket out, along with the yarn swift. She would sit a while and roll some yarn. She was in no rush to get back to the cottage, with no work pressure right now and a happy glow lingering after her evening with Matt.

Before she left the shop, she thought to tell Phoebe about the stabbed stuffed sheep incident, but Phoebe was already on a phone call with a customer. Maggie would tell her later, Lucy figured. She didn't want to hold up the sitting.

She handed Maggie her knitting bag, then sat a considerate distance away and set up the swift.

"Thanks, Lucy. Jamie told me not to get up. I'm not sure if I'll be able to do this," she added doubtfully.

"Give it a try, that's all I ask," he coaxed her.

Maggie took out her knitting and then a petal pink knitted lace shawl. She draped it over her T-shirt and bare arms. "What do you think? Hides a few wrinkles and my flabby arms?"

"You don't have any wrinkles and your arms look fine,"

Jamie insisted. He was sitting nearby, already working with a piece of charcoal in hand, the sketch pad opened on his lap. "Gloria worried endlessly about that stuff. I loved her little lines. It told the world she'd lived a full life. That was one of the reasons I fell in love with her."

Lucy appreciated Jamie's thoughtful take on female aging, but she hoped he didn't voice his opinions in front of any executives of cosmetic companies. They'd put out a contract on him, no question. An entire industry could go under if that point of view ever caught on.

"The scarf is a nice touch, Maggie. It reminds me of the one Gloria was making," Lucy noted, then realized maybe she shouldn't have said that. Jamie flinched visibly, but didn't pick up his head.

"The stitch is similar," Maggie admitted, though Lucy thought she also felt awkward with the comparison. "Gloria was working with a much finer gauge yarn and needles."

Lucy decided it was time to get to work on her yarn rolling. She opened the first skein and stretched it, then clipped the tiny strand that held it together. Then she fit the yarn on the umbrella-style wooden swift.

"Are you rolling some yarn for us? That's a good deed, Lucy," Maggie said.

"I can do something useful while I sit here a few minutes. We'll all need more tonight." She hadn't brought along her knitting, she'd left the house in such a rush.

"Too bad you can't come to Suzanne's, she's a great cook," Maggie told Jamie.

"I wish I could. But I don't want to step on the PI's toes. He told me specifically to stay away."

"How did you find him?" Lucy asked. "Did you call Dana's husband?"

"I'd planned to, then my friend Kenny told me that his brother is a cop in Boston. He knows a lot of very capable guys in this line of work. I figured a recommendation from a police officer would be reliable."

Sounded good to Lucy. Since the investigator wasn't local, he would view the situation and cast of characters with a fresh eye. That might help, too.

Jamie could be self-sufficient. He didn't always have to be led by the hand . . . a woman's hand, more specifically.

"How is it going with the estate probate? Any progress?" Maggie asked him.

"It's a long process, Maggie. Longer than I thought. Lewis is still making an inventory of Gloria's assets. And then all the property has to be appraised for its market value and all of that information submitted to the court. I've been spending a lot of time looking through records in her office, trying to make a rough estimate. Trying to figure out what she had and what she owed."

"Have you been able to get anywhere with it?"

He sounded worn-out just talking about it, Lucy noticed. He knew very little about business and real estate matters. She probably knew even less, and would have found that task daunting and the material indecipherable.

"From what I can see so far, a lot of the properties are heavily mortgaged. She was borrowing from one to make the payments on the other."

"Oh . . . that's too bad." Maggie looked surprised. Lucy felt the same.

Jamie didn't say anything, just offered her a grim smile. He paused and rubbed out a line with his thumb. Then he stared at the page a minute and flipped it in disgust.

Gloria had kept up a brave front, Lucy realized, but she

was struggling just to stay afloat financially. A woeful metaphor for her tragic death.

"I guess that's why she resorted to borrowing from those thugs. Did they ever come back?" Lucy paused with the swift, waiting for his answer.

"Not yet. But I know they will." His tone was flat and un-emotional, his fast-moving hand blocking out the sketch. "I've applied for a loan against the house. Suzanne helped me with the paperwork. That's the only way I'm going to be able to pay them off and get rid of them. It still won't be enough. I'm hoping they'll negotiate."

"But Gloria took the loan. You're not responsible for her debts," Maggie reminded him.

"Not in a court of law. Not as far as the estate is concerned. But these guys don't follow that playbook, Maggie. They have their own terms, and it's best not to ask too many questions."

The bandage on his hand was gone, but the base of his finger and thumb were still black and blue, Lucy noticed.

She snuck a peak at the sketch pad. He was good, very good. He had a distinctive style. It came as a surprise since his personality seemed so yielding and accommodating in many ways. She hadn't expected his artwork to project a bold voice.

"I didn't think about it much right after Gloria died," he continued. "I was in shock, I guess. But now I do won-der what else was going on in her private life, her business life, the part she kept hidden from me. I let her handle the finances, no questions asked. It was all her money and I didn't think I had the right to butt in," he admitted. "But, if somebody intentionally . . . hurt her," he said, when Lucy knew he really meant "murdered her," "I think it must have had something to do with her business deals. What else could it be?"

He stopped sketching and looked up at both of them. Maggie and Lucy didn't say a word in answer.

Lucy's thoughts were racing. Should they tell him about Mike Novak? He was bound to find out sooner or later if this private investigator did even half a decent job.

But Novak claimed he'd had no real contact with Gloria for months and had been at the club, in plain sight, the night she died. What good would disclosing their relationship to Jamie do now?

Maggie didn't speak, either, but Jamie continued, "I guess a big part of me doesn't really want to know the truth. I prefer to think of Gloria the way I knew her. Beautiful, strong, able to do anything she set her mind to. So loving and good-hearted. If she acted unethically in business, or was involved with some low people . . . I guess I don't really want to face it," he confessed quietly.

Maggie leaned forward, despite her orders to sit still for the sketch. "Of course not. We all have memories that we want to preserve of people we've loved and lost. But life is so complicated. No one is all good, or all bad. We still love them and we don't stop when they disappoint us, or even after they're gone. It's hard. In a way, it's a comfort, too."

Maggie's words were wise and sounded as if they'd been spoken from experience. Had Maggie found out something about her husband, Bill, after he'd died that had disappointed her? If she had, she'd never told Lucy. But that didn't mean it hadn't happened.

Jamie swallowed hard and nodded. He rested the sketch pad on a tabletop and rubbed his eyes. "I do love her. I guess I always will," he said with a sigh.

What could you say to a person after that? Maggie and Lucy didn't say anything.

"You know when I first met Gloria, I was pretty down and out, working at some crummy, dead-end jobs," he said, turning back to the sketch. "When she asked me to move in, I took a suitcase and a box of art supplies and a few canvases I didn't want to chuck out with the rest. That was it. All I had in the world. If I have to go back to living like that again, I'm okay with it. It was never about the money," he told the women, looking up at them again.

Maggie nodded, signaling she believed him, but she didn't interrupt.

"Sure, I like a nice house, a nice car . . . all of that. But it seems pretty meaningless without her. Part of me never expected it to last. I see that now. I thought Gloria would get tired of me long before I ever lost interest in her. She could have had anyone. I was lucky to have been with her even for a short time. That was, like, a gift or something." He shrugged and sighed. "Like a really beautiful flower. You enjoy it while it's in bloom, but you don't expect it to last forever."

"Nothing ever does," Maggie agreed with a sigh. "Our happiest days, or our saddest." She picked up her knitting again, the pale pink shawl slipping gracefully around her shoulders. She did look worthy of a portrait, Lucy thought.

Lucy finished winding a ball of gold yarn and set it in the basket with the others. Then she stood up and picked up her purse. "I've got to go. See you later, Mag. So long, Jamie."

"'Bye, Lucy. Good to see you." He stopped sketching for

a moment and looked up at her. "Now tonight, please tell the investigator all you know. Anything you can remember. And please let him take over now. That mess Maggie found at the front door this morning was a warning. I can't stand the idea of any of you getting hurt."

"Don't worry. We'll stay out of it now, I promise. I think we've gone as far as we could. And probably further than we should have," Lucy admitted.

Chapter Thirteen

*L*ucy was the last to arrive at Suzanne's house on Friday night. Suzanne's thirteen-year-old daughter, Alexis, answered the door. She was almost as tall as Suzanne now, with the same rich dark hair and brown eyes, but a far lankier, flatter version. She stood barefoot, her long legs topped by short shorts under a baggy T-shirt that said "Harbor Sea Wolves." With a bud from an iPod stuck in one ear and the other pressed to a cell phone, she communicated in sign language to Lucy, signaling that the rest of the group was out back.

Lucy walked through the rooms of the lovely old home, noticing some recent improvements. Suzanne had just started in real estate when she'd found the gracious colonial that was the perfect size for her family. The house's run-down condition and desperate cry for TLC put most buyers off, but kept the price in reach. The place was perfect for Suzanne, who didn't mind living in a constant state of renovation and for her husband, Kevin, who was a contractor and old home specialist.

But several years later, they had not made much progress. Kevin's clients always came first, and it seemed that one repair on the old house led to another. Still, the Cavanaugh crew managed to thrive in their chaotic, domestic work site, which blended in with the décor and general family confusion.

Lucy found her friends sitting at the big table on the cedar deck that adjoined the family room and kitchen, the area that Suzanne had made a priority for repair. The great room and kitchen had turned out beautifully and Suzanne was a spectacular cook who made the most of her professional quality kitchen.

Lucy wondered what was on the menu tonight. As her friends greeted her, she spied some tasty-looking appetizers on the table—tapas selections, it looked like—along with two bottles of wine.

Lucy took a seat near Dana and took out her knitting. "Where's Phoebe?"

"She can't make it. Josh's band is playing somewhere. You know how loyal she is to the cause," Dana replied.

"Is this his old band . . . or the new one?"

"The new one. Big Fat Babies," Maggie replied in a serious tone. "He's been writing a lot of music for them. They want to make a CD, not just stay a bar band. That's one of the reasons he jumped ship on Error Messages."

"How about Crystal? I guess she wouldn't come without Phoebe," Lucy added, answering her own question.

"Crystal is a Big Fat Babies fan, too. But she's still working on her squares," Maggie reported. "She's definitely going to contribute."

"That's good. It's always nice to turn someone on to knitting," Lucy said. Though Crystal had seemed an unlikely candidate, it just went to show. You never know who's going to get hooked, so to speak.

Suzanne came out to the deck wearing a bright red apron that complimented her dark hair. "Everything's ready. I don't want the food to dry up. I think we should eat and not worry about the investigator."

"What did you make? It's smells so good," Lucy asked.

"Paella, with chicken, chorizo, shrimp, clams, and mussels." She turned to Dana, who was a vegetarian. "Don't worry, I made you a vegetable-and-seafood-only version."

"Thanks," Dana said, "you didn't need to go to any trouble."

"Hold the pickles, hold the lettuce. Special orders don't upset us," Suzanne sang. "Not in this house, anyway."

Their hostess slipped back inside and Dana rose, too. "I'll go see if she needs help."

"I'll come, too," Lucy offered. She always liked to see how Suzanne prepared these dishes and picked up some cooking tips. The others got up, also, to clear and set the table. Suzanne, Lucy, and Dana soon returned with the paella and trimmings and Suzanne served.

"Hmm, delicious." Maggie sighed, savoring a bite. "You used real saffron, I can tell. This part, the yummy crusty edge? They call that the *sacarat*. The best part of the dish. I haven't had paella this good since Bill and I were in Spain."

This sparked a flurry of fond memories of travel and foreign cuisine. Lucy had traveled through Europe and hoped to do more. She wished she was the type of person who could just grab a backpack and set off by herself into the unknown. No reservations, no schedules, just pure wanderlust.

But she wasn't quite that type and did sometimes wish she

had someone to share these experiences with. That was a good part of the joy for her, she wouldn't deny it.

Maybe in Matt she had found that again. It was just too soon to tell.

The doorbell rang and Suzanne rose to answer it. "Must be that guy," she said and everyone understood what she meant.

Lucy didn't know why, but she felt a little nervous to meet the investigator. She felt relieved, too. She'd been wondering if it was really right to keep what they knew from Jamie. Now they could share their suspicions and knowledge candidly with the PI and he'd have to follow through.

Suzanne soon returned, followed by a tall man who seemed to be in his late thirties or early forties. He looked fit, with a square jaw, close-cropped salt-and-pepper hair, and the overall look of a former policeman. He wore a striped polo shirt and neatly pressed khaki pants. He glanced around the table and offered the group a polite smile.

"Everybody, this is Richard Dolan. He's the investigator helping Jamie," Suzanne said smoothly. Everyone welcomed him and Suzanne made introductions.

Richard Dolan sat between Suzanne and Dana, but politely refused Suzanne's offer of paella. "I'm good, thanks. But it looks delicious."

"A glass of sangria, or a beer?" she offered.

"A beer would be fine." He took a slim pad and pen from his breast pocket and set them on the table at his place. "I'm sure you all know why I've been hired by Mr. Barnett. He tells me that you were close friends with his late wife and have been concerned about the circumstances surrounding her death. I'm here to look into all of that and, hopefully, find some answers. Some answers the police may have missed in their rush to close this case."

"That's the way we feel, too. We think they just assumed it was an accident. A drunken women falls into her own swimming pool, home alone, late at night. Very cut and dry," Maggie said.

"But we don't think that's what really happened. Or, that's *all* that happened," Lucy clarified.

"I understand. Okay, then, who wants to start?" Lucy watched him flip open the pad and note the date, time, and location at the top of the page.

"I guess I should," Suzanne said and everyone knew why—because she had found Gloria's body. She explained everything she'd seen at the house that day, the wineglasses, the magazine, even the length of orange yarn tangled around Gloria's body.

She also described their phone call the night before, Gloria's upbeat attitude and the sound of the doorbell that had interrupted the conversation.

Lucy went next, describing her meeting with Gloria at the Main Street Café, what she'd said about Jamie, calling so many times to have her join him, and how she'd said she didn't want to cramp his style.

"But maybe she'd didn't go because she had plans. Maybe she knew someone was coming to visit her while he was gone," Lucy speculated. Richard Dolan didn't reply. He nodded and made another note.

Then Dana spoke, explaining Gloria's confession about her affair, how she broke up with Mike but had some conflict over that relationship once she'd returned to town. She also told him about the confrontation at the country club and Novak's response to their questions.

"We're not sure if Jamie knows about that relationship," she added in a careful tone. "Gloria came to me in confidence and we didn't think it was our place to tell him."

"I understand. I work on a lot of matrimonial cases. This kind of information can be a heavy blow to a spouse." He answered with a serious look. "I know how to handle it, don't worry."

"And I have something else to tell all of you," Dana continued. "Jack told me just before I left the house."

"Something about Novak?" Lucy asked.

"That's right. You know how he claimed he'd been at the club most of the day and all night? Eating dinner and playing cards at the time Gloria died? Well, that wasn't entirely true. He had been there most of the day, but Jack says he saw Novak leave the club sometime between ten and eleven. Jack was having dinner with a client that night and he remembers seeing Mike out in the parking lot, picking up his car without waiting for the valet. Then he drove out from a side entrance of the lot. Didn't pass the circle where everyone waits. Jack was sure it was him. He drives a silver Porsche, the only one at the club."

The detective made careful notes. "And what time did your husband say this was, approximately?"

"About half past ten. It must have been around then because Jack got home before eleven and we live about twenty minutes away."

"Very good recall, Dana," he commended her. He turned to Suzanne. "And you say your phone call took place a little before eleven?"

"I'm pretty sure. Because I was afraid to call that late, but did want to get through to her, even to leave a message."

"And it sounds like this club isn't far from Mr. Barnett's house, either," he noted.

"No, not at all. It's in the same neighborhood," Lucy said.

"So Mr. Novak could have left the club briefly, visited Ms. Sterling, and returned to join the card game."

"Easily," Dana said. "The club is crowded on weekend nights in the summer, especially the bar and restaurant. He probably wouldn't have been missed if he moved from one group of friends to another."

"That's just what I was thinking . . ." The detective was writing more notes. He looked up at them and finally offered a real smile. "You're a pretty sharp group." For amateurs, he meant. "I could use this kind of backup all the time," he joked with them.

They *were* pretty sharp, Lucy agreed.

They continued to fill in Gloria's story with all the information they had gathered, including the questionable property transfers and the strange, stabbed, ketchup-soaked stuffed sheep hanging in front of Maggie's shop door the other morning.

He didn't comment too much on that episode, but agreed it didn't sound too threatening.

The interview had taken a long time. Nobody noticed the evening passing. But they had all managed to pick up their needles and were knitting steadily through the conversation, so it wasn't a wasted night.

Lucy sat back, feeling drained. Like a sponge that had been wrung out.

"So, what do you think?" Maggie asked. "Is there enough to get the attention of the police again?"

"You've given me a lot to go on. How it all shakes out is the question. I have to follow up on these leads before we know anything for sure. I'm going to give it my full attention," he promised. "I can see that you all really cared about your friend."

He smiled again and rose to go. "Thanks for speaking with me. I may be in touch with you again. Mr. Barnett knows where to reach all of you, right?"

"He has all of our phone numbers. And you can always call my shop, the Black Sheep, on Main Street." Maggie reached out and handed him her card.

"That reminds me, let me give you a card in case you remember anything else important." He reached in his wallet and handed cards out around the table.

"You're all emotionally involved in this situation, I can see that. But you've done your part. Leave the rest to me. Further attempts to follow up on your own could really compromise my efforts. Mr. Barnett is paying me a fair wage," he assured them with a small smile. "I don't want to waste his money. More importantly, if anyone intentionally harmed Ms. Sterling, they could easily harm one of you. We don't want to risk that, do we?"

Lucy glanced at her friends' expressions and thought they were taking the warning to heart. She knew she was, too. Finally.

Lucy woke early on Saturday, feeling few effects of Suzanne's sangria, which had gone down so easily at their get-together last night. She jumped in the shower, pulled on some sweats, and took Tink for a jog downtown.

She and Tink made it all the way to the harbor without mishap, coming to a full stop only once for Tink to check her messages on a favorite fire hydrant.

A farmers' market was set up in the parking lot adjacent to the village green every Saturday morning in the summer. The area was packed with people, many toting good-smelling foods too close to Tink's sensitive nose. Lucy led the dog back up Main Street, tied her to a parking meter in clear sight, and stepped into the Schooner for a bottle of water and an iced coffee.

She took a seat at the counter, not far from the register where Edie Steiber watched over her enterprise with an eagle eye while making change at the cash register and processing credit cards.

"Table number five needs some more coffee, honey," she reminded a waitress flying by.

Lucy had been coming into the Schooner since childhood. The diner had been one of her aunt Laura's favorite places to dine out or treat her nieces to huge ice-cream sundaes on a hot summer afternoon.

Time was when Edie would be hopping around the place herself like the Energizer Bunny, a coffeepot dangling from one hand as she roamed from table to table. The way Maggie tended her garden with a watering can.

But the years of hard work—and eating from her own menu—had slowed her down considerably. She had become as much an icon and institution in the small town as the Schooner itself.

Despite her harsh opinion of Gloria, Lucy still liked Edie. Edie had lived a long time and clearly had her reasons for resenting Gloria, especially during the Thurman years. Lucy did wonder what she thought now. She hadn't seen Edie at the memorial service, nor run into her at the knitting shop lately.

"Hey, Lucy." Edie honored her arrival by leaving her post and walking over to chat. "Out getting some exercise today?"

"I'm trying. At least Tink gives me a walk every day."

"Nice dog," Edie said, glancing outside at Tink, who had

sat down in the shade of a tall tree. "Do you want a little bowl to give her some water?"

"That would be great." Lucy didn't have Tink's port-o-bowl and planned on giving the dog a drink from her hand.

Edie gave her a small plastic bowl used for takeout and filled it with cold water. Lucy also ordered an iced coffee and a water bottle for herself, to go.

"So . . . I bet all your friends are pretty broken up still about Gloria," Edie said, broaching the touchy topic as she fixed Lucy's coffee.

"Yeah, we are," Lucy admitted.

"It was a sad way to go," Edie acknowledged. "No matter how you felt about the woman, dying in a freak accident like that, sort of a waste. How is her husband?"

"He's struggling," Lucy replied.

She wasn't sure how much she ought to tell Edie about Jamie's emotional struggles and his financial ones, but she did feel Edie had the entirely wrong impression about Gloria and Jamie's relationship. Maybe it would be enlightening to her to hear that Jamie sincerely mourned Gloria, and didn't seem to care about her fortune. Or what would be left of it.

"Yeah, it's always rough to lose someone close," Edie conceded. "Part of life, I guess. He's young. He'll get over it," she added.

Someday maybe. But not that quickly, Lucy thought.

"The money must be some consolation," Edie said bluntly.

"It might be . . . if there's any left after her debts are settled." Lucy hadn't meant to disclose that information, especially to Edie, who was more efficient at spreading news than a CNN correspondent. In Plum Harbor anyway.

Lucy did take some small satisfaction in the shocked

expression on Edie's wrinkled face. "Money's all gone, too? That's a surprise. That woman was living high on thin air, I guess. A real magic act."

"I guess so," Lucy had to agree. There was a touch of magic in Gloria, anyone could see that.

"Well, I'd better get moving. Tink's tongue is dragging on the sidewalk. I think she needs this water."

"Sure, hon. You take care," Edie said in a somewhat warmer manner than usual. Feeling guilty for casting aspersions at Gloria just before she died, perhaps?

Lucy picked up her drinks and Tink's bowl.

"You too, Edie." She dropped some crumpled bills by the register and Edie nodded at her.

Tink was so happy to see her back, she jumped up on her hind legs, nearly giving Lucy a bath in the water and iced coffee.

Lucy set the plastic bowl down and let her drink. When the bowl was empty, Lucy untied the dog's leash and started down Main Street toward the Black Sheep. Tink had taken to the bowl and carried it easily in her mouth as they walked down the street. Lucy didn't even notice.

She tied the dog on the knitting shop porch and went inside. Dana and Suzanne were there, sitting at the work table in back, while Maggie roamed the shop, collecting items for her Saturday morning beginners' class.

Dana wore her slim-fitting yoga clothes and a certain Zen glow that indicated she'd come straight from the Nirvana Studio. Suzanne brandished her large, I-mean-business real estate lady earrings and a crisp white shirt under a red linen blazer. She was checking her BlackBerry, probably en route to an open house or meeting clients.

They were talking about their meeting last night with

Jamie's private investigator. Lucy walked in and sat down at the table by Suzanne.

"I felt a lot better after we vented to him," Suzanne confessed. "He seems to know what he's doing."

"Has anyone spoken to Jamie? I'm sure he wants to know how it went with Dolan," Maggie said.

"He's going into Boston today. He might have already left," Suzanne said. "I was supposed to go over there to look through some tax records with him. But he called late last night, after you guys had left. He had to meet the gallery owner today to talk about postponing the show. I guess that's pretty important, too," Suzanne added.

"At least it sounds as if he's going through with it," Dana said. "That's a good sign."

"Yes, it is," Lucy agreed.

It did sound like Jamie was going through with the show, which Lucy found a positive note in an otherwise bleak landscape. Maybe Maggie's encouragement had helped him.

"Gloria would be happy," Maggie said simply. They all knew that was true.

The shop phone rang and Maggie answered it. Lucy could tell it was Phoebe on the line, explaining that she was running a little late this morning. "All right, I understand. There's a class starting in an hour. Just get here before then," Maggie said, then hung up the phone again.

"Jamie had some more bad news yesterday from Lewis," Suzanne told her friends. "Looks like the estate is insolvent. Once all the debts are paid off, there won't be a dime left."

That was bad news, though not totally unexpected, Lucy realized.

"Poor Jamie. He's really got a lot on his plate. Is he

responsible for any debts that the estate can't cover?" Maggie asked.

"No, he's not, thank goodness," Suzanne said as she took out her knitting. "He still has the house, free and clear, and I helped him apply for a line of credit against it. He should hear back from the bank soon about that. If he hasn't heard already," she noted.

"I don't know how he's going to make it without that loan," Dana said, "unless he gets a job."

"If he can hang on until his show, he might be able to earn a living from his paintings," Lucy suggested hopefully.

Maggie glanced at her and offered a small smile. "Yes, let's hope so. I'm glad he's meeting with the gallery owner this weekend. He has to get on with his life, especially his work. Gloria would have wanted him to keep moving forward."

The bell above the shop door rang. It was still too early for customers on a Saturday and Lucy looked over to see who it could be.

A woman they all recognized walked in. Detective Marisol Reyes, from the Essex County Police. Detective Reyes had worked with Detective Walsh on Amanda Goran's murder investigation, but Walsh was not with her right now, thank goodness. She was alone.

Maggie looked at her friends with alarm, then rose quickly to meet the unexpected visitor.

"Detective Reyes . . . what a surprise." Maggie walked to the middle of the shop, where the detective stood by the counter.

"Hello, Mrs. Messina. I'm glad to find you in," Detective Reyes began politely. "I wondered if you could help me out this morning with some information?"

"Information? I will if I can . . ." Maggie offered. Lucy heard her voice trail off on a shaky note.

"This is a difficult story to relate. The body of a young woman was found late last night, on the side of the road, near Plum Beach. The police are trying to determine her identity. She appears to be in her twenties . . ." Detective Reyes paused and reached into her purse again and pulled out a small pad. "Long black hair, blue eyes, though she wore contacts that made them look darker," she added. "Medium height, thin build. Several tattoos." She read from the pad, then looked up at them. "There was one on her shoulder. A skull and a rose with the word 'dad' written underneath."

"*Dad?* I thought it said, 'bad,'" Lucy blurted out.

Detective Reyes looked confused. Her eyes narrowed. "Do you know who this girl is?"

"We all do." Lucy looked over at her friends, her gaze finally resting on Maggie.

"Her name is Crystal," Maggie continued. "She's been hanging around here a lot lately. She's friends with my helper, Phoebe. Maybe you remember her."

"I do remember Phoebe," Detective Reyes replied.

"What made you come here?" Suzanne asked the detective.

"The victim had nothing on her. No ID of any kind. But we found something in her pocket . . ." She opened her neat leather shoulder bag and took out a plastic bag that appeared to hold a folded sheet of pale yellow paper.

"I can't remove this from the bag. It's evidence in the investigation," Detective Reyes explained. "But you can see that it has the name of your shop on the top and the logo. So we assumed the victim had come here recently."

Maggie looked closer and gasped, covering her hand with her mouth. "Oh dear . . . I think I need to sit down a minute . . . I'm sorry . . ."

Detective Reyes reached out to support Maggie's arm. Dana stood nearest. She jumped up and caught Maggie on the other side. Then they helped her over to a chair at the table.

"I can look now, it's okay," Maggie said after a moment.

The police officer handed down the baggie again and Maggie looked at one side and then the other. Then she handed it back to her. "Yes, that definitely belonged to Crystal."

"What is this piece of paper exactly?" the detective asked, curious.

"It's a handout I give to beginner students. It has the basics, casting on, and the knit, purl stitches. With a few simple diagrams." Maggie sighed, unable to say more.

"And how can you be so sure that this one belonged to her?"

"She was working on a project with us. Simple squares for a blanket. I didn't have the pattern handy, so I just wrote it down for her on the bottom of the sheet. See, right here." Maggie pointed at a spot under the plastic.

"Yes, I noticed that." Detective Reyes nodded. "I wasn't sure, though, if she had written it or someone else had."

"Phoebe will be able to tell you more about her. Her last name. Where she lives and all that. She should be here very soon. She just called to tell me that she's running late . . ."

Maggie's voice trailed off. Lucy felt her stomach clench in a pile of knots. She stared around at her friends, who also looked shocked at the news. Two deaths in Plum Harbor within a few weeks was hard to take in.

"That would be very helpful," Detective Reyes said.

"Could you give her a call on a cell phone and see if she's close by?" The detective checked her watch. "If it's going to be much longer, I'll come back."

"I'll call her," Dana offered. Maggie cast a grateful look in her direction, then she turned back to Detective Reyes.

"So, Crystal is dead?" Maggie asked quietly.

"I'm afraid so. We don't now very much right now."

What horrible news. Phoebe was going to be so upset, Lucy thought.

Dana had reached Phoebe and hung up. "She's just parking her car. She'll be right in."

Lucy glanced at Suzanne. Her complexion looked as pale as her white shirt. They waited without saying a word. Only Phoebe had been close to Crystal, but they had all spent time with her and even welcomed her into their circle. News of her death—a violent death at that—was shocking and disturbing. Lucy could tell her friends felt the same.

A few moments later, Lucy heard Tink give a few sharp barks. Her happy hello bark. The dog loved Phoebe, who always gave her loads of attention.

"That's just my dog," Lucy explained. "Phoebe likes to pet her. This could take a while."

Detective Reyes waited, then turned to face the door. She was medium height, but stood very tall with perfect posture. Her long dark hair was held back in a tight ponytail, her complexion free of makeup. Her conservative outfit, a tan jacket and blue pants, was very professional and dignified. Just what you'd expect a female detective to look like, Lucy thought.

Finally the door opened and Phoebe walked in.

"Hey, Mag. I made it."

Phoebe took a few steps into the shop, then stood staring at everyone. A knapsack was slung over her shoulder and she put it down on the floor by her feet.

"What's going on? You all look so bummed."

"Hello, Phoebe. Detective Reyes, remember me?"

Phoebe suddenly noticed the detective, who walked toward her from the back of the shop.

"Sure. How are you?" Phoebe looked confused and hooked a thick lock of hair behind her ear, exposing a row of piercings. "What's up?"

"I'm afraid that I have some bad news for you, Phoebe," Detective Reyes said simply.

The detective related the gruesome story. "We found some evidence on her person that is leading me to believe she's a friend of yours, someone named Crystal?"

Phoebe nodded numbly. Lucy saw her eyes immediately fill with tears. "You did? But . . . how? Are you really sure?"

"We're never absolutely positive until the next of kin identifies the body. Without knowing her identity we haven't gotten to that stage yet. If you can sit with me a minute and answer some questions, maybe we can find her family."

Phoebe nodded. Tears that had melted her eye makeup slid down her cheeks in two tiny black streams.

"We had plans last night, and she never showed up. I left a message on her cell. But I didn't think anything was wrong. I thought maybe she was seeing her boyfriend and just blew me off."

"She has a boyfriend?" Detective Reyes asked.

Phoebe nodded bleakly. "I know there was some guy she was seeing. He lives around here. I never met him, though. Crystal said he was with someone else and she was sort of on the side. She told me that they were having some problems, arguing a lot. Then a few days ago, she said things were working out and they were going to get together soon."

"Interesting. That could be helpful." Detective Reyes rested a hand on her shoulder. "Let's sit down over here and talk a minute."

Then she led Phoebe to a quiet spot in the front of the shop, where they sat in two overstuffed armchairs. The detective took out her notebook again and began to ask Phoebe questions about Crystal and their friendship.

Lucy and her friends waited at the big table. "Poor kid," Suzanne said finally. "Both of them, I mean."

"What devastating news. How awful for her parents," Dana said. "Did she grow up around here?"

Maggie shrugged. "I don't know. I don't think so."

"Phoebe probably knows," Lucy said.

"What a nightmare." Maggie gave out a long sigh. "This is just too much. I don't think I can function after this news."

"Are you going to close the shop?" Lucy asked.

Maggie considered the question, then glanced at Phoebe, who still sat with Detective Reyes. "No, I won't close, but I'll cancel the class. Phoebe needs the day off."

Maggie found some paper and a marker on the sideboard near the table. She quickly made a sign canceling the class, then went out a moment and posted it on the front door.

By the time she came back in, Detective Reyes and Phoebe had finished talking. They walked back and joined the others.

"I'm sorry to have brought you this news. I appreciate everyone's help this morning." Detective Reyes adjusted the leather strap of the bag on her shoulder.

Lucy realized she must be armed and wondered where

she carried her gun. Not in her handbag, of course. Her loose jacket hid any sign of a shoulder holster.

The women said good-bye to Detective Reyes and she walked out the shop's front door. Lucy noticed two women had strolled up to the porch, but after they read the sign Maggie had posted, they left again.

"You must be very upset now about Crystal, Phoebe, you take the day off." Maggie reached out and tenderly brushed a strand of Phoebe's hair off her cheek.

Phoebe sighed, her head sagging. "I am. But I don't think I want to be alone all day. I'd rather be hanging out here. At least if I work I'll be distracted a little."

"Whatever you want, Phoebe." Maggie's tone was comforting. "Maybe you should call Josh and see if he'll come by and keep you company," she suggested. "He knew Crystal, too. Didn't he?"

"A little. She came to his gigs and we all hung out together a few times. Guess I'll call in a little while. I don't want to wake him up and freak him out with bad news."

"What else did Detective Reyes say?" Dana asked Phoebe.

"Not much more than she told you. She'll get back in touch once she gets in touch with Crystal's family. I told her I wanted to know what happens."

"Yes, I guess we all do," Maggie said.

A short time later, Dana, Suzanne, and Lucy left the shop to go their separate ways.

As Lucy walked home with Tink, she could only think of Crystal, who had seemed a little lost and scared, but had so much of her life ahead to figure things out. Her death seemed another cruel waste. It was unsettling to have two people she had recently met die within a short time of each other. Not her usual carefree summer.

Lucy kept herself busy for the rest of the day, finally taking on the flower beds in the backyard. Wearing a pair of old shorts and a T-shirt she reserved for house cleaning, she attacked the weeds and straggling branches that had sprouted in all directions, choking out the flowering plants. It was hot, dirty work but satisfying to see the fresh, moist earth of the beds clear of weeds and the blooming stems come to the fore.

She worked outside for several hours, taking breaks to sit under the umbrella on her patio and sip glasses of ice water, occasionally splashing the cold water on her face and head, even down her shirt. Matt was busy in his office until 5:00 and they'd planned to meet in town for dinner and a movie around 7:00.

Lucy figured she'd quit her yard work in the late afternoon, leaving time to rest and get ready. She could feel grains of dirt imbedded in her kneecaps and wondered how long and hard she'd have to scrub to get that out. But it was only about 2:00 when she heard the phone ring. She had the handset handy on the outside table and ran over to catch the call.

"Lucy? It's me," Dana began. "I just heard some shocking news about . . . about Crystal. It's pretty unbelievable."

"Did the police find her family?" Lucy asked.

"No . . . they can't find anyone. But they did go to her apartment and searched her belongings. Jack was down at the station today, to catch up with somebody about another case," Dana explained, "and he heard the whole story."

Jack had a lot of connections in the local police department, with both the village and county officers. The police, Lucy had come to see, were a tight-knit bunch, and loyal to their own. They clearly considered Jack part of the club and were pretty free in conversation with him.

"It turns out that her name isn't really Crystal Warren," Dana continued. "It's Christine. Christine Thurman."

"Thurman? You mean George Thurman's . . . daughter?" Lucy was shocked and dropped down in a chair.

"That's right. The cute little girl who left town at five years old came back. And no one recognized her," Dana added.

How could they? Lucy recalled the photograph she'd seen the night before Gloria's memorial, the one that showed George, Gloria, and George's little girl, Christine. Well, Crystal to them. A sweet-looking, fairhaired sprite, with bright blue eyes and a sunny smile. Nothing like the tattoo-covered Goth who'd insinuated herself into their circle.

"How did the police find out?" Lucy was dumbfounded.

"Phoebe had told Detective Reyes where Crystal lived. They went to her apartment and tried to find some ID, in order to locate her family. They found a passport and some other papers that showed she was living under an alias."

"But why?" Lucy was still dumbfounded. "Why come back here only to disguise herself?"

"Lucy, don't you get it? She came back to catch up with her stepmother, Gloria."

Chapter Fourteen

*L*ucy sat back and thought about Dana's revelation. Her brain was reeling. That had to be it. Why else would Christine Thurman return to Plum Harbor? She had no family or even friends here anymore.

But somehow it wasn't like those stories you hear about some child given up for adoption, who comes into town asking questions, searching for her birth mother. Gloria's stepdaughter had never revealed herself. She had gone out of her way to disguise her identity.

That didn't make sense or bode well.

"Wait, that's not all . . ." Even Dana, who rarely lost touch with her cool, calm center, sounded rattled now. Lucy braced herself for another bombshell.

"They've checked her cell phone records. There were about a million calls to Jamie."

"Jamie? She knew Jamie?" Lucy heard her voice rise in alarm. Tink, who had been sleeping in the shade under the table, jumped up and barked.

"Apparently she knew him quite well," Dana continued. "Even though neither of them let on while they were around us. The police are looking for him. He's wanted for questioning. It doesn't look good." Dana sounded bleak. "Though I suppose there could be some plausible explanation . . ."

"An 'explanation' for why they knew each other so well, but acted as if they were strangers when we were around?" Lucy asked her. "What reason could that be?"

"I really can't think of one," Dana admitted. "Phoebe said that Crystal—Christine, I mean—had a boyfriend, but he was in another relationship. That could have been Jamie, don't you think?"

"Yes, he might be the guy Christine told Phoebe about. Christine Thurman must have wanted something from Gloria and Jamie was her connection," Lucy speculated.

"Money, maybe? What else could it have been? Lucy, do you think she had anything to do with Gloria's death? . . . No, it's too horrible to imagine," Dana said quietly.

"I know what you mean," Lucy cut in quickly. "I don't want to think it, either."

Neither of them spoke for a long moment.

"What do the police think?" Lucy asked finally.

"They aren't saying anything right now. They're waiting to question Jamie," Dana reported. Lucy heard her let out a long slow breath. "I've just told Suzanne and I'm going to call Maggie next. Actually, I think I'll go over there and tell her and Phoebe in person. Maggie isn't going to take this well and Phoebe will feel even more upset now about her friend," Dana predicted. Lucy was thinking the same. "Jack went out for a late golf game. He won't be back until dark. I can stay with Maggie and Phoebe a while."

"I'm meeting Matt in the village later. I'll get ready now and come by the shop."

Lucy hung up with Dana and hurried to clean herself up. She showered and dressed quickly, then left for town with her hair still wet and some makeup and jewelry stashed in her purse for further repairs.

Jamie. . . . It was hard to believe. They had all trusted him so much. They'd flocked around him after Gloria's death, like a bunch of fretful mother hens trying to soothe him. Protect him, even. He must have been laughing at them the entire time.

She felt so betrayed and used. Maggie, who had been the closest to him and Gloria, would feel even worse. And what about poor Phoebe? Had Crystal/Christine befriended her, then used her just to keep track of what was going on at the knitting shop once she realized that Gloria's friends had suspicions about the drowning?

Maybe even to keep track of Jamie?

Thousands of questions spun in Lucy's head. She soon reached the village and parked in front of the Black Sheep, right behind Dana's little black hybrid. She saw her friends Dana, Maggie, and Phoebe up on the porch. They all looked very grim. Grim and shocked, Lucy thought. As if they'd just witnessed some horrific accident out on Main Street.

"Lucy . . . you didn't have to drop everything and run over here," Maggie said.

"I wanted to." Lucy walked over and sat down. "I'm just as stunned as you are. I never once thought Crystal could be involved in Gloria's death. Does that mean Jamie was hiding something, too?" she added quietly.

"I think so—something big. A secret relationship with Gloria's stepdaughter. It's so hard to believe. They must have had some scheme going to trick Gloria out of her money, or her house or something," Maggie said sadly.

Lucy nodded slowly. The two of them wanted to get it, one way or another.

"Jamie had us all fooled. And Gloria paid the biggest price," Maggie added sadly.

Phoebe looked as if she'd been crying again. "Crystal once told me that she grew up someplace in Florida, but I never thought about it. I mean, I never put it together with Jamie and Gloria. She once told me that she'd never had much of a family, only her mother. But her mother had died, about a year ago."

"I'd heard her mother moved down south somewhere, soon after George died," Maggie said. "The mother must have had bad feelings about the way George Thurman's estate was split, and passed that on to her daughter," she added.

"And George's ex-wife already had plenty of anger to-ward her husband and Gloria for the way the marriage broke up," Dana said. "Gloria basically stole George—and all his money—away from her. Then when he died, Gloria inherited that big house and a great deal of her husband's holdings, their piece of the Avalon Group, too."

"His daughter must have inherited some share of Thur-man's wealth," Lucy said. "But she'd been so young it must have been held in trust for her. Maybe by her mother?"

"That was probably the case," Dana agreed. "Or by some attorney George had put in charge. But you know, so many times when children inherit that way, the money gets used up by irresponsible—or even greedy—guardians."

"You mean, by the time she had control of it, there wasn't much left?" Lucy asked. "So she felt cheated."

"That could have been." Maggie's forehead furrowed in thought. "Or there may have been a good amount there, but she still felt shortchanged. Her mother may have brainwashed her with her own bitterness. And Christine might have resented Gloria for destroying her family. You never know how young kids perceive things."

"Maybe her mother's death brought all these toxic feelings to the surface and pushed her over the edge," Dana speculated.

That certainly sounded plausible to Lucy. She could just imagine the message George Thurman's daughter may have heard, day in and day out while growing up—how much better off she and her mother could have been, how much brighter her future could be, if only her evil, greedy stepmother, Gloria, had never come into their lives.

"So, at some point, she must have teamed up with Jamie and they put together a scheme to take back the fortune Christine thought should have gone to her when her father died," Dana concluded.

"George Thurman had that property down in Florida when she was little, so it wasn't hard to check and see if Gloria still spent the winter there," Maggie speculated. "Maybe they quietly stalked Gloria, figured out her habits, and Jamie found a way to introduce himself. Then started to romance her."

"She'd just broken off with Mike Novak," Dana offered, "and she was vulnerable. Though they had no way of knowing that."

"Yes, that part was lucky. Jamie swept Gloria off her feet

and somehow persuaded her to marry him." Lucy wondered if that part of the plan had been difficult because of the age difference and since Gloria hadn't seemed inclined to marry for so many years.

"I don't think he had to persuade her much," Maggie countered. "I think he just drew her in. He acted as if he needed her and she fell into a savior role, wanting to rescue him. Didn't you say that a while ago about them, Dana?" Maggie recalled.

"That dynamic was definitely going on between them, I think. I'm not sure Jamie had to fake it. I'm not sure he was even faking his attraction to Gloria. Not entirely," she added.

"Who knows? Maybe he did have real feelings for her, but got in too deep with Crystal's scheme. When I saw Gloria in town, a few hours before she drowned," Lucy recalled, "she told me that Jamie kept calling her, asking her to come to Boston for that party. Maybe he was having second thoughts about some plan he and Crystal had to kill her?"

"That is possible. I never thought of it," Dana admitted. "We still don't know exactly how they did it. They must have gotten her into the pool somehow, without a struggle. Drugged her maybe? Which is why her blood work from the autopsy came back showing a high level of painkillers."

"So you don't think Gloria took painkillers, like Jamie said?" Suzanne asked.

"I think that was just a story, to cover his tracks," Dana replied. "Including her dark moods."

"Moods we never saw," Maggie added.

"That all sounds pretty likely," Lucy agreed.

"Okay, Jamie and Crystal killed Gloria," Phoebe cut in. "But who killed Crystal?"

It was silent for a moment. The friends glanced around at one another, no one willing to guess aloud at what might seem the obvious conclusion.

Finally Dana said, "It had be Jamie. They had gone to such great lengths to kill Gloria and then found out there was no money. What a shock that must have been. The little they could salvage would have been that line of credit he'd applied for against the home equity."

"Oh, right. It must have been approved and he didn't tell anyone." Lucy recalled Suzanne mentioning that she'd helped him with the application. He should have heard an answer by now from the bank. "So he must have decided to cut Crystal—I mean, Christine—out of the few crumbs left. She was the only one who knew what they had done. Well, who knows what really happened . . . but she was the one who ended up dead and dumped in the woods. He must have killed her before leaving town with whatever money he could get his hands on."

"The money he told us he would use to pay back the loan sharks," Maggie recalled. "I'm sure now he never intended to do that. He just planned on skipping town and hoped they'd never find him."

"Now he has some really bad and angry people after him, as well as the police. Not a very smart crook, was he?" Lucy glanced around at her friends.

"They both must have thought it would be easy," Dana pointed out. "He'd marry Gloria, get his name on her will and on some of her assets, and then she'd meet with a little accident. But once they did away with Gloria, they opened a Pandora's box."

"They did, didn't they?" Maggie mused.

"They'd never imagined that Gloria had so many secrets," Lucy offered.

"And what about her secrets? Especially Mike Novak," Maggie asked. "Do you still think he visited that night?"

"Yes, I do. Obviously before Jamie and Christine arrived." Dana's tone was very certain. "There was something in his body language when we confronted him about it. Something I saw in his eyes. I do think he went to visit her, but he didn't want to tell the police, of course, once he heard that she had drowned. He may have even expected to hear from them, wondering if anyone saw his car, or put things together."

"Like we did?" Lucy asked.

"Exactly. But he managed to fly under the radar and thought it was just as well. I guess, if he *was* there, it will come out now, when the police investigate again."

"Yes, it will," Maggie agreed. "But now you've reminded me, what about that PI who came to Suzanne's house last night? Do you think he was another one of Jamie's tricks?"

"Probably an actor," Lucy guessed. "Jamie must have hired him to divert us and make us stop snooping into Gloria's death."

"I'm going to ask Jack to check it out," Dana said. "I think there was a licence number on the business card. He can find out pretty quickly if it's phony."

"Yes, have him do that if it isn't too much trouble," Maggie said. "Though I think we already know what Jack will say. . . . It's hard to believe we were all fooled so easily. And for so long."

"We weren't fooled entirely," Lucy pointed out. "We all felt unsatisfied by the story of Gloria's accident. We all felt some twinge of suspicion."

"Yes, we did," Dana agreed. "But who could have imagined such a complicated scheme?"

"It's as if we were looking at some huge project, like a big Aryan knit sweater, or even the group blanket we've been making. With your entire focus on one tiny section, it's hard to get the big picture."

"That's what Jamie was counting on," Maggie agreed. "That must be why he stayed so close to the shop, keeping up his friendship with us. So that we wouldn't become suspicious of Gloria's death—or him."

But they eventually did, Lucy realized. Though they had never really suspected Jamie, and hadn't figured out the real plot behind Gloria's murder. Yet, they'd instinctively sensed their dear friend had not died by accident. And they had tried hard to uncover the facts.

That was some small consolation, wasn't it?

Chapter Fifteen

It was Dana's turn to host knitting night on Thursday. Jack was working late. Maggie told them to bring all of their squares to the meeting. Everyone had completed their assigned number and she wanted to lay out the blanket again for a preview of the final product.

They were also going to vote on the color of the yarn they'd use to stitch together the squares and the color of the crocheted border, which Maggie pointed out, didn't have to be the same color as the stitching.

Dana was also going to fill them all in on everything Jack had heard at work during that last few days—the missing pieces of Gloria's murder. Articles had also run in the *Plum Harbor Times*, which the group had been studying closely.

The first one reported Christine's murder and her double identity.

The next reported that Jamie had been picked up in Texas on Sunday, trying to cross into Mexico. He'd been sent back up to Massachusetts and booked on suspicion of murder in his wife's death.

"He must have ditched or sold his car somewhere on the way. He wasn't driving the BMW Gloria gave him. But they caught him anyway," Dana told the group as she served glasses of chilled, organic white wine.

She had prepared a healthy meal for them, appetizers of tabouleh salad and red pepper dip with vegetable sticks and pita chips. As her guests enjoyed the starters, she put finishing touches on the main course, slices of wild salmon, grilled in a soy mustard sauce atop a bed of sauteed spinach and shiitake mushrooms, with a side dish of seven-grain pilaf.

It looked remarkably appetizing, Lucy thought, despite the abundance of health benefits.

"Wow, that looks good," Suzanne remarked. "I don't even have to break my diet tonight."

"Guilt-free dining served here." Dana smiled, beckoning them to the buffet she'd set out in the kitchen. They decided to sit at the big slate coffee table in the family room. Maggie had reserved the dining room table for laying out and viewing their blanket.

"But getting back to the guilty parties, Jamie Barnett and Christine Thurman?" Maggie prodded her. "Did Jack hear any gossip about Jamie's interrogation by the police yet?"

Dana glanced at her and nodded. Lucy could tell by her expression she'd heard more than gossip, she'd heard the whole thing.

"He didn't cooperate at first. He had a lawyer who advised him not to say anything, especially since there's not much physical evidence. Gloria's body was cremated," she reminded them. "But something must have gotten to him. I don't know,

maybe he just felt guilty and remorseful, finally?" Dana asked
the others. "He decided to plead guilty, at least to killing
Christine Thurman, and he gave the police the full story—the
plan Christine had cooked up and how Gloria finally died."
Dana had served some salmon and trimmings in her plate, but
now put it aside.

Lucy could tell it was upsetting for her to relate the story,
but at this point, she had little choice. They were all waiting
to hear it.

"So . . . what did he say?" Suzanne prodded her. She was
eating eagerly. The conversation had not quelled her appetite,
at least not so far. "How did it happen?"

"Jamie claims that even though he was part of the plan to
kill Gloria, when the time came, he didn't want to go through
with it," Dana told them. "He told the police he was trying to
put Christine off, to delay the actual murder. He tried to persuade her that he could get more out of Gloria if she was alive,
rather than dead."

"I don't understand . . . he married her to kill her and
inherit the money. Then he didn't want to kill her after all?"
Lucy asked.

"That's what he says. He said that he seduced her and
married her for the money. As part of the plot, but as time
went by . . . well, he says he had real feelings for her and
didn't want to go through with it. He claims he really loved
her." Dana paused. "But Christine had too much stored up
against him by then and was annoyed that it was taking so
long. He and Christine were lovers, too. So she was jealous
about Jamie marrying her evil ex-stepmother . . . even though
it had all been her idea."

"Wow, is that twisted. I can't imagine how she put up with

the arrangement in the first place," Suzanne said, swallowing a mouthful.

"She was desperate, I guess. You might even say obsessed with getting revenge on Gloria," Dana guessed. "Christine had a record. Petty stuff, shoplifting, bad checks. There had been some complaints filed against Jamie, too, which the police didn't see immediately because he'd been living in Texas under a different name for a while. He'd never quite been pinned down for fraud but wasn't above accepting gifts, or even money, from his girlfriends, many of them older than him."

"Okay, so he was the perfect man for the job," Phoebe cut in. "How did he meet Crystal . . . I mean, Christine Thurman?"

"She had some medical training and was working as a home health aid for an older, wealthy woman in Boca who was diabetic. Jamie was the woman's younger boyfriend. Christine Thurman's obsession with Gloria was pretty much what we imagined. She felt shortchanged by her father's will and the money that was left for her in a trust fund was depleted by the time she became legally entitled to it. Then her mother died and she felt unhinged even more," Dana explained. "So she meets Jamie while working at this house and her employer is a woman a lot like the memory of her long lost stepmother."

"And Christine gets the inspiration for her plan," Lucy finished for her.

"Exactly," Dana answered. "Or maybe she'd had the idea for a while and was just waiting for a guy like Jamie to come along."

By now the knitters had mostly finished their meal and Dana picked up a few plates and carried them over to the sink.

"So how did they finally . . . do it?" Maggie asked quietly. "Did he confess that, too? Since Gloria's body was cremated, there are no remains to exhume and reexamine," she pointed out.

"The police got a pass on that one. Jamie told them exactly how it happened. He was supposed to come back from Boston in the middle of the night, meet Christine at the house, and finish off Gloria. He thought that if he didn't come back, Christine would lose her nerve and wouldn't go through with it. So he called Christine from Boston on the designated night, and told her he couldn't return. He didn't want to go through with killing Gloria and they had to think of a better plan. He thought he had persuaded her to put it off."

"That's why he kept calling Gloria, asking her to meet him in Boston?" Lucy asked.

Dana nodded. "I guess in a twisted way, he was trying to protect Gloria. He claims he was sure he'd dissuaded Christine from killing her. Didn't believe she would do it without his support. So he didn't bother to come home."

"But Christine went ahead anyway on her own," Suzanne filled in. "Boy, she really hated Gloria, didn't she?"

"That's what he says," Dana replied. "Jamie says Christine came in through the back gate, which was never bolted around midnight and found Gloria asleep in her chaise longue by the pool. She often fell asleep knitting or reading at night, while Jamie was working, so that was part of their plan. She saw a wineglass nearby and thought, all the better, assuming Gloria had been drinking. So she snuck up on her and quickly injected her with a huge dose of painkiller. With her medical training, she knew how to find a spot that wouldn't be obvious in an autopsy. Probably between her toes. Jamie had already given her the name of a pain medication that was around the house, a prescription Gloria had been given by her dentist a few weeks ago. So they were covered on that end of the story, too," Dana reminded them. "So the mix of alcohol and drugs in her system rendered her defenseless."

"So there was poor Gloria, knocked out on her chaise longue. Totally helpless." Suzanne described the image they were all imagining.

"That's right. Christine rolled the chaise to the edge of the pool and dumped her in," Dana continued.

"That's why the chaise wasn't in its usual spot when I found Gloria in the pool," Suzanne cut in. "But of course, the police wouldn't have thought anything strange about the longue chair being on the far side of the pool, where the sun was so strong."

"They had no idea of Gloria's habits. And their suspicions were not aroused," Dana replied. "Poor Gloria may have never woken up before she was dumped in the water and drowned. And if she did wake up, she was too disoriented and uncoordinated to save herself in time."

"That's why the police found her knitting in the pool. That beautiful scarf. It was almost completed. She must have had it on her lap," Maggie said glumly.

"That's right," Dana agreed.

"And Jamie claims he had no part in this? He didn't even want it to happen?" Lucy asked again.

"That's what he told the police. He does have witnesses for his entire time that night in Boston. He was out partying in different bars until early morning, well after the time Gloria was killed. So that claim seems true."

"What about Christine? He did kill her, right?" Phoebe cut in.

"Yes, he made a full confession. He says his only regret now is that he didn't walk away from the beginning, before Gloria could ever get hurt. But he did say he'd never really planned on killing Christine, it happened during an argument. He was still angry that she'd murdered Gloria when he told her the plan was off. She was pressing him to get whatever money he could quickly so they could leave town. She was worried that he was losing his nerve. He says she showed up at the house just as he was packing up to go away without her. They argued and . . . he strangled her, then dumped her body on his way out of town."

"I guess he'd totally freaked out by then," Phoebe offered.

"Everything fell apart and he must have panicked," Dana agreed. "He didn't even try to hide the body very well."

"He never seemed like the sharpest needle in the bag to me," Suzanne added. She carried a few empty dishes to the sink, helping Dana clear up so they could start their knitting.

"He did seem too good to be true." Lucy smiled and sighed. "Just goes to show, you can't trust a man who cooks, knits, and claims he loves to give pedicures."

"Right, the pedicures. That should have tipped us off." Suzanne laughed. "He just looked so darn cute in his barbeque apron," she recalled, "and fumbling with his knitting needles."

"We were all taken in. Yours truly included. I'm sure now that dire need to paint my portrait was just a ploy to stay close to us. Another excuse to hang around the shop and make sure we didn't meddle anymore in Gloria's murder . . . and to encourage more sympathy," she added. Maggie opened her knitting bag and took out a thick stack of knitted squares.

"He was good at that," Dana agreed. "A real master. He

was so close to us, acting so vulnerable and needy, we had no chance of seeing his real colors. Or intentions."

"He was an illusionist," Lucy offered. "Drawing our attention in one direction, while carrying on some dirty tricks with the other."

"A con man, you mean," Suzanne clarified. "And Gloria was the biggest victim of his game."

"Yes, she was, poor soul," Maggie said sadly. "But you know, in spite of everything, I think he really did care for Gloria. I think he may have even loved her. She was the only person in his life who ever took care of him and believed in his talent. That must have counted for something. Of course," she added quickly, "we'll never know, will we?"

"No . . . we won't," Lucy said. But she tended to agree with Maggie. Jamie had been a complete fraud and the worst kind of social parasite. But no one was all good, or all bad.

If Jamie Barnett had possessed a shred of decency, she tended to believe that he'd come to care for Gloria in a way he'd never expected. Gloria had been his protector and champion and only saw the best in him. Maybe he'd started off acting the part of her true love and surprised himself, by actually falling in love with her.

"Is this a cautionary tale, about older women and younger men?" Dana asked her friends.

"Not necessarily. That situation can work out perfectly for some people. It really depends on the couple, don't you think? But most of us probably have a better shot at a good relationship with someone who's age appropriate," Maggie added. "Like me and Nick Cooper, for instance."

"Nick Cooper?" Lucy was surprised to hear that name again. "I thought he had his chance, and that was that."

"He did. But I had second thoughts. We're going to a jazz brunch at a pub in Newburyport this weekend."

"Nice of him to ask you out again. He doesn't give up easily. I'll say that for him," Dana noticed.

"I'd say that for him, too. But I asked him this time," Maggie confessed. "I thought about it and decided I'd been a bit . . . stubborn or something. And I would like to know him better."

Maggie turned and headed for the dining room. Lucy glanced at her friends. There was a bit of eye rolling and exaggerated faces, but no one dared to make further comment.

As Maggie calmly laid her squares on the table, according to the pattern she'd sketched and now held in her hand, Suzanne, Lucy, Dana, and Phoebe produced their own contributions and then helped arrange them.

A few minutes later, they saw their nearly completed blanket, practically all the squares filled in, even the special one made in honor of Gloria's memory in the middle.

"Wow, that looks great." Suzanne was the first to deliver a review. "It's even prettier than I imagined."

"It does look good. I like the colors we chose," Dana said.

"Me, too. Nice mix," Lucy agreed.

"And our squares came out very even. Well, most of them," Phoebe added.

"Yes, they did. It's come together nicely. But I do have one suggestion," Maggie told the others. "I think we should keep the square I made to honor Gloria. We can make a border for it, and hang it in the shop, to remember her."

"Great idea, Maggie. I felt sad about seeing that star go and didn't realize why," Dana admitted.

"I did, too," Lucy said. She picked up the square with the shooting star and smoothed it out with her hand. "I think we should hang this someplace where we can see it all the time and remember Gloria's strong spirit. I have a feeling she's near, watching over us while we knit."

And was hovering nearby, while we were figuring out the real story of her death, Lucy added silently.

"I'm sure she is near, in spirit." Maggie took the star square from Lucy's hand and set it aside. "I'll just knit something new for the middle. Maybe a heart or a flower?"

"A heart is a good idea." Suzanne held up a strand of plum yarn to visualize a border. "It sends a message of caring to whoever gets our blanket."

"We still need a few more squares," Phoebe reminded them. "The ones Crystal was supposed to make. I can do that," she offered.

"Don't be silly. We can each do one right now." Lucy sensed that Phoebe felt responsible for bringing Crystal—Christine, rather—into their group, a wolf in lamb's clothing. A Goth wolf, rather.

But how could Phoebe have known? Christine had been using her. Using all of them. They'd all been fooled by her, too.

"Lucy's right. We'll just polish those off tonight and be done with it," Maggie suggested.

Maggie stepped back and gazed down at the blanket and then looked back up at her friends again. "Well, this one's a wrap. But I have a few new ideas to show you."

Notes from the Black Sheep Knitting Shop Bulletin

To All Our Knitting Friends Who Remember Dear Gloria Sterling—

Thank you all so much for your cards and notes. They've been a great comfort for those of us who were closest to our wonderful friend Gloria.

Some of you have asked Maggie about the project Gloria was working on before she passed away, the beautiful mist lace scarf. I was interested in making it also and just finished a version in creamy white merino.

I easily adapted the pattern, making it slightly wider and longer, so that it's more of a summer shawl. But you can wear this scarf just about anytime, or anywhere.

The pattern was designed by Lisa Dykstra for Crystal Palace Yarns and is available for free on the Crystal Palace Yarns website. There are lots of other great patterns there. It's definitely worth a visit.

Here's the link:

http://www.straw.com/cpy/patterns/scarves/kidm-mist-lace-scarf.html
http://www.straw.com/patterns

I'm sure Gloria would be flattered to know that we all admired her good taste and sense of style so much.

Fondly,
Dana Haeger

Hey Everyone,

Here's the lowdown (no pun intended) on those socks I just made for Matt.

I definitely scored some major girlfriend points and they were frighteningly easy to make. (Please don't tell Matt I said that.) A perfect "quickie" fun project or gift.

I found the free pattern online at www.wendyknits.net

Here's a direct link to my choice, Sprucey Lucy Socks. I couldn't resist that name, though there are dozens of sock patterns there to choose from:

http://media.wendyknits.net/media/sprucey-lucy-socks1.pdf

You can also find some great patterns by this designer, Wendy Johnson in her book, *Socks From the Toes Up*.

I now totally understand Phoebe's foot fetish and will *never* tease her about it again.

Lucy

Everyone has been asking me about the blanket that the Black Sheep knitters just made for Warm Up America! So I thought I'd post this information for you.

As we all know, the joy of knitting is not in receiving, but giving our handmade work to others. That's what Warm Up America! is all about. Warm Up America! collects handmade items from knitters like you—blankets, blanket squares, hats, socks, toys, etc.—and distributes them to those in need, such as hospice and nursing home residents, the homeless, or families who have lost their home due to a fire or flood. You don't need to make an entire blanket, either, but can contribute any amount of hand-knit squares that will be joined with contributions from other knitters.

Project Linus is another wonderful organization that provides love, security, and comfort to traumatized and needy children with hand-crafted donations from "volunteer blanketeers."

You can find more information about Project Linus and the Warm Up America! Foundation—and instructions for the blanket squares and many other useful projects that are easy to knit—at the links below:

www.projectlinus.org
www.WarmupAmerica.com

Stay well, count your blessings . . . and keep knitting!
Maggie

Recipe
Jamie's Coconut Macaroons

We'll Always Have Those Macaroons to Remember Him By!

Okay, the truth is out. If we only knew then what we know now . . . and all that.

Yeah, maybe we should have known that Jamie Barnett was too good to be true. :(I guess his cooking—and other attributes—distracted us.

I was cleaning off my desk the other day and found this recipe that he gave me for those scrumptious coconut macaroons. Remember the ones he used to bake and bring to the shop all time?

Just like dear old Jamie, the instructions are deceptively simple . . .

Enjoy (and watch out for those charming younger men . . .),
Lucy

Jamie's Too Good to Be True Coconut Macaroons

1 pound bag of shredded coconut
1 teaspoon vanilla extract
1 can (14 ounces) sweetened condensed milk
Optional: ½ bag semisweet baking chocolate
Parchment paper
Cookie sheets (flat without rims are best)

Heat oven to 375 degrees.

Line cookie sheets with parchment paper.

In a large bowl, mix together coconut, sweetened condensed milk, and vanilla extract until ingredients are completely blended.

Drop in spoonfuls onto parchment-lined cookie sheets, about 1½ to 2 inches apart.

Bake about 10 minutes, or until tops are golden.

Chocolate Dip

Melt chocolate in a small bowl in microwave or on stovetop, according to package instructions.

For a Jackson Pollock effect, dip a spoon into the melted chocolate and drizzle over the entire sheet of thoroughly cooled macaroons.

Or you can dip the top of each macaroon into the bowl and place the tray in the fridge to harden the chocolate.

Recipe
Pasta with Roasted Asparagus, Artichokes, and Pesto

Hey Everyone,

I keep getting rave reviews for my roasted asparagus pasta and know you all want to try it. Lucy made it for her boyfriend and he practically proposed on the spot. (Only kidding, Lucy . . .)

It's pretty easy to whip up if you have a little spare pesto in the fridge, but it will still taste good without pesto. Just add a little more onions and grated cheese.

You can buy prepared pesto in the store, but if you can find fresh basil, it's not hard to make. I put that little recipe at the end for you. Sometimes I mix spinach fettuccine with the regular semolina kind, or whole wheat. The two colors of pasta look pretty on the plate. Italians call that "straw and hay" . . . or something like that. To make this dish a little heartier, add a few slices of sautéed and crumbled prosciutto or some grilled shrimp or grilled chicken breast. Sounds good? You bet your crochet hook it is.

If I'm not knitting, I'm eating. What can I say?

Love and hugs,
Suzanne

Pasta with Roasted Asparagus, Artichokes, and Pesto

1 pound pasta

4 tablespoons olive oil

Coarse salt and freshly ground pepper

Large bunch (1 pound or more) fresh asparagus

1 can artichoke hearts packed in water

1 medium onion, chopped

2 garlic cloves, diced

4 tablespoons olive oil

$\frac{1}{4}$ cup (or more, to taste) fresh or store-bought
pesto sauce (recipe below)

Freshly grated Parmesan cheese

Heat oven to 425 degrees.

Cook pasta to package directions. Set aside when done.

Wash asparagus and trim hard ends (about 2 to 3 inches from bottom).

Set in one layer on a cookie sheet, drizzle one tablespoon oil, and shake pan to coat spears.

Bake in preheated oven, 7 to 10 minutes, shaking pan to rotate spears.

Spears should be soft and golden brown. Sprinkle with coarse salt and freshly ground pepper.

Cool and cut into pieces.

In a large heavy pan (large enough for the pasta), heat

one tablespoon or so of oil. Drain artichoke hearts completely. Lay flat side down in heated oil. Cook until golden brown and turn once. Heat briefly and set aside.

Add two tablespoons more of oil to pan and heat. Add chopped onion and diced garlic cloves.

Cook onion until clear and soft. Add asparagus, toss lightly. Lower heat so vegetables don't overcook.

Add cooked pasta, in thirds. (You may not need all of it.) Add about one-quarter cup pesto sauce (or more to taste) and turn. Add artichokes on top (and any extras such as grilled shrimp or grilled chicken). Serve with freshly grated Parmesan cheese.

Pesto Sauce

There's no right answer to pesto. Some people like more garlic, or less. More cheese, or pine nuts. Or walnuts, or no nuts at all. Feel free to adjust your ingredients accordingly.

—S.C.

1 large bunch of fresh basil, about 2 cups of leaves, loosely packed
3 to 4 garlic cloves, coarsely chopped
Olive oil
4 tablespoons toasted pine nuts
one-quarter cup freshly grated Parmesan cheese

Remove basil leaves from stems. Wash leaves and dry thoroughly on paper towels or dish towels. (Make sure the leaves are dry or this recipe will not work out, believe me.)

In a blender or food processor, mix leaves with chopped garlic and blend, drizzle in olive oil. Add nuts and cheese, mix again, and add a little more oil if necessary. Sauce should have a pasty consistency.

Refrigerate to use within a week, or store in freezer.